FIFTY PERCENT ILLUSION

FIFTY PERCENT ILLUSION

MIRANDA MACLEOD

Apple Blossom Press
Boston, MA

Fifty Percent Illusion
By Miranda MacLeod

Copyright © 2017 by Miranda MacLeod

All rights reserved.

This is a work of fiction. Any resemblance of characters to actual persons, living or dead, is purely coincidental. The author holds exclusive rights to this work. No part of this book may be reproduced in any form or by any electronic or mechanical means, including information storage and retrieval systems, without written permission from the author, except for the use of brief quotations in a book review.

ISBN: 9781548101916

Find out more:
mirandamacleod.com
Contact the author:
miranda@mirandamacleod.com

ALSO BY MIRANDA MACLEOD

Telling Lies Online

Holly & Ivy (cowritten with T.B. Markinson)

Love's Encore Trilogy:

A Road Through Mountains

Your Name in Lights

Fifty Percent Illusion

Americans Abroad Series:

Waltzing on the Danube

Holme for the Holidays

Stockholm Syndrome

Letters to Cupid

London Holiday

Check mirandamacleod.com for more about these titles, and for other books coming soon!

ABOUT THE AUTHOR

Originally from southern California, Miranda now lives in New England and writes heartfelt romances and romantic comedies featuring witty and charmingly flawed women that you'll want to marry. Or just grab a coffee with, if that's more your thing. She spent way too many years in graduate school, worked in professional theater and film, and held temp jobs in just about every office building in downtown Boston.

To find out about her upcoming releases and take advantage of exclusive sales, be sure to sign up for her newsletter at her website: mirandamacleod.com.

ONE

THE POTTED PALM in the investigator's office surely had seen healthier days. Rorie couldn't stop staring at the tips of its shriveled leaves, cracked and spotted with brown, as if by concentrating hard enough, the plant might somehow spring back to life. It didn't, but Rorie continued to observe it anyway. It kept her mind off why they were there in the run-down waiting room. More accurately, it kept her from dwelling on the uncertainties that roiled within her, because she hadn't a clue why they were there. All would become clear soon enough. Hopefully.

Beside her, Cecily sat on a chrome chair, the orange upholstery reminiscent of a cast-off from an auto mechanic's lobby. It creaked and groaned as her partner thumbed through a magazine that, judging by the plump turkey that graced its cover, was at least 6 months out of date. Cecily projected a soothing calm, but that stood to reason. It wasn't *her* missing sister they were there to find out about. She had less on the line.

The waiting room that surrounded them seemed unaccustomed to guests. Aside from the two of them, the room was empty, and the mountain of papers and boxes on the receptionist's desk was a dead giveaway that the P.I. firm hadn't employed a receptionist in quite some time. A less dedicated potential client might be inspired to turn around and go elsewhere. Somewhere with comfortable furniture and in-season reading material. But none of this mattered to Rorie.

Despite outward appearances, when it came to finding people, Murray was the best in the business. Rorie's attorney, Helen, swore by him. Runaway kids, deadbeat dads—you name it, Murray could flush them out from wherever they hid with the efficiency of a bloodhound. His success rate was second to none. He found his mark every time.

When it came to keeping his appointments running on schedule, Rorie noted silently, and without a trace of charity, that he was considerably less reliable.

"How much longer will he keep us waiting?" Rorie didn't expect an answer, but Cecily glanced at her watch and gave Rorie's hand a squeeze.

"He'll be ready for us soon. You're sure he didn't give you any hint about what he'd found when you spoke with him on the phone?"

Rorie mulled over the conversation one more time. It had been brief. The call had come over the weekend as she and Cecily sat at the diner while movers emptied the Orange County apartment of boxes and prepared to move them to Rorie's house in Westwood. Her head had been immersed in the details of the move and on their new future, without a single thought for a sister she'd never met. Murray's call had sent her in a tailspin. Was there something he'd said then, some detail shared that she'd forgotten?

She shook her head, frustrated. "Nothing. Just that he had news, and it was better if he delivered it in person." She pressed one hand to her abdomen, smashing the dark, silky fabric of her tank top against her skin, as if somehow the pressure would keep her fluttering belly from flying away. "That can't be good, can it?"

"You don't know that." Cecily's hand tightened like a vice around her fingers. Rorie welcomed the pressure, an anchor to keep her from flying to pieces. "It could just be too complicated to discuss on the phone."

Squeezing her lids shut, Rorie nodded in agreement, but the unyielding lump in her gut betrayed her uneasiness. What *good* news could Murray have discovered about her sister that couldn't have just as easily been shared over the phone? Rorie couldn't think of a single thing. But bad news? The options were plentiful. Her mother's younger daughter could be in debt, or in jail and in need of some money from her big sister to bail her out. Isn't that what these things usually boiled down to? In Rorie's family they did.

The thought of money sent a new wave of nausea through Rorie's troubled insides. Her efforts to reunite with her family had already cost her a pretty penny. Who was to say this new sister of hers wouldn't turn out to be the same? She might end up being no better than the imposter who'd pretended to be her mother while draining Rorie's savings account dry. True, this time Rorie was the one seeking her out and not the other way around, but it still paid to be cautious. People weren't always what they seemed.

Agitated, Rorie opened her eyes and stared at the closed office door. There was still time to slip out, unseen. Maybe it would be a better choice. She had her father and mother back in her life, and Cecily and Tyler, too. How much more family did she need?

Despite common sense urging her otherwise, she remained in her chair. No matter the outcome, she at least needed as many answers as Murray could provide about this elusive sister of hers.

The office door cracked open and the sound of muffled voices bled into the waiting area as Murray, a short balding man in a beige suit, bade his previous clients goodbye, then turned his attention to the two waiting women. It was too late to run now. They'd made eye contact. She was committed.

"Miss Mulloy?"

His eyes darted from Cecily to Rorie as he attempted to apply his superior investigative skills to suss which of them was his client. Success escaped him, and a red flag waved in Rorie's subconscious. How good an investigator could this guy be if he hadn't bothered to Google her before they met? She had a whole page on Wikipedia for chrissakes. Never mind that the woman next to her was an Emmy-nominated actress whose picture had been splashed across every newspaper and magazine for the better part of a year. *Does the man not watch television, or eat anything fresher than the contents of a takeout container, that he hasn't seen a recent grocery store tabloid?* Or was she just inclined to find fault today, no matter the reason?

Rorie stood, sparing him further effort. "Yes. I'm Rorie Mulloy. And this is my partner, Cecily DuPont." The curious twitch of an eyebrow as the investigator pondered her words gave Rorie pause once more. He couldn't be confused by her meaning of partner, could he? *Please tell me you get the gist of it, or will I have to explain?*

"Yes, of course," he said finally, and left it at that.

Rorie's nerves settled slightly as he shepherded them into his jumbled office without further discussion. He pointed to two chairs whose stuffing, thankfully, appeared to be a few decades newer than the ones up front. "Ms. Mulloy," he said when they were seated, "you hired me to locate your sister, Rebecca Courville."

✦

His statement of this obvious fact could have elicited another heaping serving of derision, but now that they were seated in the office with the answers to her questions so close, Rorie found that the only reaction she could manage was breathless anticipation.

"There's no sense beating around the bush. I'm afraid I have some difficult news."

"I thought you might." As her heart plummeted, Rorie realized that Cecily's pep talk earlier must have had more of a buoying effect on her spirits than she'd expected. Despite her pessimism, some small part of her had foolishly been hoping for the best, and was about to be cruelly disappointed. She swallowed hard and waited for Murray to continue.

"As you know, due to your mother's recurring mental illness, your sister was in and out of foster care since birth." Rorie nodded perfunctorily, as Murray had gone over this information before. "As she got older, she ran away a lot, and the state records get a little fuzzy as to her whereabouts after 2001. She dropped off the radar completely in 2003 when she turned eighteen. But I was finally able to trace Rebecca to a town outside Memphis, Tennessee, near the Mississippi border."

"Mississippi?" Rorie was unaware of any other family ties to the state.

"Looks like she went up there from Louisiana with a boyfriend, a musician. In fact, they both played guitar and sang in some of the country-western bars around Memphis."

"And that's where she is now?" She could feel her heart grow lighter. Hearing her sister's journey was beginning to bring back some hope. An aspiring singer in Memphis? That didn't sound so bad.

Murray's lips formed a tight, thin line. "I'm afraid not.

You see, Ms. Mulloy, your sister passed away about a year ago."

"She's dead?" Hope disappeared as a chill swept over her, making her body shake uncontrollably. Her sister had only been in her early thirties, more than a decade younger than Rorie was. Of all the unfortunate scenarios she'd imagined, her sister being dead had never occurred to her. Her concern had only extended as far as self-protection, a realization that under the circumstances filled her with guilt. *How could I have been so selfish?*

She felt Cecily take her hand, the warmth from Cecily's fingers penetrating the iciness of Rorie's flesh. She looked straight ahead at Murray and willed herself to stay strong, knowing that if she turned her head and saw the concern that was surely on her girlfriend's face, she'd break down and never make it through the rest of the meeting. *But, dead?* This wasn't at all how things were supposed to play out.

Murray's head was down, his eyes scanning the file in front of him. "An accidental overdose, according to the police report. The boyfriend's mother got worried and came by the apartment. Found both the bodies."

"Both?" The word weighed on her. "Her boyfriend, too, you mean?"

"Yes," Murray confirmed. "Which brings me to the difficult part, the reason I thought it best if we did this in person."

"Okay." Rorie swallowed roughly, her throat like sandpaper. As if discovering the depth of her capacity for self-absorption was just a walk in the park? Or finding out her sister was dead, for God's sake, wasn't the *difficult* part? Something between panic and blinding rage bubbled up inside. At this point, Cecily's grip on her fingers was the only thing keeping her from jumping out of her own skin.

"There was a daughter, Bryn Alexander."

"*Was?*" *Dear God, don't tell me anyone else is dead.*

"Sorry, is. Incidentally, that's why your sister was so hard to find. She'd been living under the name Rebecca Alexander, though there was no record of a marriage or any indication she'd legally changed her name. Makes a private investigator's life difficult when people go and do that."

Rorie tapped her foot against the leg of the chair as he launched into a lecture on the finer points of proper names and identification. Given the extent of his discoveries, she was willing to give him the benefit of the doubt when it came to his investigation techniques, but his interpersonal skills needed some finessing. This hardly seemed the time or the place for a lengthy discussion of proper name etiquette.

Finally, she cleared her throat. "I'm sorry, but can we get back to the child you mentioned for a minute? Are you saying I have a niece?"

"Bryn. She's four years old. I still have a few calls out to state agencies in DeSoto county, trying to determine her exact whereabouts, but I thought you'd like to know where everything stood right away."

"I don't think I understand where things stand at all." Rorie frowned at her own obtuseness. There was a message in his words that she was failing to grasp.

"Her guardian, Ms. Mulloy." Murray's own brow wrinkled, mirroring Rorie's expression. "That is to say, her lack thereof. You see, none of my research has turned up any next of kin, aside from her father's mother. And let's just say that the apple didn't fall far from the tree when it came to drug use in that family."

Realization weighed upon her. "So, the grandmother's an addict, too?"

"With the usual rap sheet to go with it. She spent a little time in jail for drug possession, has more misdemeanor charges than I can count. She claims to be clean now, but her past is more than enough to make a judge deem her unfit to raise a child." He shrugged. "To be fair, it's not so much a reflection on her character, I'm sure. The opioid epidemic's hit that region pretty bad. But with no other relatives in the area that I could locate, most likely your niece is in a foster home."

Rorie stared blankly as the information seeped into her brain. She wasn't sure what to say.

"A foster home can be a good thing, though, right?" Cecily offered, clearly trying to salvage the situation in whatever way she could. "Perhaps she's with a family that's interested in adopting her."

Murray pursed his lips. "Sure. I guess that happens sometimes." It was clear that his experience led him to think otherwise, and given the little she knew about their country's broken foster care system, Rorie was inclined to take his view. "Oh, here," Murray added. "I've got a picture of her, if you'd like to see."

Rorie held out her hand and took the photograph of a smiling, round-faced cherub with sandy ringlets that stood out in tiny ponytails on either side of her head. Bryn appeared to be about two years old in the photo. The family resemblance was strong. Her skin and hair were fairer than Rorie's, but their eyes were unmistakably the same.

The picture was wallet-sized with ink stains around the edges, as if it had been carried around in someone's purse. Rorie wondered if it had belonged to her sister, if she'd carried her little girl's picture with her wherever she went. Her heart wrenched with the sudden, jarring loss of a sister she would never know, and the child they had yet to find. "You're still searching for my niece?" Hearing herself identify the child in this way made finding her take on an increased urgency, as if in some way this little girl *belonged* to her, even if she didn't know her yet.

Murray nodded solemnly. "I should hear something in the next few days."

"Call me as soon as you do."

With both of Bryn's parents gone and no other relatives to come to the rescue, it dawned on Rorie that she might be the only one who could help, the only person the child could rely on. Rorie choked back a laugh. What an absurd situation to be in. She was about the least equipped woman she could think of when it came to children. She wouldn't know a maternal instinct if it bit her on the ass. Just how far was she prepared to go for this orphaned niece of hers, cute little ponytails notwithstanding?

She glanced nervously at Cecily, who had taken Bryn's photograph from her and was studying it with eyes downcast and unreadable. Cecily was the motherly one, but they'd discussed it before and she'd made it clear that her child rearing days were done. If it came to it, how much would Cecily be willing to do for a child who wasn't even her own blood?

They left the office in pensive silence, headed back to the home they had shared for all of a single weekend. After years in a bad marriage, reaching the point where she was ready to take a step as small as moving in together had been difficult enough for Cecily. No matter how ready they were to make the commitment, Rorie knew the transition wouldn't be smooth. Cecily hadn't even unpacked yet, and now there was the prospect of a four-year-old child being thrown into the mix. How could Rorie ask this of her so soon?

You're getting way ahead of yourself. Murray hasn't even found her yet.

But somehow, deep down, Rorie knew that he would.

Sure, she'd doubted him in the beginning, but no longer. For all his oddity, he delivered results. Helen wouldn't have recommended him if he didn't. There was no reason to think he wouldn't this time, too. And for all their optimism that the child might already be in a loving home, she felt in her gut that it wouldn't be as easy as that. When the child was found, there would be choices they'd have to make, and at this point, Rorie had no idea what those decisions would be.

TWO

A STACK of moving boxes greeted them in the hallway when they returned to Rorie's Westwood home that afternoon. Despite the shock the morning had dealt, Cecily felt a thrill at the sight, a reminder that this was her home now, too. It would take some time for it to truly feel that way, but at least the transformation had begun. Some favorite throw pillows were piled on a sofa in the living room, the heavy glass vase Tyler had given her for Mother's Day was on the coffee table, and her clothing hung from the extra rod in the master bedroom's walk-in closet. It was a start.

The weekend's move had been overshadowed by the call from Murray, but every so often the magnitude of her decision to move in with Rorie shone through and made her smile. She'd hesitated to make that final step for over a year, needing to be sure. That was her biggest hang up, that for too many years she'd allowed what other people needed or wanted dictate her choices. She'd grown unaccustomed to making her own decisions, and this had been one choice that she knew she had to get right. Too much was at stake to get it wrong.

But finally, she'd been sure. Now, for better or worse, they were in this together for good.

For better or worse. The phrase conjured up images of matrimony that made her shudder. Her commitment was absolute, but marriage was a road she couldn't travel again. Still, she was ready to face whatever life threw at them, though if she was honest about it, she hadn't expected the first test of their partnership to come quite so soon. A dead sister, and a parentless child out there somewhere, waiting to be found? It sounded like a movie, and while it would have been heartbreaking to hear a story like this about strangers on television, having it happen to someone she loved was a shock.

The investigator's news had shaken her deeply, but what she felt was nothing compared to how Rorie must be taking the news. She just wished she knew exactly how that *was*. Cecily looked past the fortress of brown cardboard boxes, searching Rorie's stoic features for a clue to her girlfriend's state of mind as she paced the living room. She'd inherited that trait from her father, and in typical Mulloy fashion, the deeper the emotions, the faster she put up a wall to hold them in. It was Rorie's strategy to process how she felt in her own way and time. Eventually, Cecily had learned, she would ask for the help she was willing to accept and the barrier would come down. But if the wall developed cracks too soon? *Watch out.*

While Rorie's face betrayed little, there were storm clouds in her eyes. Rorie was a master at holding in her worries, but Cecily could see through her facade better than most, and knew that she was close to her breaking point but still stubbornly clinging to her resolve to sort out her emotions on her own. It would never work. No wall was strong enough for this. Cecily would have to step in without being asked, and hope Rorie would understand why.

Rorie stopped in place, appearing cautious but filled with yearning, as Cecily approached. She didn't really want to go it alone, and Cecily felt a wave of relief. She was doing the right thing by not letting her. Wrapping her arms around Rorie's shoulders, Cecily pulled her close before she had the chance to shut herself off again.

"I'm so, so sorry about Rebecca." Within the safety of her embrace, she felt Rorie's body shudder as her defenses weakened.

"I didn't expect...I know I never met her, but—" With a sound somewhere between a sob and a gasp, the tears began to flow. "I thought she'd need money, and I was ready to hold that against her. What does that say about me?"

Cecily's heart lurched at the look of guilt and sadness on Rorie's face. Her suspicions about her sister had been more than natural, and ones that Cecily, too, had shared. Neither of them could've guessed the truth. The last thing Rorie needed was to start blaming herself for things that couldn't be helped.

"It says that you're human, that's all. Anyone would feel that way, especially given what your search for your family has already put you through."

Rorie nodded silently, too drained to speak. It was plain to see that a fog of blame still engulfed her. Cecily's words might not have helped now, but she would keep repeating them to her every day until they did, until the look in Rorie's eyes told her that she believed them to be true.

"Sweetheart, you look exhausted. Why don't you go rest while I sort through these boxes and try to tidy up? We can talk about it all after you've had a nap and a cup of tea. It's easier to think with a clean house and a rested brain."

Once Rorie retreated from the room without argument, Cecily picked up a box with a label marked 'office supplies.' Rorie's house wasn't overly large, but there'd been a small extra bedroom that she'd cleared out for Cecily to use as a work space. Eventually she would have a real office at her fledgling production company, Sapphicsticated's, new studios, but that was several months away. Until then she would work from home.

The room was empty except for an old desk, which Cecily had planned to use in the interim, until she found something new that she liked. She set the box on the desktop and reached into her pocket for her keys, sliding them across the tape seal until the flaps sprang free. Inside were notebooks and pens, stationery and envelopes, and all the other things that would fill the desk drawers. She pulled one drawer open as she reached into the box, but as her fingers closed around a cup of pens, she stopped and looked around again with a frown.

It felt all wrong. The reason for that nagged at her, poking at her brain and daring her to put it into words, but she resisted. For nearly twenty years, every step in her relationship with Rorie had been slow and measured. Too slow, Cecily could admit, and too much time wasted. But *this*. This threatened to move at lightning speed. She wasn't ready so much as to think the words.

Taking in her new space, Cecily attempted to summon up the excitement she'd so recently felt. She'd spent the past few weeks pouring through catalogs, trying to decide how best to furnish the space. Robin's egg blue on the walls, perhaps, with furniture in chocolate brown. Or maybe something lighter, airier. So many options to explore.

But as she studied the room now, those plans left her feeling hollow. *Wouldn't this room be...* She shut down the thought before it was complete. It wasn't time for that yet, but it also wasn't the right time to unpack. Withdrawing her empty hand from the box, she folded the flaps in on themselves and pushed it aside. This room could wait just a little longer.

Wouldn't this be—

She squeezed her eyes tightly shut but the thought wouldn't stay silent.

Wouldn't this be just the right size for a little girl's bedroom?

And there it was, out in the light of day. They hadn't discussed it yet, what exactly they would do about Bryn. It had been clear from her distress that Rorie needed to process the loss of the sister she'd never known first, before trying to take on any other issues. At least, that was what Cecily had told herself as she studiously avoided bringing it up on the drive home. But the implications of Murray's news were obvious. Bryn had nowhere to go, no family except them. Cecily knew they'd need to talk about that fact very soon, and figure out what it meant.

Bryn. Her mouth twitched at the corners. *Such a cute little thing.* Her mind conjured up an image of the little girl in the picture, so real she could almost see her standing in the room. That mop of sandy blonde curls and those sun-kissed cheeks, like she'd spent the day chasing waves at the beach. And those glacier-blue eyes that were exactly like her aunt's. If Rorie had ever had a baby of her own, it might have looked just like Bryn. A rush of tenderness toward the child overtook her at the thought.

But by her own admission, Rorie had never seen herself as the motherly type. They'd already discussed the possibility of children and decided against it, and had both been satisfied with that plan. Moving in together was one thing, a very permanent thing as far as Cecily was concerned. Marriage and children, on the other hand, were not supposed to be in the cards.

But when it came to the question of Bryn, what else could they do but play the hand they'd been dealt? If it turned out that Rorie's niece needed a home, they'd have little choice but to step in. Bryn was family. Of course, stepping in could be accomplished in a lot of ways. It didn't necessarily mean Cecily having to abandon the idea of her home office in favor of a nursery.

Providing for Bryn financially was not a problem. Clothing, food, her education, all of that Cecily would happily fund if some other willing relative stepped up to take her. *A grandparent maybe?* Except Rorie's mother, though doing better since her move to California, was in no condition to raise a child. And apparently the same was true for the child's father's, too. Most likely, there was no one else.

It was one thing to commit to financial help, and a whole other to offer Bryn a home. Yet that was what the child needed most. If it came to it, were they up for the challenge? Was *she* up for doing it all over again?

The first day of kindergarten. Visits from the tooth fairy. Saturdays spent at soccer games, parent-teacher conferences. Learning to drive. First dates. Cecily's memories whirled. She cherished every one of these moments with Tyler, but bringing a child into their lives would change everything. Though it felt like they'd been together forever, she and Rorie were only barely starting to get used to living together as a couple. What would introducing a child to the mix mean for them?

Cecily looked up as a tapping noise reached her ear, and smiled as she saw Rorie leaning against the open doorway, holding two steaming ceramic mugs. "I thought you were napping."

"Tea sounded so good, I thought you might want a cup,

too." She held it out as she entered the room, and Cecily took it gratefully. "How's the unpacking coming?"

"Delayed." Cecily took a deep breath, battling with herself whether to bring it up now or wait a little longer. Perhaps Rorie needed more time to recover from the day's news. Perhaps she did, too. But she knew the longer they put it off, the harder addressing it would be. "Sweetheart, we need to talk about Bryn."

"I'm not sure what to say." Rorie tapped her fingernail nervously along the rim of the mug. "I think I'm still in shock."

"You have every reason to be. But Murray's a pro. He's bound to find her soon. We need to know what our plan will be when he does."

"She might be in a perfectly good home, just like you said, with loving parents, and her own room, and a puppy." Despite her best effort, Rorie clearly didn't believe a word she was saying.

"If so, we'll still want to help however we can. Set up a college fund, send her presents at Christmas. Whatever you want. But what if she's not?"

Rorie shut her eyes and sipped her tea. "There's boarding school, I guess. Maybe not at age four, but in a couple of years..." Her voice trailed off into a long sigh.

"True." A small part of her leapt at the suggestion, like being offered a lifeline out of the blue. Boarding school, though? The thought of banishing such a tiny thing to a boarding school made her feel like a villain straight out of a Dickens novel. She'd never go through with it. "Is that what *you* want?"

Rorie's shoulders slumped. "No. But I know that you said—"

"Never mind what I said. That was before. Neither one of us anticipated this."

Rorie crossed the room to set her tea on the desk. As Cecily followed with her eyes, she once again appreciated the room's full potential. "With some new furniture and a coat of paint, this could be a nice bedroom for her, don't you think?"

Rorie slipped her arm around Cecily's waist. Her expression remained guarded, but Cecily thought she saw a flicker of hope in her eyes. With a sigh, Cecily nestled her head against Rorie's shoulder. *Whatever you want to do, just tell me. I'm here for you.*

"Shell pink walls and a canopy bed," Rorie murmured, "with gingham and lace curtains."

Cecily turned her head and stared at Rorie, mouth agape. "Shell *pink*?" She hadn't been expecting *that*.

Rorie grinned. "What?"

"It's just so..." Cecily considered for a moment. "It's a bit of a departure from your usual neutral palette."

Rorie shrugged. "Maybe so, but it's exactly like the room my cousin had in Boston. It made me so jealous as a kid, I thought I would die. All the military housing and apartments we lived in had plain white walls, and we were never in one place long enough to decorate. All I could do was try to imagine it looking like something else."

"That's probably why you're such a good set designer," Cecily mused.

"Huh." Rorie's eyebrows scrunched as she seemed to contemplate this possibility. "You might be right. I never thought about it that way."

It was a detail about Rorie's childhood Cecily had never heard before, and another reminder of how different from one another their childhoods had been. Though she could have been dismayed at how much she still had to learn about Rorie, that wasn't where Cecily's thoughts were focused. Rorie had dropped her defenses in record time, and that memory and the emotions it stirred had come straight from her heart. *That's real progress.*

"Shell pink and gingham." Cecily shook her head as she took in Rorie's signature monochromatic clothing. "Never in a million years would I have guessed that one."

"If she doesn't like it, we can always repaint." Rorie kissed Cecily's cheek. "Are we really going to do this?" she whispered close to Cecily's ear.

"I think we really are." A shiver coursed through her as she embraced this leap of faith that they were preparing to take together. A decision so large and yet, because it was with Rorie, one that Cecily found easier to take. "As soon as Murray finds her, we'll do everything we can to bring her home."

Arms still entwined, they exited the bedroom, and Cecily paused in the hallway to switch off the light. "For now, all we can do is wait."

THREE

"WELCOME to the Sapphicsticated World Headquarters, ladies!" Cecily beamed as her friends entered the echoing warehouse. *World Headquarters* might be overstating the current situation, Cecily admitted to herself. It wasn't much to look at yet, that was for certain. Her broad smile faded to embarrassment as Frankie stumbled on a rough patch of concrete. "It's sort of a work in progress right now, so watch your step."

The new arrivals swiveled their heads to take it all in, seemingly unperturbed by the chaotic surroundings. Like Cecily, they grasped the creative potential the space offered and were suitably impressed. Sunshine filtered through dusty windows twenty feet overhead, illuminating a spacious interior that was easily large enough to house everything a young production company might need: offices, a generous recording studio, and even a small soundstage.

She'd only recently closed on the property and was still working with her architect to finalize the renovation plans before construction could begin in earnest. Though it still mostly resembled an abandoned storage warehouse, the presence of blueprints and power tools hinted that a transformation was in the works. It wouldn't approach the scale of Grant Studios, but it was an excellent start. Soon, this would be the home of Hollywood's newest production company, dedicated to bringing positive lesbian stories to the world. It was that mission, rather than the still somewhat rough outward appearance of the space, that brought such appreciative grins to the assembled women's faces.

"It won't be completed for several weeks, but I just couldn't wait to show it to you, and to hold our first official meeting of the board of directors." Cecily motioned the group toward the far end of the warehouse. "Come back this way and we'll have a seat in the 'boardroom.'"

Her fingers traced quotes in the air as she said it, and the reason soon became clear. At the far end of the massive space was a fifteen-foot-long metal table, centered on a piece of blue industrial carpet, and surrounded by a dozen chairs. Lacking even walls, it wasn't really a room at all, but with a little imagination, it was easy enough to pretend.

Dee tapped her knuckles on the rusting monstrosity of a table that dwarfed the corner. "Did you buy this little gem here, or did it come with the space?"

"Trust me, it was here when I bought the place," Cecily replied with a good-natured shrug. "It'll be out of here as soon as I can find enough strong backs to lift it."

Dee's wife, Peggy, chuckled. "It does look like it would be more at home somewhere else. Like maybe in Hitler's bunker." A seasoned accountant at a major Hollywood studio, Peggy had left her job to join Sapphicsticated as the head of finance. Her arms were piled high with reports, which she allowed to flop onto the table's surface with a loud *thwack!* As she sat. "At least it's solid."

The others nodded. In addition to Cecily, Rorie, Peggy,

and Dee, their friends Lu, Frankie, and Rhonda were also in attendance. Together they formed the board of directors, though only Cecily and Peggy would be employed full time to start. Lu, formerly a writer on Rorie's show, would be in charge of soliciting and evaluating scripts on a part-time basis, and tackling any rewrites. The rest would lend their expertise and moral support in a less official, and—on strict orders from watchdog Peggy—entirely *unpaid*, capacity.

"Well, here we are!" Cecily's stomach fluttered as the women took their places around the table, and the reality of the situation hit her full force. *I'm going to be a Hollywood producer!* But what, exactly, did a producer actually do? She gulped. Better shut the door on that thought before it induced full-scale panic. "I have to confess, I've been dreaming about this for a while, but now that we're actually here, I'm not sure how to begin."

"First things first," Rhonda said from the far end of the table. "I think congratulations are in order for a certain someone's Emmy nomination!"

Cecily blushed as an enthusiastic smattering of applause broke out from the group. The nomination was a thrill, to be sure, though with all the upheaval in her and Rorie's personal lives the past several weeks, it felt more like something that had happened in a dream. Only the three canvas sacks of fan mail that her agent's office had sent over provided tangible proof that it was true.

"Really, y'all. Thank you." Her cheeks tingled with added heat at the reemergence of her old southern accent, but it was beyond her control, the type of thing that was most likely to sneak past her filter when her emotional guard was down. Like it currently was. The fact that it had been Rhonda who made the gesture made it that much more touching. It had taken a long time for the makeup artist with a string of unlucky love affairs to be able to look beyond Cecily's history of being married to a man long enough to warm up to her. Cecily was grateful now to count her as a friend.

Looking around the table, her spirits were dampened by the wistful look on Rorie's face, as well as Dee's. It was a reminder that despite critical acclaim and a strong fan base, their own show had been snubbed for a second award season in a row. Cecily's heart broke for her partner, who had such a strong professional history of winning. She knew Rorie saw it as a personal failure. After not getting a single Emmy nod, rumors were flying all around town that the show could face the chopping block by the end of the year.

With all the other changes they were facing, including Cecily's move, the new company, and the possibility of Rorie's niece coming to live with them, Cecily worried that the uncertainty at work was adding considerably to Rorie's stress. That's why it was even more vital that Cecily hit the ground running so that her new company wouldn't heap any additional concerns on Rorie's already overflowing plate.

"According to everyone I've talked to," Cecily said, ready to get down to business, "the most important thing to tackle is choosing our first project. Lu, do you have any prospects to report?"

Lu straightened her glasses at the mention of her name. "I do. Thanks in part to the added press you've been doing leading up to the Emmy's, scripts and proposals have been flooding into the company email nonstop." She passed a stack of papers around the table as she spoke. "A lot of them are about as bad as you are probably imagining, but I've compiled summaries of the best ones for us to consider, and a few are extremely promising."

"So, what are we thinking?" Rhonda asked, leafing through the handout. "Television series? A movie?"

"Why not all of it?" Frankie asked with a grin. "I'd be happy to star in any one of these." Laughter erupted around the table at their friend's shameless ambition. "What? It would be nice to finally play a role that was guaranteed not to get killed off. No one dies in any of these, right?" she added, scowling at the list of projects.

"Nope," Lu reassured her. "I weeded those out first. Rule number one of Sapphicsticated, Inc. is no lesbian dies on our watch."

"Great!" Frankie said. "Then let's do them all!"

"Hold on a minute." Peggy gurgled in obvious fiduciary distress. "Optioning them is one thing, but as the money person, I'm going to suggest a more manageable start in terms of projects to produce. What about a web series?"

"Just a web series?" Rhonda raised an eyebrow as she looked toward Cecily. "I thought Miss Moneybags was bankrolling this operation."

Cecily laughed, though the full extent of the costs involved in running the operation had been a stark revelation to her when Peggy first explained it. "I'm investing in the facilities and payroll, but even I don't have the funds to spring for most of what's on that list all by myself, at least not that I can risk on my own. Do you know how much a feature length movie costs to produce? We'll need investors for anything bigger."

"And where do those come from?" Rhonda's brows knit together. "I mean, I love you guys, but I don't have a lot of cash to spare. Just sayin'."

Cecily fidgeted in her seat, hesitant to admit that she wasn't exactly certain herself. It was one of the many aspects of her new role that she would be learning on the job. Try as she might, she'd been unable to locate a book for dummies on running a production company.

"We could try crowdfunding." All heads swiveled to look at Lu, who had voiced the suggestion. "A friend of mine wrote a screenplay and was able to raise most of the money to produce it that way."

"I've heard of that, too," Peggy added. "You offer incentives for different donations, like for fifty dollars you send them a movie poster, things like that."

"That's a great idea!" Cecily smiled broadly, her spirits lifting as she pictured them all gathered around the table rolling posters one Saturday afternoon. "We could easily do that."

"What about renting out the soundstage when it's not in use?" asked Frankie. "An online friend of mine just mentioned a friend of theirs who's some hotshot indie filmmaker. I don't know all the details, but she's looking for a place on weekends for a new project. I *do* know she's willing to pay."

"As long as we're not using it," Cecily said with a shrug, "I don't see why not. Put her in touch with Peggy to work out a fee. Sounds like some easy income."

As the group discussed which projects to pursue, the sound of a door slamming echoed from the far end of the warehouse, followed by the clicking of two sets of shoes on the concrete floor. Cecily looked up to see her friend and fellow voice actor, Stephanie, making her way toward them. She'd invited her to join the meeting to offer advice on sound equipment, but Cecily was surprised to see she'd brought a guest, a tall, professional-looking woman who seemed vaguely familiar, but Cecily couldn't quite place her.

"Stephanie!" Cecily stood and embraced her friend. "Everyone, this is Stephanie. We worked together at Grant Studios."

"And do you remember Jill?" Stephanie asked, motioning to the woman beside her.

"Jill Davidson," the woman said, holding out her hand.

"Yes, of course!" Cecily shook her hand, suddenly recognizing her as an associate producer from Grant Studios. They hadn't worked on the same show, but Cecily was certain they'd been introduced at some point.

"I hope you don't mind me tagging along," Jill added, "but when Stephanie mentioned your new production company, I was intrigued. I thought maybe you could use some advice."

"Oh, thank God," Peggy piped up from across the table. "Someone with actual experience. No offense, Boss," she added as Cecily's mouth dropped in mock offense.

Jill laughed. "Don't worry. I'm not trying to step on any toes. I've got more than my share of commitments at Grant. But your mission is of personal interest to me. I'd like to help, if I may."

Personal interest? Cecily lifted her brows in mild surprise. *So, she's one of us, then?* She hesitated. Pride told her she could manage alone. The knowledge that her browser history contained seventeen variations on a search of 'what does a Hollywood producer do?' argued otherwise. She glanced around the table, reminding herself of how many people were counting on this venture to succeed. *This is no time for vanity.*

Finally, she replied. "Thank you, Jill. We can use all the help we can get."

"Well, tell me what you have planned so far." Jill nodded with interest as Cecily touched on the highlights of the meeting, but visibly blanched at the mention of a crowdfunding campaign. "Let me stop you there. Do you know what's involved with that type of thing?"

Cecily felt a nervous tickle in her belly. She'd never heard of the concept before today. Though it had sounded like a good idea, she had a feeling she wouldn't like whatever Jill had to say about it. "Not entirely. But some of the others said they've heard of it being successful."

"Yes and no. I'm not saying they can't raise money, but they can be more of a headache than they're worth. Do you have a distribution arrangement with a major studio?" Cecily shook her head, uncertain even what that would entail. "That's what I figured. Which means you'll be responsible for processing all of the rewards to donors yourself. DVDs, posters, memorabilia... I'm guessing that none of you have had the pleasure of getting several hundred small donations only to realize that by the time you pay to print and ship movie posters, you've basically used up the money. And that's only if you're willing to spend every weekend for months rolling and stuffing the tubes yourself."

Cecily winced. In her imagination, they'd finished the work in a single day. She had enough obligations to worry about without spending all of her free time, too. "What would you suggest?"

"Something much less amateur."

"Uh huh." Cecily bristled at Jill's choice of words, but bit back any further response.

"You'll want to start with a few major donors, handpicked, with a personal stake in seeing your project succeed."

That was, of course, precisely what Cecily dreamed of. There was just one problem. "Where exactly do I find people like that?"

"I'll send you a few names. You'll have to make the pitch, but these are people I think will at least be interested in hearing what you have to say."

She said it with such assuredness that Cecily nearly swooned. Even in her casual weekend attire, her brown hair pulled back into a ponytail, Jill was statuesque and perfectly put together. She radiated confidence, and the validity of her credentials was bolstered each time she spoke. Cecily's insides grew cold with a mix of envy and self-doubt. In short, Jill Davidson was everything that Cecily was not.

The buzzing of the front door bell announced the arrival of the sandwich delivery, so Cecily adjourned the meeting and invited Jill and Stephanie to join them for lunch. As she finished setting out the platters on the oversized table, she felt the warm press of a body behind her, and all her built-up tension drain away as Rorie's strong thumbs massaged the sore spots in her neck.

"So, what do you think?" Cecily murmured, marveling at her partner's instinct for finding just the right spot like a pro.

"I think you need to relax, Cici. Your back's so tied up in knots, I'm surprised you can stand upright. You've got a good group here, and you're off to a solid start. Enjoy it a little."

"How about that Jill?" Cecily's neck stiffened just saying her name, and she grimaced as Rorie's thumb dug into the new knot.

"She seems to be the real deal. I think you should learn what you can from her."

Cecily grunted, though it was true. "I guess I can't decide whether I'm jealous of her, or developing a crush."

Rorie snorted.

Cecily glared. "What?"

"Nothing."

Cecily eyed her suspiciously until Rorie relented.

"Okay, fine. It's just that you don't seem to be the only one here in danger of developing a crush."

Rorie gestured with her chin toward the far end of the table where Rhonda and Jill seemed deeply engaged in conversation, their sandwiches sitting untouched on their plates. Jill must have said something particularly amusing, because just then Rhonda giggled, flipping her fiery red hair behind her shoulder in the most blatantly flirtatious way.

Cecily's eyes widened. "You don't think…"

Rorie's lips twitched. "Are you kidding? Did you not see the way she was staring at her from the minute Jill walked into the room?"

"No. I was too worried about all the ways I was going to screw up my new business."

"Well, I saw it. In fact, I think there's still a puddle of drool on the table where Rhonda was sitting."

Cecily stole another glance at the women. "Is Jill her usual type?" Her insides were even more jittery now than before, and she couldn't put her finger on why.

"Not really. But maybe it means this time it would have a shot at working out."

Cecily nodded, knowing all too well Rhonda's unfortunate history of dating women only to be left high and dry, usually for a man. It had warped her romantic views considerably. Their friend had all but sworn off love, but it was pretty clear watching her now that Rhonda was falling fast and hard, and that this new woman seemed to return her interest.

Cecily felt a warning twinge. She knew next to nothing about Jill, but something about the idea of her with Rhonda was making her nervous. This match could turn out well, or be a disaster waiting to happen, one that she might end up in the middle of. Or worse, be blamed for.

Maybe I should tell Jill no thank you after all. Her insides churned at the prospect of going it alone after the unexpected gift of Jill's offer to help. Cecily longed to succeed, but she lacked the expertise to guarantee it would happen. Her only choice was to accept her offer, and brace herself for the consequences.

FOUR

AFTER THE MEETING ENDED, Cecily remained to sign off on work orders for the construction crew that would start on Monday. The sky was a deep indigo with just the faint glow of orange and pink in the west when she arrived home. Though she was excited to see the plans for Sapphicsticated coming together, her body dragged with fatigue as she searched her purse for her keys.

Inside, Rorie was stretched out on the couch watching television. "Dinner's on the counter!" she called out the moment Cecily's foot hit the entryway floor.

After years of being the one who stayed home to make sure dinner was on the table, Cecily felt disoriented by the announcement. Had she ever come home to a hot meal that someone else had cooked? Not that she could recall. But though her stomach rumbled, guilt weighed on her. Rorie worked full time and had already spent most of her day off at the board meeting. She didn't need to cook, too.

"I'm sure I could've made do with some leftovers. You didn't need to make anything."

"Don't worry, I didn't. I ordered a pizza. Grab a slice and come watch a movie with me."

Now that's my favorite kind of cooking. She should have known Rorie would know the best way to handle the situation. She surveyed the box with amusement. A partial piece of Rorie's favorite extra meats special sat beside four pristine slices of garden vegetable, light on the cheese. Oh, how well Rorie knew her.

While she wasn't as hard on herself over her appearance as she'd been while a regular on *Portland Blue*, the prospect of squeezing herself into a designer dress for the Emmy's next month had inspired Cecily to start watching her figure again. She'd been doing it quietly, as she knew Rorie worried when she got too obsessed with her weight, but clearly, she couldn't put anything past the woman she loved.

Cecily considered her low-calorie half of the pie and made a face. She doubted any of the women at today's board of directors meeting would torture themselves by eating a pizza with almost no cheese, Jill included, and they all looked just fine. What a relief it would be to leave the most hyper-image-conscious aspects of the Hollywood scene behind her for good when her trip down the red carpet was over. But for now, she would persist. She was already an actress 'of a certain age', and the tabloids could be brutal. No need to give them ammunition.

It was the price of fame. She wasn't sure she'd ever stop worrying about what people thought of her appearance completely, but at least she looked forward to a day she could feel less like a specimen under a microscope. Until then, she would have to be content to slide a single slice of pizza onto her paper plate, and try not to think too longingly of the taste of thick-sliced pepperoni and spicy sausage smothered in three-cheese blend.

A blast of icy air hit Cecily's bare shoulders as she passed beneath the living room vent. It had been a typically hot August day, but as the sun set, the air-conditioning was finally gaining the upper hand. As she sat on the corner of the couch, Cecily looked longingly at the lightweight blanket that Rorie had draped across her legs. Perhaps sensing her gaze, Rorie lifted the corner of the blanket and beckoned for her to climb under.

Rorie sucked in her breath as Cecily's feet made contact with her bare skin. "Your toes are cold!"

Ignoring her protests as always, Cecily buried the offending toes further beneath Rorie's warm calves and snuggled the rest of her body in close. Rorie didn't really mind, she just liked to tease.

The plate in Cecily's hand was little more than an accessory at this point. She'd already scarfed down most of the pizza on her walk to the living room, and a final bite polished off the rest. She hadn't realized how much of an appetite a full day of work could produce, or at least how hungry she could get when the workday was spent without the benefit of a studio catering department. *God, I'm spoiled. I'd better learn how to be a normal working woman, and fast.* She thought of Jill, confident and knowledgeable. That's how she wanted to be. If she had to spend every minute on it, day and night, she vowed someday to achieve it.

She tossed the plate onto the coffee table and settled back with a satisfied sigh as Rorie let her arm fall loosely around Cecily's waist.

"What are we watching?" she asked as Rorie aimed the remote at the television screen.

"Whatever's next in the queue."

Cecily shrugged. She didn't really care. Their weekend ritual of watching a movie had mostly become an excuse to spend a few lazy hours together. Snuggled in each other's arms, half the time at least one of them was asleep by the time the credits rolled. But not tonight.

An electric shock coursed through her as Rorie slipped her fingers beneath the hem of Cecily's top, tracing tiny circles with the tips of her nails against Cecily's bare flesh. Her whole body tingled. *Not sleepy tonight, Darling?*

Music blared as the movie began, but it mattered even less than usual what was playing on the screen. Judging by the way Cecily's body was responding to Rorie's caresses, neither of them would be giving it the least bit of attention past the opening credits.

Cecily closed her eyes and tried to clear her mind of everything but the gentle pressure of Rorie's fingers on her back, innocent enough now, but holding the promise of more. Despite the waves of pleasure washing over her, flashes of the day invaded her thoughts, shattering the peacefulness she was trying so hard to cultivate.

"What's wrong?" Rorie's hands worked the knots at the base of Cecily's neck. "You're even more tense than you were at the meeting. Aren't you happy with how it went?"

"I am. It's not that. It's just, I keep thinking about Jill. And that's not what I meant," she added, anticipating whatever teasing response was forming on Rorie's lips about her having a crush, and nipping it in the bud. "I just keep thinking about her and Rhonda." She winced as she considered the ways in which what she'd said sounded just as risqué as her first statement.

"Oh. Yeah, Rhonda sure seemed smitten."

"Yeah." She was relieved that Rorie had given her a pass, just this once, on her unintended innuendo. What she had to tell her wasn't a joking matter. "There's something else. I had a chance to chat with Jill after everyone left, and I kind of got the same vibe from her. Her ears perked up like a curious puppy every time I so much as mentioned Rhonda's name."

"That's good, right?" Rorie pressed her lips against the spot on Cecily's neck that she'd finished rubbing, the wet warmth of contact sending a delicious shiver down the length of Cecily's spine. Rorie's hands, no longer occupied with her neck, glided beneath her shirt, skimming her abdomen until they reached her breasts and once more began tracing delicate circles along the lacy fabric of her bra.

"Yes. I suppose so." She closed her eyes again and tried to relax into the caresses, but couldn't quite manage it. The confusing memory weighed heavily on her. "It's just..."

"It's just what?" Rorie murmured as she nibbled Cecily's earlobe.

"It's just..." Cecily's words trailed off momentarily, unable to form words through the pleasure that was making her insides contract. "I remembered something from when I was still working at Grant last year. There was a reception one evening, for my show and several others. That's where I recognized Jill from. I was introduced to her there."

"Uh huh." Rorie's teeth grazed the sensitive flesh behind Cecily's ear.

"And," Cecily continued, sucking air between her teeth as she struggled to keep hold of her train of thought in the face of Rorie's latest distraction, "and, I'm not completely sure, but I could have sworn I met her date, too. And it was definitely *not* a woman."

"Oh." Rorie's low groan vibrated against her neck.

Cecily nearly groaned, too, at the fact that her revelation had brought Rorie's attentions to a halt when she was *so* close to the edge. But the moment had eluded her for now, so she might as well finish her thought. "Given Rhonda's history, I'm wondering if we should warn her."

Rorie's breath still warmed the back of Cecily's neck, but the fact that her lips had gone completely still hinted that she was deep in contemplation. Finally, she replied. "No. I think we should leave it alone."

"Are you sure?" Cecily rolled her body to face Rorie. "She's been through this so many times before."

Rorie gave her head a vigorous shake. "But she really hasn't. Not the way you're thinking. Rhonda has a type, and I told you before that Jill isn't it."

"But maybe she is, if it turns out that Jill's bisexual…"

"Think about it, Cici. Why should that matter?"

Cecily frowned. It shouldn't, of course. She knew better than to buy into the hateful old stereotypes that suggested bisexuals were unfaithful by nature. But Rhonda was certainly convinced it was true, and she told her story so persuasively that Cecily was embarrassed to realize she'd begun to believe it without question.

"Jill's sexuality, or anyone else's for that matter, has nothing to do with it. The girls she flirts with have one thing in common, they're all immature and self-indulgent little starlets, looking for 'experiences' to add authenticity to their acting. And Rhonda's all too willing to help them mark off the lesbian box. I've tried to convince Rhonda of this before, except she's too stubborn to listen."

"Then what do we do?"

"Nothing. This is a lesson Rhonda needs to figure out on her own. Besides," Rorie's gaze drifted down toward Cecily's top, which had gone askew as she turned and now exposed the better part of her little rounded belly. Rorie's eyes glinted with mischief. "I have more important things to think about right now."

Heat consumed her as Rorie's palms skimmed her torso, taking the errant shirt with them. She grinned as the fabric cleared her head and went sailing behind her, likely landing somewhere in the vicinity of her discarded paper plate. Her lacy black bra followed swiftly after. She settled with her bare back against the soft upholstery as Rorie hovered above her, just far enough away that Cecily could anticipate the heat of her body but couldn't quite feel it. Her nipples formed taut peaks against the chilly air.

"Should we move to the bedroom?" Cecily swallowed hard as Rorie's tongue seared the hollow of her throat. "I doubt we're going to be paying any attention to the television."

Rorie shook her head as her lips trailed down Cecily's chest. "We've got the whole place to ourselves. We can do whatever we want, anywhere we want. Kitchen. Living room." She punctuated each location on the list with a kiss. "On a bear skin rug in front of the fireplace."

Cecily giggled in part from the mental image that created, and in part because Rorie had arrived at the most ticklish spot at the top of her tummy. "We don't have a bear skin rug. Or a fireplace."

"Minor details." She continued her descent despite, or perhaps spurred on by, Cecily's gleeful squirming. Skirt and panties soared across the room to find their friends.

Cecily's body rocked gently, her heels massaging the muscles of Rorie's back, who was slowly working her lips up toward Cecily's center by way of her goosebump-covered thigh. Cecily raised her buttocks so that Rorie could position a throw pillow beneath her. One of her favorites, she noted for no real reason beyond trying not to lose control as the fabric brushed against her most sensitive parts. Her bottom wiggled eagerly. With no place to be and no one to interrupt, they could be here all night. *Time to settle in and get comfortable.*

Rorie's cell phone, which apparently had quite a cruel sense of timing, chose that moment to ring. Rorie tensed. The hand she'd been using to knead Cecily's breast paused midstroke. Her breath remained so tantalizingly close between Cecily's thighs that the second ring made Cecily curse out loud.

"Shit! Do you need to get that?" If Rorie didn't answer it, she might, and the caller probably wouldn't like what she had to say.

"Nope." Her fingers resumed their rhythmic motion across Cecily's nipple. "They can leave a message."

At least, Cecily was fairly certain that's what she'd said. It's what she thought she'd heard in that fraction of a second that her brain was allowed to process the conversation before Rorie's determined mouth made contact and she lost all ability to think. Ringing phones, fire alarms, minor nuclear explosions—none of them would have made a lasting impression after that.

It was several hours later before either of the women gave another thought to the phone call. Somewhere in the midst of their encounter they'd had the presence of mind to turn off the television, which by the time they noticed it had moved onto a movie neither of them remembered even putting in their queue. And so now the room was dark, except for a single blinking light trying to alert Rorie to an unheard voicemail.

Eventually, its persistence paid off. Stifling a groan, Rorie rolled her body away from Cecily's and picked up the phone. She listened to the message once through, then replayed it on speaker.

"Ms. Mulloy, this is Murray. I've found Bryn. She's living in a group home in Mississippi. The next move is up to you."

Cecily's pulse raced. She reached for the switch on a nearby lamp, bathing the room in sudden illumination and revealing the full range of emotions that played across Rorie's face.

"A group home. I guess that means there's no foster family in the picture."

Cecily nodded. "Just us." She opened her arms and Rorie relaxed into her embrace. Cecily thought she could feel Rorie's heart pounding as wildly as her own. "It's late now. You can call him tomorrow and get things rolling."

She closed her eyes, soaking in the quiet intimacy of the moment as if it was their last. It might well be. If her years of parenthood had taught her anything, it was that pretty soon, their life together was going to change completely. Again. But the newly improved and confident version of Cecily welcomed the challenge.

FIVE

"I LOOK LIKE A POODLE." Cecily grimaced at her reflection in the limousine's tinted window, which was streaked on the outside with droplets from the falling rain. It was at least her dozenth complaint since they'd left the house, and she knew that she fully deserved the eye roll Rorie gave her in response. She was even annoying herself.

"No, you don't."

"I do. This weather is making it frizz."

"Don't talk to me about frizz. If I hadn't spent six hours having new braids put in for this grand occasion of yours, my hair would be sticking out a foot in every direction."

"I should have just insisted the woman at the salon put it up in my usual style."

"I don't think a ponytail held in place with a twenty-year-old scrunchy is entirely appropriate for the Emmy's."

Cecily stuck out her tongue. "That's what you said about my yoga pants. I hate this dress."

"You love that dress. It's a custom-made Christian Siriano." The heat was palpable as Rorie's gaze traveled the length of Cecily's figure. "Plus, you look sexy as hell in it."

Cecily's cheeks tingled and burned. Rorie was right. The dress *was* amazing. When she'd bought designer labels in the past it had been more about warding off the Mean Mom Brigade than actually liking the style, but this dress was easily the most fantastically glamorous thing she'd ever worn in her life. She might wear it daily, if it came three sizes bigger. "But I'm wearing so many layers of Spanx that I can't breathe."

She eyed Rorie's black tuxedo jacket through a green fog of envy. When she'd told her what she planned to wear, Cecily had urged Rorie to have a gown made, too. Her girlfriend preferred a muted palette, but she didn't usually trend so masculine in her style, so the choice had been a surprise. Rorie had argued that it was so Cecily could shine extra bright on her special day, but sitting in the backseat feeling like a stuffed sausage, Cecily guessed the more likely truth. With no chance that she would be called on stage to accept an award of her own, Rorie had opted for an outfit that didn't pinch or bind, and did so without a modicum of regret. *Smart woman.*

The fact that Rorie hadn't been nominated for her role as production designer for her show was still enough of a sore topic that Cecily worried about the effect today's ceremony would have on her. It wasn't the award itself. Rorie had won plenty of things before, including an arguably more prestigious Academy Award. She was grieving over the difficult news that her show's upcoming season would be its last. While they didn't rely on the income to live on, Rorie loved her work, and finding a new job was always a stressful period of transition even for a sought after talent such as her.

Cecily assumed this to be the reason for the scowl on her girlfriend's face now, until she caught sight of the phone in her hand. Rorie had started going through her emails as they inched with excruciating slowness closer to the red carpet drop off, and whatever she'd just read seemed to have upset her.

"What is it?"

Rorie filled her cheeks with air, letting it out in a sudden burst. "Red tape. I swear to God, the state of Mississippi has apparently never processed an out of state guardianship request before."

Cecily's mood soured even more. Paperwork had been flying back and forth between Rorie and her attorney, Helen, and the foster care home Bryn was in, for weeks. It was turning into a perfect nightmare of inefficient bureaucracy. "What happened this time?"

"They say my birthdate is in the wrong place on my driver's license, and do I have a different one. Like what, one from *Mississippi*? California puts the date where they put the date! How am I supposed to change that?"

"I'm sorry, sweetheart. Maybe it's time I called my dad?" Cecily's father, the longtime senator from Louisiana, had shown surprising acceptance of his daughter's relationship despite his conservative political leanings. She believed he might be motivated to pull some strings with acquaintances in his neighboring state on Rorie's behalf if she asked him nicely.

Rorie had rebuffed previous suggestions of the sort, and did so again. "No. I know how tense things are between you and your family. I'll just call Helen tomorrow and have her try to deal with it."

"The problem's not Daddy, you know. Never has been. It's my mother." Anger bubbled up at the memory of how her mother had wavered between chilly politeness and complete neglect during the almost two years since Cecily had announced she was a lesbian. The fact that she'd done it at the Thanksgiving table in front of a few dozen political and business associates might have had a little to do with her mother's reaction... but it still stung. Cecily was far from ready to let bygones be bygones.

"But they're a team, aren't they? He'll have to run it past her. You know how it is. She'll insist on having her say."

It was true. Her father had stood up to presidents, but even he feared the Dragon Lady of Baton Rouge. "I don't care. This is important." That wasn't to say that Cecily wasn't still brainstorming ways to get around her mother. She just hadn't discovered one that would work yet.

At last, the driver pulled into the staging area and it was their turn to make a grand entrance. For a moment, all other thoughts subsided save for the thrill of walking down the red carpet on Rorie's arm. Lights flashed as photographers snapped pictures, and the crowds gathered behind velvet ropes waved and cheered. But once they had reached the tented area reserved for participants and media, the fuss quickly died down and Cecily found herself standing off to one side while talk show hosts and reporters rushed to interview much bigger stars than her.

"I feel like I'm back in gym class," she said to Rorie with a pout, "waiting to be chosen for a dodgeball team and afraid of getting picked last."

"It's not as bad as that. The people from E! asked you about your dress as soon as we arrived."

"That was fifteen minutes ago." Cecily couldn't help but think that Rorie was grasping at straws to cheer her up. The woman who'd interviewed her hadn't even remembered her name. Just as she'd suspected all along, her nomination was a fluke, and the character she'd played long forgotten.

Cecily's pulse quickened as she spied a gentleman in a classic black tuxedo who was trying to catch her eye. She smiled broadly, but his gaze shot past her and came to rest on

Rorie. Cecily's shoulders slouched. "I think that guy over there is trying to get *your* attention, though."

Rorie glanced in the direction she had pointed. "Oh, Max. I worked on one of his shows a few years back. I heard he's got a new pilot in the works for next season."

"Should you go talk to him?"

Rorie looked uncertain. "I don't want to leave you by yourself."

"Don't be silly." Cecily put on a brave face that she hoped did not convey how much she wished she were back at home watching the Emmy's on TV rather than participating in the affair, and gave Rorie a nudge. "You need to be networking. Maybe he has a lead on a new project."

Without Rorie beside her, Cecily felt even more awkward than before, and still none of the reporters showed the least bit of interest in approaching her. *Not even the tabloids*, she thought ruefully. A year ago, they would have tripped over themselves trying to get a comment from her about her former co-star, Brad Perris. And she would have loathed every second of it. Now she watched them with the expression of a puppy at a shelter hoping to get adopted. *What a pathetic business this can be.*

Her stomach rumbled so loudly that she could hear it even through the five layers of spandex that encased it. She'd skipped lunch in an effort to look as slim as possible in her dress. It was a serious miscalculation. Not only did no one here seem to give a hoot how she looked in her dress, but she was pretty sure she might pass out before she had a chance to grab her first appetizer at the after party. The only consolation was that if she actually did keel over, it might make the front page of the entertainment section.

Spotting a refreshment table off to the side made her giddy, even though it was somewhat picked over and the choices were limited. Cecily wondered in amusement how many other women had made the same mistake she had. The cheese platter had been reduced to crumbs, and the fruit salad was little more than garnish, but there was some sort of pink mousse on a cracker that looked promising. Cecily popped one in her mouth, delighted at the delicious explosion of salmon flavor on her tongue. She eyed the platter greedily and shoved two more in her mouth as Rorie reemerged from the crowd.

"You have something pink on your upper lip," Rorie pointed out as she used her index finger to remove the blob and wipe it on a cocktail napkin.

"Oh, great. If any of the paparazzi were going to take a picture of me tonight, I'll bet that's the one they got."

"Who cares? You hate those rags anyway, right?"

Cecily pondered this for a moment. "Funny thing about that. Apparently, tabloid reporters are much more attractive once they've lost all interest in you."

Rorie laughed. "Isn't that how life always works? Come on. You're an Emmy-nominated actress. You're hardly a nobody."

"But look around this place." From where Cecily stood, she could count half a dozen stars who were household names. Not to mention years younger. "I mean, I was on *Portland Blue* for less than a season, and I'm only here tonight because I died convincingly. The show's moved on so much since then, no one remembers who I am."

"That's not true."

"It is. Just a few months ago, I got at least a bag of fan mail a week from my agent. Now they trickle in one by one." She pouted. "It just makes me question why I'm here tonight."

"Because you're talented and you gave an Emmy-worthy performance." Rorie's tone was matter of fact. She wasn't trying to bolster Cecily's ego, just reminding her in case she'd forgotten.

Cecily was surprised to feel a genuine smile on her face as some of her gloom lifted. "Thank you. I *am* really proud of that scene. But you know who I really think should win? Martha Jones."

"Oooh." Rorie nodded appreciatively. "She really is good."

"Right? She's the Meryl Streep of television. Plus, you know who she's dating? Brad Perris!" She grinned as Rorie's jaw dropped.

"No! Your ex?" Rorie teased as Cecily's face flushed scarlet at the memory of the made-up tabloid love affair between her and her former co-star.

"Stop it." Cecily glared. "Isn't that ironic, though?"

Rorie smirked. "Hey, you know how to get all these paparazzi to notice you, don't you? Go find Martha and whisper something mysteriously in her ear. It'll be front page of the tabloids tomorrow. Brad's ex threatens his new lover with death!"

"That's just... so wrong." Even so, Cecily's spirits were buoyed by a reminder of the upside of no longer being worthy of tabloid attention. Sometimes she hated how much the trappings of Hollywood still mattered to her. "Come on, it's time for us to find our seats. Let's get this over with so we can go home and eat pizza in our pajamas."

They were seated in the VIP section. Despite the afternoon's media snubs, at least the organizers had remembered that Cecily was an award nominee and deserving of certain perks. Once seated, Cecily could no longer complain that no one was taking her picture. There were camera crews everywhere, recording every minute detail in extreme close-up. The sudden increase in attention made her belly rumble and twist.

As the lights dimmed and the show began, the camera crews moved on to other stars. Cecily relaxed into her seat to watch the show, but her stomach continued to churn. She tugged discreetly at the elastic of her undergarments, desperate to make room as her insides seemed to expand and push against the waistband. A series of quiet belches provided temporary relief as she squirmed in her seat.

Rorie turned, a funny look on her face. "Are you okay?" she whispered.

Cecily nodded unconvincingly. "Nervous, I think. And a little warm. Is it warm in here to you?" Even as she asked it, she could feel beads of sweat forming along her brow and at the base of her neck. Incongruously, a chill shook her bare shoulders with such force that all her muscles tightened in protest.

"I thought I'd seen your stage fright at its worst, but I've never seen you *this* nervous before. Did you prepare a speech, like I suggested?"

"Of course." While she doubted her chances of walking away with the award tonight, it would be just her luck to win and have nothing prepared, so she'd taken Rorie's advice and jotted down some thoughts on a notecard the day before.

She opened her mouth to explain this to Rorie, but released another belch instead. "Oh. God."

Rorie's eyes filled with concern. "You're not looking well."

"My stomach's a little off," Cecily whispered, as if it weren't readily apparent. "I'll be okay." Taking note of where they were in the program, Cecily glanced at her watch. They were maybe ten minutes away from the announcement of her category. A sharp pain jabbed her beneath the ribs. *Ten minutes?* She could make it that long, but only just.

Finally, the announcer approached the podium to list the

nominees for best supporting actress as a clip of each person's performance ran on giant screens. A spotlight blinded her. Cecily knew all cameras were fixed on her face, which by now had to be glowing in a slick sheen of sweat. A wave of dizziness hit full force as her pupils contracted in the blinding light.

"Cici?" Rorie hissed into her ear over the din of applause. "You're white as a sheet!"

Her insides flipped and groaned, and Cecily could manage nothing more than a curt nod in response. The announcer held the envelope and a tiny whisper in her head told her that if she could just hold out a minute longer, the winner was about to be read. Meanwhile in her mind, a chorus, complete with marching band, sang out that if she didn't make it to the bathroom immediately, she would in all likelihood die right there on the spot.

Jumping from her seat, Cecily barely registered the horrified expression on Rorie's face or the harsh murmurs of the audience as she tore down the aisle toward the exit. All she knew was that she had to get out of the auditorium before disaster struck. She prayed she would make it through the door in time.

ONE MINUTE Cecily had been sitting beside her, the next minute she was a flash of red satin racing toward the back of the auditorium at breakneck speed. Rorie's heart raced as she bolted from her seat and chased after her. She wasn't entirely sure what was wrong, but to make a scene like that in front of half of Hollywood, it couldn't be good.

Pushing her way past the photographers and camera crews that blocked the aisle, she reached the foyer perhaps a minute after Cecily, but her girlfriend was nowhere to be seen. The space was empty except for a security guard who wore a startled expression on her face.

"I'm looking for Cecily DuPont. Have you seen her?"

The security guard gave a shaky laugh. "She was kind of hard to miss. Just a minute and I'll see where they've taken her."

Taken her? An image flashed in her mind of Cecily being wheeled away on a stretcher. Melodramatic, yes, but then again, this was Cecily they were talking about. She wouldn't have it any other way.

After a brief conversation over a walkie-talkie, the woman motioned for Rorie to follow. "She's in my boss' office. This way."

They passed from the elegant lobby through a nondescript door and into a long, plain hallway. The guard removed a key ring that jangled from her belt and unlocked a door about halfway down. Inside the small office sat a bedraggled Cecily, her makeup smeared. She was wearing a set of janitor's coveralls in place of her gown.

"Cici!" Rorie lunged the distance from the door to Cecily's chair and knelt beside her. "What happened?"

Cecily left out a moan. "I threw up."

"Oh, honey—"

"All over my Christian Siriano gown!" Cecily let out a wailing groan. At that moment, another security guard appeared in the doorway, holding out a transparent plastic trash bag that appeared to contain the sad remains of Cecily's designer dress. Cecily broke down in tears, and with no idea how to make things better, Rorie wanted nothing more than to curl into a ball until it all went away.

"I've called your driver," the guard offered sympathetically, "but he's completely parked in. It could be half an hour before they can move enough cars for him to get out."

This was typical of Hollywood awards shows, so the news wasn't a complete surprise. Because of the limited space, arrivals and departures were a highly-choreographed affair. Limousines were carefully parked according to the approximate time their corresponding celebrity was expected to leave. As a nominee, Cecily would normally have lingered for photos and interviews after the show, and her car had therefore been assigned one of the last time slots to pick her up for the circuit of after parties. Understanding all of this, however, did not improve Rorie's sense of helplessness.

"We could call you an Uber?"

"Yes, thank you." Rorie looked once more at the sobbing, frizzy-haired, makeup streaked Cecily. She would die if anyone saw her like this. "Is there a backdoor where it could meet us?"

"Of course. And don't worry about the coveralls. They're hers to keep."

Not that anyone would want them back.

The look on the guard's face mirrored her own helplessness. She was just as out of place as Rorie was next to a now sobbing-and-hiccupping Cecily. When the woman's walkie-talkie beeped, summoning her back to the lobby, Rorie thought she'd never seen someone exit a room so fast.

After the guard departed, Rorie turned to Cecily. "Do you think it was just nerves, Cici?"

Cecily clutched her stomach with a grimace and shook her head vehemently.

"Maybe something you ate?"

"I think it was the salmon mousse," Cecily answered with a pathetic whine.

"Seriously?" Despite her partner's obvious distress, Rorie couldn't help but laugh. "The salmon mousse?"

Cecily's eyes narrowed. "What? Why is that funny?"

"You don't remember the Monty Python sketch from college?" Rorie shook her head at Cecily's confusion. "Come on, it's a classic. I really thought I'd taught you better than this. Remember, it's the one where the Grim Reaper shows up at a dinner party with all these obnoxious guests, and everyone died from eating the salmon mousse?"

"That sounds terrible." It was clear that in that moment, Cecily quite literally could feel their pain.

"You're only saying that now. Trust me, it's hilarious."

Cecily responded with a noncommittal harrumph. Seconds later her face took on a greenish tinge and she raced out of the office and down the hall. Rorie cringed at the loud flushing sound that emanated from behind the closed bathroom door. She had to admit that in this particular context, there wasn't anything remotely funny about salmon mousse poisoning.

It was exceedingly good luck that Cecily made it through the drive home without further incident, though twice the driver had to pull over due to false alarms. When the car stopped in front of their house, Rorie helped a weakened Cecily to the front door, the cuffs of her too-long coverall catching beneath her bare heels and soaking up rain water from where it had puddled on the driveway. By the time they reached the living room, she looked ready to collapse.

"Go sit on the couch while I make sure the bed's clear," Rorie directed. She bundled up bits of clothing and accessories that had been tried on and discarded that morning in their rush to get ready for the awards, and was heading toward the closet when the doorbell rang. "Just a minute, I'll get it."

"It's okay," she heard Cecily's voice call weakly from the living room. "I've got it."

"If it's the Grim Reaper, don't let him in!" She felt a little guilty, knowing how miserable Cecily was, but the worst of the symptoms had subsided so that it felt funny again, and the joke was just too much for her to resist. How often did someone actually get poisoned by salmon mousse, after all?

The sound of voices, Cecily's and an unknown female's, echoed down the hall into the master bedroom. It must be a neighbor stopping by after watching the Emmy's on television. Rorie frowned, realizing she had no idea if the person had come to offer congratulations or condolences. In all the confusion and haste to get Cecily home, neither of them had bothered to ask who won.

Shoving the armful of odds and ends into the closet to be dealt with in the morning, Rorie heard Cecily enter the bedroom. Her muscles clenched in apprehension at the haunted look on her partner's face.

"Cici, what is it now? You look like it really was the Grim Reaper."

"Worse," Cecily replied, her tone hollow. "It's my mother."

SIX

CECILY'S PALM scraped along the wall as she crept down the hallway, occasionally stopping to lean against it for support. It was shortly after sunup and the night had been a rough one, both emotionally and physically. The physical provocations from her food poisoning had mostly subsided before dawn. Though her body was weak, the prospect of breakfast seemed a welcome idea. The cause of her emotional distress, on the other hand, had yet to be addressed. She was most likely sitting at the kitchen table at that very moment, with a cup of coffee and a newspaper, in exactly the same manner as her mother had greeted every morning for longer than Cecily had been alive.

Sure enough, her mother looked up as she entered the room, coffee in one hand and paper spread open across the table in the breakfast nook.

"My goodness. Don't you look a fright."

"Morning, Mother." Keeping the *go fuck yourself* out of her tone was especially challenging in her current state, but she thought she'd mostly pulled it off, thanks to her many years of training. As if she didn't know, even without looking in a mirror, how awful she must look. *Not that she can resist a chance to point it out.*

Somehow, the woman was already dressed in a pantsuit without a single crease in it, her dyed blonde hair perfectly coiffed and makeup fully and artfully applied. She looked, Cecily thought, just exactly like the leader of an alien race that she'd always secretly suspected her mother to be. If it were ever revealed there'd been a mix-up at the hospital and Cecily wasn't really Margaret DuPont's child, she wasn't sure which of them would feel more vindicated.

"Looks like that Jones girl won."

Cecily's beleaguered brain, deprived of both fuel and caffeine for much too long, spun uselessly at this information. "Won?"

"I assumed you might not have heard, given your sudden departure from the auditorium. Unless what it says in the papers is true?"

"What it says..." Cecily gave up trying to make sense of the words and sank into a chair. "Could you start over, please? Am I understanding you correctly that Martha Jones won for best supporting actress last night?" She managed a weak chuckle as she realized that the question of who won had never once crossed her mind during the previous night's ordeal.

"Yes. They managed to resume the show and make the announcement shortly after your *episode*." Her disapproval of her daughter's *episode* couldn't have been plainer. Food poisoning, along with most other human bodily functions, didn't exist in her world. Cecily reckoned that a mix-up at the hospital was in fact impossible because she'd actually been delivered by stork, regular childbirth being much too undignified and messy.

"Well, that's lovely for Martha. She really deserved it."

"Then what happened had nothing to do with jealousy over her dating Brad Perris?"

"Brad Perris?" Cecily's eyes widened. "Why would you—"

Her mother tapped one perfectly manicured finger on the newspaper in front of her. Squinting, Cecily recognized it not as an actual newspaper but as one of the many celebrity tabloids that she'd been desperate to have notice her less than twenty-four hours before. And there she was, on the cover after all, her face literally arranged in a triangle alongside Martha and Brad with an oh-so-not subtle heart behind them. *Careful what you wish for.*

"Mother, how many times do I have to tell you those papers are fake?" It was the one glaring anomaly to her mother's otherwise perfectly patrician facade. The woman devoured trashy magazines from the supermarket checkout line with an insatiable appetite, and believed every word.

Her mother sniffed. "Well, I know you and Brad were *close* and—"

Cecily bristled at all that her tone implied. "I don't know how you think you know that, since I never so much as mentioned him to you. We were coworkers. Anything you may have read beyond that is as real as those fifty different times Jennifer Aniston was having a baby, or all those diets where you can lose fourteen pounds in one week from eating cheesecake."

"I just thought..." Her voice trailed off and her expression became defensive.

"You thought that maybe I'd been *cured* by finding the right man?" Cecily seethed as her mother's face told her that was exactly what she'd hoped, but had had just enough sense not to say out loud. "I'm in love with Rorie, Mother. Just like I have been for the past two years. Hell, the past twenty years. We live together. We're—"

About to adopt a child, she'd nearly said, but bit back the words just in time. That was a conversation best left for another day. And preferably one she could conduct through email once it couldn't be put off any longer, possibly using her father as a proxy.

"We're happy," she concluded instead, annoyed at her own cowardice and deciding to take it out on her mother. "What are you even doing here?"

"You were sick last night, so I came over early today to check on you. That's what mothers do."

No, that's what normal mothers do. "Fine. But what were you doing here last night?"

"Well, after I saw on television how you rushed out of the auditorium, naturally I was concerned."

Cecily gritted her teeth. "You didn't rush right out from Baton Rouge and magically manage to get here ten minutes after we got home. I meant, what are you doing in LA?"

"Business."

"For Daddy's campaign?" It was the most likely answer. Her mother viewed keeping Senator DuPont in office as her own full-time occupation.

Her mother sat uncharacteristically silent, fidgeting with the handle of a teaspoon. "If you must know, I was consulting a divorce attorney."

"That's totally unnecessary, Mother." Cecily seethed at this further evidence of her mother's inability not to interfere in her affairs. "Chet and I finalized the papers just fine on our own, ages ago."

"Not for you. For me."

Cecily stared, uncomprehending. "For you?"

"Well, dear, you made not being married seem so appealing." Her mother gave an airy laugh that failed to be convincing. "I thought I'd give it a try myself. Why not? Everyone's doing it."

"Give it a try?" Stunned, Cecily searched her mind for anything that might help to combat her mother's sudden madness. "What about marriage being a sacred institution? What about Daddy? What," she added, appealing to the highest authority of all, "what will the voters think? It's less than two months until the election!"

A shuffling of slippers on the tile behind her announced Rorie's arrival. Befuddlement was etched across her face from whatever parts of the conversation she'd gleaned.

"Mother's just informed me that she's divorcing Daddy," Cecily said, filling in anything Rorie may have missed. "And apparently, I inspired her to do it!"

"I'm very sorry to hear that, Mrs. DuPont." She sounded sincere, but her expression telegraphed a desperate desire to escape the conversation immediately. "Perhaps I should—"

Oh no, you don't. "Sit." Cecily's command was gentle but firm. There was no way she was being left alone at a time like this. "Have some coffee with us, Sweetheart," she added in a belated attempt not to sound like she was scolding a puppy at obedience school.

"Right. I'll just sit, then." Rorie finished filling her mug and pulled out an empty chair. "Great idea."

"Mother, you can't be serious."

"Of course I am." She said it as if it were the most mundane decision in the world, yet something about her eyes made her words ring less than true.

"After forty-five years together? You two have been a couple since college!"

She shrugged. "Times have changed a lot since then. You have no idea, Cecily." Her eyes narrowed at Rorie. "Or, maybe you do. The point is, a woman today doesn't have to be married."

She agreed one hundred percent, and from anyone else, Cecily might have applauded this burst of feminism, but not coming from her mother. "You love Daddy, don't you?" she demanded instead, her insides quivering as if her life's foundation depended on the answer.

"It's complicated," her mother replied, looking away so that Cecily couldn't read her expression. "Besides, I don't appreciate the double standard. If *you* decided to try the single life, I don't see why *I* shouldn't be able to do something new, too."

"But, I... I didn't just decide to try something new. You do understand that, right?" She regarded her mother in disbelief. "I wrestled half my life with whether to leave Chet before I realized I had no other choice." With a folded paper napkin, she dabbed beads of sweat that had formed along her hairline. The conversation had left her feeling flushed and queasy. "We'll discuss this later. I need to get ready for work."

"Absolutely not," her mother and Rorie said in unison.

"But construction's just wrapped up and today's our first official day working in the new space." Even as she said it she had a sinking feeling that she would be absent for opening day. She might be able to sweet talk one of them into letting her go, but with two such formidable women united against her, she was doomed.

"Peggy and Lu can manage just fine on their own. You're going to finish your toast and head back to bed." The good news was, if they ever managed to gain custody of Bryn, Rorie was well on her way to mastering the motherly scolding. She'd even used her pointed index finger to emphasize the beat of her words. The only thing missing was an emphatic *young lady* at the end.

With Cecily's mother nodding in agreement, she admitted defeat. Popping the last bite of toast into her mouth, she made her way slowly back to the bedroom and felt only the barest twinge of guilt at leaving Rorie to face her mother alone. *Serves her right for wagging a finger at me.*

GOOSEFLESH FORMED on Rorie's forearms, as if the temperature of the room had dropped with Cecily's departure. Across the table from her sat Margaret DuPont, like a scene from one of her nightmares. Her nemesis, the woman responsible for keeping her and Cecily apart for so many years. She didn't blink as she returned Rorie's stare, her face a composed mask of calm that didn't betray a single hint of emotion, like she'd been engineered that way just to keep you guessing.

After all this time, here she was with her—what, exactly? Not mother-in-law, nor was she ever likely to be, given how Cecily reacted to the topic of marriage. She shivered again. She wasn't sure precisely what they were to each other, other than strangers stranded at the breakfast table together with no idea what came next, now that possibly the only interest in the world the two of them had in common had just left the room.

"So, you're the *friend*, then."

Rorie drew a sharp breath at the way she said it, but tried to let it slide. They'd been made aware of each other's existence the night before, but it hadn't been what might be called a proper introduction, what with Cecily dashing away halfway through to throw up. Who could blame her? Rorie wished she could do the same now.

Regardless, the situation at the time of Cecily's mother's

arrival hadn't exactly lent itself to formalities. Rorie offered up the best she could now, using every scrap of good manners she could muster. "It's nice to finally meet you, Mrs. DuPont."

"I'd say that Cecily has told me a lot about you, but she really hasn't."

"I see." Rorie pursed her lips to refrain from pointing out that the oversight was probably more a reflection on Cecily's strained relationship with her mother than anything to do with Rorie. No need for *both* of them to be rude.

"I'm not even certain what to call you. Girlfriend? Partner?" She flinched at each option, not trying to hide it. "You're not planning to get married, I assume."

"I—"

"My daughter made her feelings on the topic of marriage very clear on my last visit to Connecticut. Though I won't pretend to understand why y'all put up such a fuss over being able to get married and then don't bother doing it."

Y'all? What do you think I am, some sort of ambassador for all of lesbian-kind? Rorie cleared her throat, blessedly cutting off the woman's diatribe. Her marriage prospects were just about the last thing she wanted to discuss right now. "Why don't you call me Rorie."

She noticed that Cecily's mother was not quick to suggest calling her by anything less formal than her surname. Being invited to call her Mom was a stretch, but surely it wouldn't kill her to be addressed as Margaret by her daughter's partner. *Does she have a nickname? Maggie? Madge?* She choked back a laugh at this preposterous idea. No one would dare. Even Cecily couldn't manage to call her anything more endearing than *Mother*.

"How long are you in town?" Rorie hoped her face didn't give away how desperately she wanted the answer to be 'not long.'

A shadow of uncertainty crossed the older woman's otherwise confident face. "I should probably be heading home, but…"

Remembering what had just been said about divorce, it struck Rorie that the reason for her hesitation may be that she no longer knew where home was. In what might have been a moment of triumph over the unlikeable woman, she felt an unaccountable pang of empathy instead. "Surely you'll stay in town to visit Cecily, at least for a few more days?" she suggested, offering a graceful retreat from the stark truth, like an olive branch.

"I suppose I could extend my stay at the hotel a few days, at least until she's feeling better," Mrs. DuPont declared, her poise returning. Rorie hoped the lack of anything biting or nasty in her retort signaled her acceptance of the truce.

Rorie opened her mouth to reply, but the appearance of her lawyer's face on her cell phone stopped her short with a spasm through her gut. "I'm sorry, I need to take this call." As Cecily's mother rose from the table and busied herself with making a fresh pot of coffee, Rorie greeted her attorney. "Helen, any news on Bryn?"

"More of the same, I'm afraid. That's why I'm calling."

"What do they need now?"

"It's not so much what they need as why, Rorie. This is the sixth request for missing papers that I know were sent, or information that they already have. It's starting to look deliberate."

Rorie frowned. "I don't understand."

"Even though you're applying for custody on your own, Cecily's information is part of the home study, and given her celebrity, you're not exactly a low-profile couple. I'm worried the judge might be buying himself some time, hoping for a

Supreme Court ruling that will give him some wiggle room on denying custody to a same-sex couple."

"You're kidding me." Rorie felt bile rise in her throat at the lawyer's blunt assessment. "Can he even *do* that?"

"I'm going to do everything I can to fight it. But I thought you should know."

Rorie let out an exasperated sigh as she ended the call, and Cecily's mother turned toward her with a look that said that though she would deny that she'd been eavesdropping, nevertheless she'd heard every word.

"Frustrating news from my lawyer," Rorie needlessly explained.

Mrs. DuPont arched an eyebrow at the mention of a lawyer, and with talk of divorce lawyers still floating in the air, Rorie realized it would be in her best interest to explain further. "I have a young niece. She's in Mississippi, you see. In foster care. Both her parents recently passed, and we're hoping to give her a home here."

"Give her a home... you mean *adopt* her?" Half a dozen conflicting emotions seemed to race across the woman's face. "But Cecily never mentioned..." Her voice trailed off as, for perhaps the first time, it became apparent just how little she knew about her daughter's life.

"Well, it isn't set yet. And according to my lawyer, we may be fighting an uphill battle because some bigoted, backward judge has decided that we're not suitable parents."

"That's ridiculous! Cecily is an excellent mother. Why would anyone say otherwise?" Rorie gave her a look and Mrs. DuPont had the decency to appear flummoxed as it dawned on her precisely why the judge would say that, and that she herself had probably said something similar dozens of times in the past. "Mississippi, you said? I'm sure Cecily's father will straighten this out when she tells him. We know people there."

Though she'd left no doubt that those people were very important people, Rorie felt the need to set the record straight. "Actually, I've asked Cecily not to bring the senator into this."

"Why on earth not?"

"I know that the senator's personal views may have softened on certain issues, but I doubt the same can be said for the Louisiana electorate. I won't ask him to take that risk on my behalf. Besides, it's a family matter, Mrs. DuPont. And I always take care of my family. I don't need anyone's help in doing it."

Rorie feared she'd crossed the line by turning down her offer, but as Cecily's mother studied her silently from behind her coffee mug, there was a glimmer of something in her eyes that almost resembled respect. Finally, she gave a curt nod. "Very well. And please, do call me Margaret."

SEVEN

SIX O'CLOCK IN the morning was far from Cecily's preferred time to arrive at the office, but she'd been dodging paparazzi ever since the Emmy's. Ridiculous as it seemed to her that anyone would care about or lend any credence to rumors regarding a middle-aged woman's love life, the tabloids were still running strong with the story of a sordid Cecily, Brad, and Martha love triangle.

Since even the most tenacious photographers tended to stay in bed until after sunrise, for two solid weeks, Cecily had made her way to work several minutes shy of the crack of dawn. At first, the routine had allowed her to dodge her mother, too, who had taken up temporary residence in their guesthouse. But her mother caught on quickly and could be found seated at the kitchen table by the time Cecily rolled out of bed the third day. The one bright spot was that her mother's addiction to the tabloids gave her an easy way to keep tabs on the story. As soon as her name faded from the headlines, she'd reset her alarm for seven o'clock, like a normal person.

Entering Sapphicsticated, Inc.'s newly completed offices and studio space, Cecily drew in a deep breath. The air still smelled of freshly cut pine and new paint. It was a smell forever associated in her mind with backstage at the theater. Images of Oakwood, and the college shop before that, flooded her memory.

She sucked in her breath, pressing a hand to her chest. The weight of melancholy that accompanied those memories hit her with unexpected force. She'd given little thought to the theater since leaving for California the year before. The allure of Hollywood was infinitely brighter than the footlights from a stage, and she'd found success that matched her dreams. Yet surrounded by everything she'd worked so hard to achieve, there was a dull ache in her chest that surprised her.

Of course, settling into her new role as a producer hadn't been the most natural fit. Doubts plagued her at every turn. Was she choosing the right scripts to option? Would she find an audience who appreciated her vision? At her worst moments, she wondered if she possessed a unique creative voice at all, or if she was just a fraud.

The worst of her nervousness had subsided as more of the details of the web series they'd chosen as their first project fell into place. She'd approved the initial script and narrowed the field down to two potential directors. Casting would start the following week, and assuming she could rope one or two investors into coming on board, production would begin before the end of October. It was supposed to be an exciting time... so why did she feel so blue?

Cecily glanced into the small soundstage as she shuffled past. She frowned at an assortment of props piled haphazardly. When she'd left on Friday it had been empty space. The web series hadn't begun filming yet, so their presence was puzzling. She clenched her fists. Who was messing with her space? Then she remembered the indie filmmaker that

Frankie had mentioned at the board meeting. Had they arranged to use the studio over the weekend?

It's my company. This is something I should know. But try as she might, should couldn't recall if she'd signed a contract for the space. There'd been so much paperwork, and so much time spent chasing down agents and lawyers just so they could produce even more. Letters to potential investors, queries about the availability of actors for potential roles. Sheafs of paper with indecipherable words on them haunted her dreams. She made a mental note to ask Peggy for more information, and to have a talk with the person in charge about leaving the space clean.

A fresh mountain of papers greeted Cecily as she perched on the edge of her chair. Her heart sank as she surveyed her desk. There were contracts to be signed, scripts in one pile with rewrites awaiting approval, and in a second pile to be considered for optioning. There was a budget report from Peggy, along with the list she'd left herself of more prospective investors to contact. And this was a light workload compared to what it would be once their first project was underway, yet it was already daunting.

Cecily could almost feel her blood pressure tick upward under the stress of this one-woman operation. Well, two women, counting Peggy, but she had her hands full just wrangling the numbers. Despite needing to keep the budget lean, Cecily reckoned she would have to hire a few more hands. *An assistant to answer phones, at the very least*, she thought as her voicemail service informed her she had fourteen new messages. She pressed her overheated forehead against the smooth, crisp surface of the topmost manila folder on her desk. Why had she thought she had the smarts to run a production company on her own?

A sound in the hall sent her head snapping back upright

in alarm. It was only a little past seven, and Peggy wouldn't be in for another hour. She braced herself for a camera flash, suspecting an overly ambitious tabloid reporter had sneaked in through the unlocked rear door. She cursed herself for forgetting to lock it behind her, but then relaxed as she recognized the figure of Jill Davidson outside her open office door.

"Jill? What brings you here this early?" Relief added a chipper lilt to Cecily's tone, though it was mostly at not being stalked by paparazzi. Seeing Jill reminded her of the multitude of questions she'd been unable to find answers for herself. Begrudgingly, she'd added them to a list in her notebook to ask when she got a chance. She was already five sheets in. She felt a little sick at the thought.

"I'm checking in on a location shoot in the neighborhood and wanted to drop by."

"Do you have a few minutes? I have some questions." But just as the words were leaving Cecily's mouth, Jill announced that she could only stay for a moment.

Her disappointment tasted bitter. She'd been counting on using Jill as a resource, but she realized now that her hope had been premature. Jill wasn't serious about offering any real help, just playing cheerleader with the occasional words of moral support. Finding the answers to her questions was something Cecily might need to tackle on her own.

"Well, actually, I had a question for you," Jill said, looking uncharacteristically unsure of herself.

"Okay?" she said, but inside she thought, *For me?* Cecily stifled a laugh. What could she possibly know that Jill didn't?

Jill took a deep breath. "Look, let me just get right to it. I'd like to work with you."

"Work... here?" Cecily blinked. That was not what she'd expected Jill to say.

"I've been at Grant Studios for almost ten years. I like my

work, don't get me wrong, but ever since Stephanie told me about your new company this summer, I just keep thinking about it. Plus, I'm basically maxed out at the associate producer level there until someone dies, and—" She stopped, biting her lip. "That is, I don't mean to presume..."

Presume? Acknowledging herself as the expert in the room was hardly presumptuous on Jill's part. Cecily nibbled the lipstick from her bottom lip. "You want to be a producer, here, with us?"

Jill nodded. "I do."

Her first instinct was to say no. After all, this was her company, and Cecily could do it on her own. But a glance at her desktop made her rethink. *I've got enough work here for twenty people, and not nearly enough know-how to get it done.* She swallowed her pride. "Jill, I would love to have you." She shifted nervously. "That is, if we can afford you."

Jill grinned. "We'll work something out. I meant what I said the last time we met. I believe in what you're doing, not just on a personal level— I think you've got a good chance of hitting the market in a big way. I want to be a part of it, and I'm willing to take a long view on the returns."

After Cecily had shown Jill out with a handshake and a hug, and promises of Peggy being in touch as soon as possible with an offer, she returned to her desk with the weight on her shoulders noticeably lighter. There was still a lot to do, but with the promise of Jill joining her as a co-producer, it felt more manageable. A smile tugged on her lips as she dove into the stack of paperwork with renewed energy, confident that her vision for Sapphicsticated, Inc. would soon become a reality.

UNDER JILL'S GUIDANCE, it took no time at all to turn the daily operations at Sapphicsticated, Inc. into a well-oiled machine. Begrudgingly, Cecily had to admit that hiring Jill was the best decision she'd made. By the middle of October, it was clear that their first web series would be on schedule to start filming at the end of the month, just as Cecily had hoped. Disappointment that she hadn't accomplished it herself had to take a backseat to the fact that the job was getting done. The only question that remained was what to do about the indie film that rented the studio on weekends. It was proving to be a stickier situation than Cecily had ever anticipated.

Though she hadn't found the time to vet the project herself, she'd gathered from talking to Frankie that the filmmaker's work was known for having a strong feminist message at its core. Cecily was, in theory, all for helping get that type of positive message out to the world. It was one of the reasons she'd been so inspired to start her own production company to begin with, and so offering the use of her studio in this way should have been an ideal partnership.

In practice, however, Cecily's patience was wearing thin. Despite repeated warnings, there had been ongoing issues with things being left out of place. Little things, to be sure, but the studio was like Cecily's baby and even the smallest mess pained her. Plus, once their own project began, the situation was bound to grow more intolerable by the week. Seeing no other option, Cecily steeled herself for the difficult task of breaking the news that their contract would not be renewed for November.

As a general rule, Cecily didn't go into the office on the weekends, which was the only time the indie film crew was on the premises. As a result, tracking the director down during the week to tell her about the contract face to face turned out to be more challenging than she would have liked. When a full week passed without successfully delivering the news, dropping by the office on the weekend became her only choice.

On Sunday morning, Cecily was driving with her mother to meet up with Rorie at a favorite downtown restaurant for brunch. The route past the studio would take them only a few minutes out of their way, so she had the idea to stop by and catch the director between takes.

"Just wait in the car, Mother," Cecily said as she pulled into the space beside her usual parking spot. The other cars in the lot were a clue that the film crew was on site. The shiny SUV that had flagrantly parked in the space with her name stenciled on it helped reinforce her decision to send them packing. "This will just take a minute."

"So, I don't get to see where you work, then."

Her mother muttered the statement under her breath, so Cecily chose to pretend she hadn't heard. It was a technique that had served her well in surviving her mother's unexpected and extended stay, which was approaching the one month mark and showed little sign of coming to an end. She would make it up to her another time with a full VIP tour, but this meeting had the potential to be awkward, and she preferred to face it alone.

Despite the cars in the parking lot, the interior of the building felt strangely devoid of life. Since Jill had joined the team, the office had quickly become populated by a full-time administrative assistant and two interns who had followed her from Grant Studios, plus the cast and crew of the web series who were on hand several days per week as production ramped up.

She'd become so used to the hustle and bustle of people constantly coming and going that walking through the empty halls, Cecily felt eerily alone. Shadows seemed darker, and the echo of her footsteps made the hairs on the back of her neck stand up as she imagined someone following behind her. The warehouse district where the studio was located was safe enough on workdays, but its isolation outside normal business hours gave her a serious case of the creeps.

A sudden, loud moan sent a chill down her spine, a shot of adrenaline charging through her veins, and set her feet to racing. The closer she came to the soundstage, the louder the terrible sound became, until a woman's glass-shattering scream prompted Cecily to launch herself the final few steps and wrench the door open, pulse pounding in her ears like a kettle drum.

Her brain fizzled and popped at the sight that awaited her inside. It was horrifying. So many limbs, bare and tangled. She froze in place, having lost the ability to move as her mind struggled to make sense of what her eyes beheld.

This wasn't the first time in her life that Cecily had walked in on two women having sex. That distinction belonged to her old nemesis, Polly, and her frizzy-haired best friend, Amanda. Just the recollection of it made her shudder. It was, however, the first time that the intimate act in question was in the process of being filmed. And this was no cheap, homemade sex tape, either. This appeared to be a top-notch affair.

The soundstage had been decorated to look like a medieval castle, with a faux stone wall made of foam and a light behind it shining through an arched window covered with flimsy plastic printed to resemble stained glass. As a piece of scenery, it was masterfully done. From the bits of expensive-looking clothing strewn on the floor around a sumptuously draped canopy bed, it appeared that one of the women had at one point been dressed as a knight and the other as a princess. Neither was wearing a stitch of clothing now, that was for certain.

An equally naked camerawoman was busy filming the tryst, while they were coaxed on with helpful stage directions from the fourth naked woman in the room. At least, Cecily was fairly certain she'd counted four naked women altogether. The shock of so much exposed flesh and what was being done with it was making her vision unsteady. She might have started seeing double. Why the crew felt the need to be naked was a mystery too great to fathom.

The camera continued to roll, and the women on the bed carried on with their impressively acrobatic love making as though Cecily didn't exist. The director, a middle-aged woman with graying hair whose pendulous breasts were —*absolutely not something I should be looking at!*—glanced up at the door, also seemingly unperturbed by the interruption. She held up a finger to indicate both *Quiet, please,* and *I'll be with you in a minute,* and then went back to the task at hand.

Cecily was too astonished to do anything but comply. She pressed her lips together and her eyelids firmly shut, though one lid fluttered open defiantly from time to time. No matter how hard she tried, she couldn't stop herself from peeking, despite the painful burning of her scarlet cheeks each time she did. *They really seem to be into it, I'll give them that.* Under different circumstances, she might even have found some of the actresses' actions *inspiring,* so to speak. Under very, very different circumstances.

When the scene was done and everyone in the room had mercifully donned their robes, the gray-haired woman approached. "I'm Jada Larkin, the director. Can I help you?"

"Cecily DuPont. Founder and CEO of Sapphicsticated, Inc. And your landlord." The recitation of her entire CV probably sounded snooty, but she didn't care. She'd meant it to be. Being pompous was her only defense against mortification.

"Oh, Ms. DuPont! I didn't realize." She grasped Cecily's hand and gave it such an enthusiastic shake that Cecily immediately regretted her sour attitude. "We're beyond grateful for the opportunity to film here. It's such a pleasure to meet you! And, I'm sorry, you are?"

But, I just told you who I am. Cecily's brow wrinkled as she contemplated the odd question, until she realized that the woman had been addressing someone else, someone who had slipped in behind her. Dread mounting, Cecily turned to face their uninvited guest.

EIGHT

DEAR GOD, how long has she been standing there?

Time ground to a halt. Though her heart was surely fluttering at the pace of a hummingbird's wings, the space between each beat seemed to last an eternity. Cecily's body trembled as her mother's saucer-like eyes told her that however long she had been there, it had been more than long enough.

"You were supposed to wait in the car."

For perhaps the first time in her adult life, Margaret DuPont stood speechless. Their eyes locked, and Cecily prayed a merciful god would allow the earth to crack open and swallow her whole. *Or Mother. I'm not picky.* Instead, her mother pivoted on one foot and scurried away in the direction from which she had come, looking for all the world like a mouse who's been caught in an unsavory alley.

Mortified, Cecily turned her attention back to Jada Larkin, who was watching the scene with a look somewhere between surprise and amusement.

"Ms. Larkin, what on earth is going on here?" Her voice shook, rage building as the situation became clearer.

"We're making a film."

"You're making pornography! In front of my mother!"

Jada Larkin bristled visibly. After all... *all* of her was visible. "We are absolutely not making pornography. We are reclaiming our matriarchal heritage through the feminist reinterpretation of classic folk literature."

Cecily blinked. *Reinterpreting the what?* She spied a shining red apple on the floor near the bed, and the explanation clicked. "Fairytale porn?"

"Please, again with the pornography. If you must, we prefer the word *erotic*. And, yes. Erotic reinterpretations of fairy tales are *all* the rage right now, ever since the *Compendium of Erotic Childhood Classics* was released on audiobook last year. People can't get enough of them. It won a Grammy, you know."

Cecily stared, dumbfounded. An audiobook collection of erotic fairy tales? She thought back to the naughty files she'd been sent the previous year, the project that had ended her painfully brief career as a voice actor. *It can't be...* Then despite the deadly serious nature of the moment, a giggle burst from her lips, because it *had* to be one and the same. How many other audiobooks like that could there be?

The director pursed her lips, clearly confounded by Cecily's reaction, then continued. "Just so you understand, we are committed to tastefulness and the highest quality production values in the industry. Which is why the use of your studio has been such a blessing. In fact, we're wrapping up ahead of schedule, so I don't think we'll need to renew the contract for November."

"Well, that's..." The serendipity of the revelation sent Cecily into another fit of laughter. "That's great. I'm glad it's all worked out." All her anger had fizzled into mirth. For once, things were working out with ease.

It was absurd, but it had ended well and with the minimum of confrontation, which Cecily considered a win. She was still chuckling as she emerged into the sun-filled parking lot, until the sight of her mother sitting stiffly in the passenger seat of her car reminded her of the much scarier situation that she still needed to face.

How will I ever be able to live this down?

"I'm very sorry about that," Cecily said with sincerity as she started the car. Her stomach knotted as her mother continued to look stoically ahead.

"Cecily, can you explain something to me?" Her mother's voice was clipped in the way that made Cecily instantly feel as if she were five years old.

And, here we go. "Look. Those people have nothing to do with our studio, Mother, I promise. They rent the space, nothing more. I had no idea they were making..."

Up to that point, her words had tumbled out in a rush, but Cecily caught herself about to say the word pornography and stopped. Apparently, that was an offensive word, or so she'd been told by Jada Larkin. But more to the point, it was a word she simply couldn't bring herself to utter in the presence of her mother.

"I'll admit I was surprised to find out what kind of films you're making, but that wasn't my question." Her mother seemed oddly sheepish, given what had happened. Cecily had expected to be torn to shreds by now.

"Then, what?" Cecily's fingers twitched nervously on the steering wheel. Normally, her mother was the type of woman who took command of a conversation. Her pussyfooting around left Cecily increasingly apprehensive.

"Those two women, on the bed." Her mother cleared her throat brusquely, as if steeling her resolve to continue. "They seemed very *intimate*."

"You could say that." Cecily snorted, some of her tension subsiding. Leave it to her mother to resort to Victorian-era euphemisms. "People usually are when they're having sex."

Her mother nodded slowly. "So that *is* what they were doing, then." She said it without a trace of irony.

With a shock, Cecily realized that her mother wasn't joking. "Well, yes. What else could they have been doing?"

"I just wasn't sure," her mother responded, her tone prim and crisp as a school marm.

"You weren't..." Cecily gaped. How could a woman in her late sixties with two grown children not recognize sex when she saw it?

"I just didn't realize that's how it was done. With girls."

"How it's *done?* My God, Mother, how did you think it was done?" Her snarky attitude evaporated as soon as the last syllable escaped her lips and the very real possibility loomed that her mother would decide to tell her what she'd thought. *Please don't answer that. Please, please, don't answer that!*

"It's not like I spend my time pondering that sort of thing, young lady," she responded tartly. Cecily had never been so relieved to see her mother's usual personality returning. "I truly couldn't make heads or tails of it, you know. Shocking, really."

"I mean, all they were doing was—"

Snippets of the encounter flickered through her memory, causing her to pause. For all that it had caught her off guard, Cecily realized that in retrospect, what the actresses had been doing had been pretty run of the mill. A finger here, a tongue there. Not a single handcuff or strap-on in sight. Aside from the enviable limberness of youth, when it came to the actual sex, it didn't get much more plain vanilla.

Was she really that shocked?

Given the vigorousness with which Cecily's mother

fanned her reddened face, it appeared she really was. "I couldn't imagine your father ever doing anything like *that*."

Thanks to her mother's comment, her parents doing *that* was now pretty much all Cecily *could* imagine. In fact, that's all she could see in her head for the length of time it took to drive three city blocks. Her parents. Orally pleasuring each other. On an endless loop from Hell.

She just prayed her mother's imagination was less vivid when it came to picturing her own sex life. The more she thought about it, the more she squirmed. Her mother and Rorie had a tenuous relationship. No need to complicate it with too much thinking about sex now that they'd reached a point of civility that everyone could live with. Cecily didn't think she could bear it things became tense between them at home. If her mom wanted to live under the delusion they were having an extended elementary school slumber party, that was fine with her.

"Let's just try to forget this happened, okay?" she suggested, pulling into a parking space in front of the restaurant. "I know it must have been disturbing to you, and I apologize."

Her mother nodded silently, giving Cecily hope that the whole ordeal was over, but then she opened her mouth to speak. "Actually, it was sort of..."

The whole sentence was a quiet mumble, with the final world trailing off into oblivion, but Cecily could have sworn her mother had said it seemed nice. Despite all the surprises the day had offered, none could top the shock of that. Had her mother, the self-declared captain of the morality police, actually witnessed two women engaged in lesbian sex and declared it to be *nice*?

Is Mother having a stroke? Early onset dementia? Concern rattled her as they strode through the restaurant door. For her mother to have such a drastic change of heart, there must be *something* wrong. Or, at the very least, she'd best prepare herself for some harsh judgment to come, because it was a well-known fact that Margaret DuPont did not change her mind.

Rorie was already seated at a table set for three in the back, and as her face came into view, Cecily was startled to see her mother lift her hand and give a little wave. *What is going on?* So far during her stay, Cecily's mother had been as polite to her daughter's girlfriend as good southern manners required, but this had been something more. That little finger waggle was downright *friendly*. If she didn't know better, she'd almost think her mother was verging on expressing approval for her chosen life partner.

She'd honestly thought that the day she inadvertently exposed her mother to lesbian pornography would go down in history as the biggest disaster of all time. How could it not? But instead, for the first time in her adult life, Cecily had a glimmer of hope that they were on the verge of the type of breakthrough in their relationship that she'd never thought possible.

Could it be? Her heart skipped a beat. *Could my mother's hardened veneer actually crack to reveal a genuine human person inside?*

"I THOUGHT YOU'D GOTTEN LOST!" Rorie flashed a relieved grin as Cecily and Margaret finally appeared.

She'd had an early morning meeting with a producer at Paramount that Max had referred her to, who was considering her for the role of production designer on his new film. She'd rushed straight to the restaurant after, but was running late and was sure it would be one more thing that Margaret would chalk up against her. Instead, she'd been waiting twenty minutes and was starting to worry that she'd messed up the details completely.

Cecily gave a weak smile. "The stop at the office didn't quite go as planned." She slid into the semi-circular booth beside Rorie, brushing her fingertips against Rorie's knee in lieu of a hello kiss. Neither of them felt comfortable with public displays of affection when Cecily's mother was nearby.

"Oh?" Rorie frowned, concerned that the director Cecily had been meeting with had caused her trouble. "What happened?" Rorie slid her half-finished Bloody Mary toward her across the crisp white linen. Knowing how Cecily hated confrontation, she just might need it.

Cecily's cheeks flushed until they matched the liquid in the glass, which she drained rapidly. "I don't want to talk about it. Ever."

Rorie raised an eyebrow as she took in Cecily's scarlet face and noted the way Cecily's mother fidgeted with the handle of her fork and avoided eye contact. Had Margaret been the source of the upset? If she had been, it would hardly come as a surprise.

When Rorie had invited the woman to stay in the guest-house, she'd hoped it would give Cecily a chance to smooth things over with her. Having experienced the joy of reconciling with her own family, Rorie couldn't help but wish the same for Cecily. But she'd had no idea the woman would decide to stay for a month, nor had she counted on how uncomfortable her presence would make them both feel.

Though she'd softened a little over the weeks, Rorie still felt the disapproval lurking just beneath the surface with Margaret. Even the woman's invitation to brunch this morning had set Rorie on edge as she searched for the catch.

As much as she dreaded it, Rorie feared she would soon need to have a conversation with Cecily about bringing her mother's visit to a close.

"How was your meeting?" Cecily asked, the effects of the Bloody Mary apparently having kicked in enough for her to make small talk.

"Good, I think." Rorie smiled tentatively, recalling the meeting. It was always hard to know, but she'd had a positive feeling that the job would come through, and just in time. The work on her current show would be wrapping up within the next week, and the prospect of not knowing where she was going next filled her with anxiety. "He said he liked my vision for it, and he's been wanting to work with me for a while."

Cecily nodded encouragingly. "That sounds promising. And it starts production in January?"

Rorie nodded. "And it's mostly filming in the LA area, so I won't have to travel. I just wish—" Her throat constricted, closing off her words. "I thought we'd have heard something from Helen by now. With all the time off I'll have between now and the new year, it would be the perfect time for Bryn to settle in with us."

She met Cecily's gaze and saw her own yearning reflected back. The comfort of Cecily's hand touching her knee radiated through her, and for a moment they were the only two people in the world. Until Margaret cleared her throat.

"There's something I've been meaning to tell you."

You're heading home on the next train? Guilt over the knee-jerk reaction pricked her conscience, but she couldn't help it. The spot on her thigh where Cecily's hand had been was already growing cold after she'd snatched it away. It was her instinctive response to her mother's voice, and thanks to the woman constantly popping up around every corner, that small bit of contact was the most Rorie had enjoyed in days.

"I know you didn't want any help," Margaret continued, blissfully unaware of Rorie's ill-wishes, "but I made a phone call."

"Mother, you called Daddy?" Cecily's tone was scolding, but she couldn't conceal a touch of hopefulness that her parents were back on speaking terms, and it broke Rorie's heart to hear it.

"No, not your father. The judge's wife."

"The judge?" Rorie frowned, confused. "You mean Judge McCarthy, the one in Mississippi?"

"I didn't realize you knew the McCarthys," Cecily added, also looking puzzled.

"Well, I don't. Not exactly. But I happened to look them up, and when I did, I discovered that Mrs. McCarthy is a fellow Kappa girl. Mississippi chapter, but still."

While Rorie remained mystified, Cecily nodded as if she understood. "Oh, of course. Mother's sorority from college," she added for Rorie's benefit.

"And yours, as well, don't forget." Margaret wagged a finger at Cecily. "You could have cleared this whole thing up yourself ages ago, if you weren't so stubborn."

"I don't feel comfortable using connections like that."

"*Pshaw!* You had no compunction about calling your father for help from his political connections. I don't see how asking a Kappa sister for help is any worse."

"I guess it isn't," Cecily countered, "but then again, Rorie specifically asked us not to interfere in this. So, it isn't any better, either, is it Mother?"

"Rorie?" Margaret looked to her for vindication.

Rorie squirmed under Margaret's gaze, deeply divided. On the one hand, the woman had way overstepped by making that phone call after Rorie'd made it clear that she didn't wish to use personal connections to game the system. Then again, her lawyer had worked for weeks through every publicly available channel and gotten exactly nowhere. How angry could she really be, if a simple phone call meant Bryn would be coming home?

"I guess in this case..." She left the rest implied as a small concession to her pride. "Though I don't think I'll ever understand how this sorority bond works. I can't imagine what you could have said to the judge's wife that would make a difference."

"I simply told her that the state of Mississippi would be hard pressed to find better candidates for fostering this child than my daughter and her partner, and if her husband wanted to make some kind of a political statement, he would be wise to find a different case to do it with. Leave good people out of it," she concluded with an emphatic nod. "The judge should be giving your lawyer a call on Monday."

Rorie struggled to keep her jaw from dropping to the table. Margaret's change of heart might be far from complete on the broader social issues of same-sex marriage or adoption, but her declaration of Rorie as both a *good person* and *partner* was both unexpected and deeply touching. She felt Cecily's fingers searching for her hand beneath the table, and could tell that she, too, recognized the positive step her mother had taken. It wasn't perfect, but it was a damned good start.

Swallowing the lump in her throat, Rorie nodded. "I appreciate it, Margaret."

Though still not thrilled with the prospect of a long-term residency in their guesthouse, Rorie's heart softened. Maybe having the woman around a few more weeks wouldn't be so bad. It seemed only right that Margaret should stay long enough to meet her new granddaughter.

Whether Margaret would ever truly think of Bryn in that way was another matter. Only time would tell, and despite the morning's progress, Rorie feared they would encounter many more bumps along the road ahead. That worry was shoved away, though, as the most important part of Margaret's revelation hit her.

Monday. If what Margaret had said was true, Bryn would be joining them. Soon. With a start, Rorie realized she had much bigger things to be concerned with now.

I'm about to become a mother.

NINE

MONEY FOR PAYROLL?
Check.
Completed contract from the director?
Check.
Equipment delivery scheduled?
Check.

Cecily nibbled her lower lip, scanning the list again and again. She'd been over it a hundred times. Though everything appeared to be in order, Cecily couldn't shake the feeling she was forgetting something. Something only she, as senior executive producer, could do. Something that, if she left town without it being done, would reduce her whole enterprise to smoldering ruin.

Stop being so goddamn melodramatic. It's a week in Mississippi, not a year on safari.

After her mother's call to Judge McCarthy's wife, the final approval for Rorie to become Bryn's guardian had come with lightning speed. Even knowing her mother's knack for moving mountains in the world of politics, the immediacy of it came as a shock. The call had come Monday morning. It was done, every signature signed and rubber stamp in place. She and Rorie had been given exactly two days to board a plane to Memphis, drive to Mississippi, and bring the little girl home.

We've never even met her. Cecily tried to ignore the dull tension headache that had been omnipresent since the Monday, clouding her thoughts. Meeting her was a formality. It's not like meeting her first would somehow make them change their minds, right? They were ready, right down to decorating the bedroom, thanks to a crew of miracle workers from the set department at Rorie's show who had pulled an all-nighter to make sure Bryn would have a bedroom fit for a princess when she arrived.

Cecily pressed a hand to her chest, her heart palpitating. It was just such terrible timing. Filming for her long-awaited web series was due to start this week, and she couldn't be in two places at once. She knew Rorie and Bryn needed her more, but she missing the first week of production was like trusting her firstborn child to a new nanny. What if something went wrong that only she could fix?

What am I forgetting?

"Jill?" she called, poking her head out her office door. "Did we get Mike the deposit check yet?"

"Sent it last week!" Jill called back.

Some of Cecily's tension eased. Of course, Jill had done it. She did everything perfectly. Jill was no untested nanny, she was fucking super nanny, with a bottomless satchel filled with tricks, dispensing spoonfuls of sugar everywhere she went. She'd resent the hell out of her, if she weren't so damned good at it, and working on her behalf. With Jill in charge, Sapphic-sticated, Inc. was in the most capable of hands. *Including mine.* Though she'd come a long way, the learning curve had been steep, and Jill came to the rescue over something virtually every day.

It's going to be fine. The world won't end while I'm away.

Nevertheless, her eyes returned to the top of the list once more. She was deep in thought when the sound of someone approaching her office door broke her concentration.

"Hey, Cecily?"

She looked up to see Rhonda peering tentatively through the doorway. Though glad to see her, Cecily frowned. Tentative and Rhonda were not things she associated with one another. "What brings you here?"

"Rorie wanted to make sure you had a copy of the itinerary for your flight tomorrow, and I was passing this way so I said I'd bring it over." She held out a printed sheet of paper.

"Oh. Well, thank you." Cecily skimmed the page. It was the same itinerary she had in her email inbox, and hardly a priority worthy of hand-delivery. *So why are you really here?* Cecily thought she might know.

"Hey, you don't know if Jill's around, do you."

Cecily fought back a grin. *Bingo.* Her guess had been correct. "She's in her office."

Cecily chuckled at the eager clicking of Rhonda's heels as she trotted down the hall. Poor Rhonda was crushing hard. This was the third time since Jill came to work at Sapphicsticated that her friend had created an excuse to come by. Each time she claimed it was on her way home, but Cecily knew for a fact the office was at least twenty minutes out of her way. What she hadn't figured out yet was whether Jill returned Rhonda's interest. The memory of Jill in the company of a male companion still threw her.

"Hey, Cecily?" It was Rhonda's voice again, this time calling to her from the administrative assistant's desk that separated her office from Jill's. It was after five o'clock and the office staff had already headed home for the day, so the space was empty save for a pile of mail. It was to this pile that Rhonda was pointing excitedly, specifically to a brightly colored pink box. "How did you get this?"

Cecily shrugged at the odd question. "The mailman, I assume."

Rhonda treated her to one of her more exasperated looks. "I meant, what are you doing getting a package from Jada Larkin?"

"You know who that is?"

"Uh, yeah." Rhonda shook her scarlet curls with an air of disbelief. "Everyone knows who Jada Larkin is!"

Jill's head popped out from her office. "Did you say Jada Larkin?"

Cecily's head swiveled from Jill to Rhonda. "Am I the only one who doesn't know what the big deal is?"

"Jada Larkin is a *legend* in erotic entertainment," Rhonda explained, with more than a little reverence.

"Generally, of the female to female variety," Jill added. "Erotic literature, short films—it's all on her website."

"Along with a curated collection of toys and sexy apparel, all packaged in her trademark pink boxes, just like the one you're holding in your hands." Rhonda's expression grew sheepish under Jill's and Cecily's matching raised-eyebrow gazes. "What? So, I indulge in the occasional e-commerce."

Jill clapped her hands together, unable to contain her excitement. "I can't believe Jada Larkin has actually heard of us! Do you know how big that is?"

"She's done more than just hear about us," Cecily replied. "She was the indie filmmaker I told you about, the one who was renting our sound stage on the weekends."

Jill's mouth gaped. "Seriously? How could you not mention who it was?"

"Well, I—" Truth be told, she'd wanted a few projects that were hers alone, and that one had seemed to easy to screw up.

Cecily fidgeted, starting to feel a little embarrassed at being the only one out of the loop. Before moving to Los Angeles, she'd made it a point to watch as many lesbian films as she could find, but she was beginning to understand that there was a whole uncharted world beyond the LGBTQ section of Netflix. Apparently, she still had a lot to learn. "Honestly, I had no idea she was such a big deal."

Rhonda's eyes widened. "You're killing me."

"What, because my former life as a soccer mom didn't expose me to a lot of lesbian erotica?"

"No," Rhonda looked about ready to burst. "Because you still haven't opened the box!"

"I'll admit, I'm pretty curious myself." Jill shrugged. "So many good things come in a Larkin Pink Box."

She sure seems to know a lot about it. Cecily narrowed her eyes, contemplating her business partner. They'd been working together for several weeks, but Cecily had yet to get to know her very well on a personal level. She was still almost certain that Jill had been dating a man while at Grant Studios, and she hadn't had a chance to bring it up yet. Not that she'd know where to begin. But despite Rorie's wisdom on the subject, she wasn't convinced it wouldn't be better to know one way or the other, for Rhonda's sake.

Both Jill and Rhonda were bouncing with anticipation, eyeing the package. She forced her mind to stop wandering and reached for a letter opener to slice through the tape. *Well, one thing's for sure—if Jill ever lived the life of a suburban housewife like I did, her choice of sex education was much more comprehensive than mine.* With a toss of her head, Cecily dismissed her concerns.

Inside the box, resting atop a cushion of pink tissue paper, was a large square envelope of the same bright and shiny hue as the packaging. Cecily broke open the seal, pinching a heavy pink card between her fingers and lifting it out. "It looks like an invitation. Oh," she added, noting a few lines of scrawling handwriting on the back, "and there's a note."

She read silently until Rhonda cleared her throat with an impatient cough. When her eyes refocused from the card to her companions, both Rhonda and Jill looked ready to pop. "Oh, sorry!"

"So, what does it say?" Rhonda demanded.

"She says she's very grateful for the use of our studio, and she's sent two tickets for Sapphicsticated to attend a private screening of some of her work at her beach house in Santa Barbara." Cecily's face fell as she spied the date. "Oh, but it's this coming weekend. I'll be in Mississippi."

"I could go." The sound of Jill's voice saying this caught Cecily by surprise, mostly because she'd expected Rhonda to beat her to it. Jill blushed. "To represent the business, I mean. Obviously our styles are very different, but there's a lot of market crossover with her audience."

"Of course." Cecily snorted. Part of her bristled at handing over yet another task to Jill, but she knew it was pettiness that caused her to feel that way. Besides, if Jill went, she'd come home with a few million potential investor contacts, without a doubt. "Fine. And will you be bringing a guest?"

"Um, no. I'm not, uh—" Her eyes slid furtively in the direction of Rhonda. "That is..."

At least that answered one question. Jill was as smitten as Rhonda. *Could these two be any more obvious or clueless?*

Cecily seized on the chance to play matchmaker. "How about you, Rhonda? Any big plans for Saturday night?"

Rhonda, uncharacteristically speechless, simply gulped and shook her head.

"Good. Then you should go, too. You're a founding member, after all, and obviously familiar with Ms. Larkin's work. So, it's a date."

She sucked in her cheeks to hold back a maniacal cackle as Rhonda and Jill eyed each other shyly at her invocation of the word date. If she was going to miss the party, she could at least take a moment to be amused by their awkwardness. After all, a solid love life might be the only thing she had going for her that Jill lacked. That realization lessened some of the jealousy she'd felt toward her new business associate. Jill was a whiz at work, but Cecily'd had enough years of unhappiness in the love department to know she had the better end of the bargain.

She scooped up the package and pivoted in the direction of her office, pausing at the injured protestations of her friends.

"Don't we get to see what's in the box?" Rhonda whined.

"Nope." Cecily tossed her the envelope that contained the invitation. "You get this, but whatever is in here, it's for me."

"Oh, come on!" Rhonda pleaded. "It could be anything—lingerie! Sex toys!"

"Which is why I plan to open it alone in my office."

"You're killing me!" Rhonda's face did, indeed, reflect the agony of her curiosity, and it amused Cecily to see that Jill sported a similar look. *What a cute couple they'll make!*

Without a backward glance, Cecily continued to her desk, shutting the door with a chuckle as the protestations continued from the hall. It wasn't that she was teasing them on purpose, but she'd caught enough of a glimpse of what was under the tissue that she knew she'd prefer to open it alone.

A note tucked beneath a scrap of lace explained that this was an unused costume from the film Larkin had been shooting in their studio. She hoped Cecily would find a good use for it, either for herself or as an addition to Sapphicsticated's wardrobe collection, and that there was something else for her to consider, as well.

Her brow furrowed as she read the note a second time. Under the circumstances, someone might think the note hinted at an indecent proposal, but Cecily hadn't gotten that vibe from the filmmaker when they'd met. Whatever the something more was, Cecily suspected it was business related. *Intriguing.*

Though an argument could be made that the extra costume was also business related, Cecily recalled enough of the scene she'd walked in on to be wary as she parted the paper to reveal a swath of buttery, smooth fabric beneath. The prospect of becoming scandalously embarrassed by the gift, even alone in the room, made Cecily's fingers tingle as she lifted the garment from the folds of pink tissue.

The full-length robe was sheer and silky, and much more tastefully made than Cecily had at first feared. In fact, it was clearly a high-end piece that was evocative of the best of Hollywood glamor, like something that Greta Garbo might have worn to lounge on set between takes.

A dozen legitimate professional uses flooded Cecily's imagination, from the upcoming web series to the feature film she hoped to make in the next year. But when she closed her eyes and brushed her fingers across the fine fabric, she knew she'd be bringing it home for herself. Cecily wasn't naive about the toll that adding a child to a household could take on a relationship. Having something like this tucked away in the lingerie drawer could offer a welcome remedy.

A scrap of white showed beneath the tissue, and Cecily lifted a corner of the thin paper to reveal a thick stack of bound paper. A script. Her earlier excitement ebbed and her stomach twisted, dreading the call she'd have to make to tell the renowned filmmaker 'no.' Erotic movies, even of the high caliber that Jada Larkin allegedly produced, weren't exactly part of her vision for her company's future.

I could get Jill to break the news to her instead. Cecily steeled herself against the tempting thought. *No.* It was her company, and her job to do the dirty work. She'd take the script along on the plane, give it a quick read for politeness' sake, and let Jada know in a few weeks that it wasn't a good fit.

Faith in her own leadership restored, she left the script in the bottom of the box and went to replace the robe on top of it to take home. As she folded the garment back between the sheets of tissue that had covered it, she spied the lacy scraps that had held the note, and were now lying on the floor. She'd assumed it was part of the packaging, a lacy bow to wrap the gift, but scooping them up, she realized how wrong her first impression had been. Her heart fluttered wildly as she examined the micro-sized panties.

She balled them into her fist, her first impulse to throw them in the trash with the extra paper. A middle-aged woman, even one in relatively decent shape, had no business wearing something like this. But she paused mid-toss, imagining Rorie's face if she saw her in them. Her cheeks burned, but not unpleasantly. In fact, she mused, she was looking pretty damn good right now. Her tummy was as flat as it would ever be, and aside from a pound or two, she hadn't regained the weight she'd lost for the Emmy's yet, probably due to the stress of her mother's extended visit. *Well, maybe I could...*

She and Rorie had a trip coming up, after all. It wasn't exactly a vacation, but they were booked into a nice hotel in Nashville the first night before the drive to Mississippi, and with a four-year-old in tow, it might be the closest thing to a romantic getaway they'd see in quite some time.

She tucked the panties deep into the silky softness of the robe. Better to take them along. *Why the hell not?* With a wicked grin, she clamped the box beneath her arm and headed home to pack.

TEN

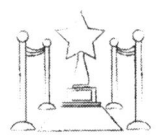

"WHOA!" Rorie's jaw dropped, as Cecily opened the bathroom door and swished her way into the hotel room, her pale peach, floor-length silk robe fluttering to offer a peek here and there of creamy skin beneath. Heat consumed her as her heart thudded wildly, blood rushing to all the right places. Was this gorgeous woman really hers?

She shivered as she ran a finger along the silk. "Where did *that* come from?"

"This old thing?" Cecily giggled, coiling the knotted belt around her fingers. "You know what it reminds me of? That last night in college. Remember?"

Remember? How could she forget? After a semester spent waiting and teasing, Cecily had met her at the hotel room door after the opening night of their show, wrapped in a robe, with nothing beneath. "I remember unwrapping you like a Christmas present, if that's what you mean." She could still recall the thrill of desire coursing through her veins, and the agony of waking up the next morning alone, though that was a memory better forgotten. "I'm afraid I don't remember much about the robe. It wasn't that one, though. That one, I would remember."

"Actually, this one was a gift." Cecily paused for a beat. "From Jada Larkin."

"Jada *Larkin?*"

"Oh, do you know who that is?" Cecily flashed a knowing grin, and Rorie realized too late the clever trap she'd stumbled into. Anything she said would definitely be used against her. Though Cecily no doubt intended to make it worth any torture in the end, Rorie wasn't about to make this *too* easy for her. "No need to answer. Your silence speaks volumes."

Rorie sputtered in protest as Cecily gloated.

"If you didn't know *exactly* who Jada Larkin is, you wouldn't have known not to answer."

"Fine, Miss Smartypants. So how do *you* know Jada Larkin?"

"Remember that indie film that was using our studio on weekends? Turns out that was her film."

Rorie gaped. "You're only telling me this now?"

"I honestly didn't know. Besides, I sort of walked in on them the other day during the middle of a particularly intimate scene, and I didn't want to reminisce about it afterward."

"Why not? Sounds like the perfect thing to relive, especially with the right company."

"Including the part where my mother walked in right behind me?"

"Oh, God." Picturing the horrified expression Margaret must have worn, Rorie couldn't help but laugh. "Is that what happened the other day before brunch to make you both act so weird?"

Cecily gave an exaggerated shudder. "And it wasn't until a few days later that I even found out who Jada was. At the time, she was just some woman directing porn in front of my mother. Now do you see why I didn't mention it?"

"That must have been traumatic. I have an idea." Rorie's gaze traveled along the sheer fabric of the robe, her fingers itching to untie the belt and send it slipping to the floor. "How about we erase all those bad memories right now?"

"And how do you suggest we do that?" She gave a playful tug on the edge of sheer silk that covered one breast. Clearly she knew that whatever Rorie had in mind would involve ditching the robe as quickly as possible.

"Oh, I don't know." Heat shot through Rorie's core, and she struggled to maintain a cool facade. "I think maybe you should give me a little preview of this new movie. So I won't be jealous that you got to see it first."

"A preview?"

"It's not every day Jada Larkin makes a new movie. You're going to need to walk me through the scene you saw, step by step."

Cecily's mouth twitched and it was clear she was also having trouble keeping up the pretense of seriousness. "Oh, really? Do you want a description, or should I show you?"

Rorie swallowed roughly as the conversation turned in the direction she'd hoped. "A demonstration is *definitely* in order."

"Fair enough. Do you want to be the knight or the princess?" She batted her eyelashes in mock innocence. "What, did I not mention that the movie is an adaptation of a sizzling collection of naughty fairy tales?"

She paused, tilting her head. "Why does that sound familiar?" Rorie frowned at the memory that sat just out of reach. "Wait, not like the ones from those books—"

"The very same. Apparently, the series hit number one on

the audio best seller list for twenty-four weeks. And won a Grammy."

Rorie paused to let the information sink in, then burst into hearty laughter. "That might be even funnier than Margaret watching lesbian porn. Who would have guessed that if you hadn't passed on that and gone on to be nominated for an Emmy, you could've been up for a Grammy, instead?"

"Yeah, maybe I would have won that one." A lingering disappointment crept into her tone.

Though Cecily had shrugged it off and been happy for the winner, Rorie's heart ached for the part of her that still wished the shining gold statue had come home with her. She knew how losing felt, and was still bitter that her show hadn't even made it to the nomination stage. "Oh, Cici..."

"And then I would forever be known as that raunchy bedtime-story girl, so I'd say I probably dodged a bullet," Cecily quipped, her moment of self-pity firmly behind her. The woman in front of her in the scandalous, sheer robe had come a long way from the Cici whom Rorie'd encountered in Connecticut. Her ability to let go and rebound was nothing short of inspiring.

"Is it wrong how much that thought turns me on?" Rorie slid one hand beneath Cecily's robe, easing it off her shoulder.

"Definitely." After a faint giggle, Cecily sucked in her cheeks and attempted a serious look. "So, which one will it be, knight or princess?"

Still up for making this a game? Rorie was happy to play along. "I'll opt for the knight, my princess."

Cecily rolled her eyes. "We have *got* to work on the dialogue."

"These films aren't really known for their dialogue, you know. So, what happens first?"

"Well, the scene opens with the knight placing her hand on the princess, like so." With a light touch, Cecily guided Rorie's hand from her shoulder to her waist, untying her belt with her other hand and pushing aside the silk so that Rorie could reach the skin and lace hiding beneath.

"What is this?" Rorie ran the tips of her fingers across the unexpectedly tiny wisps of lace that comprised the robe's matching panties.

"Mostly dental floss, I think. They're kind of ridiculous." Cecily winced in obvious embarrassment, the part of her that remembered she was not a porn vixen clearly having chosen that moment to rise to the surface. "They're so tight around my giant hips, you might have to tear them just to get them off."

"And ruin a Larkin original?" Rorie caressed Cecily's hips, kneading her fingers gently into the flesh, which unlike Cecily, she thought was of exactly the perfect proportion. "I may be a knight, but it doesn't mean I'm a brute. Unless it's part of the script," she added. "I'm all for authenticity."

Cecily shook her head, a bemused smile on her lips. Pulse quickening, Rorie eased the useless bit of lace over the swell of her hips and allowed gravity to do the rest. "Where were we?" she asked as the not-quite-panties floated to the floor.

"Right about here." More forcefully this time, Cecily grasped Rorie's hand and positioned it between her thighs.

With a thrill of surprise, Rorie realized that the whole area was completely and sinfully smooth. Clearly someone had planned ahead, including a trip to the salon before their trip. Her own body tingled as she massaged the bare mound, teasing her fingers along the edge of Cecily's dampened crease.

"And how long does this part of the scene continue?" Rorie whispered.

"Uh, about an hour, I think," Cecily replied, breathless and distracted. "Maybe...um maybe longer."

Rorie cocked an eyebrow, while her hand continued to circle. "Exactly how long did you and your mother stand there watching?"

"We're improvising. Just go with it." Her voice was husky, her body already quivering with barely contained pleasure that overflowed seconds later.

"Are you sure they were shooting a feature length film?" Rorie waited to speak until the point where she thought Cecily might be able to focus on her words, although the response was nothing more than a look of heavy-lidded confusion that made Rorie laugh. "An hour? More like a minute, if that."

"Yes dear, you're very talented." Her words were accompanied by an exaggerated eye roll. No need to brag. "Anyway, there's plenty more to come, fair knight," she added, alert enough now to slip back into the game. She plucked at Rorie's shirt playfully. "But you'll need to get rid of all this chainmail first."

Reclining naked on the bed, Cecily watched as Rorie stripped away her clothing, the intensity of her gaze sending ripples of anticipation through Rorie's body. Cecily stretched her limbs along the sheets and motioned for Rorie to join her. As Rorie settled alongside her on the cool fabric, she reveled in the familiar sense of their bodies melting together, and the sweetness of Cecily's lips as their mouths met. No matter how many times they kissed, it was a taste she would always crave.

She knew she should say something to keep up the illusion of the game, but as Cecily's fingers brushed through her tangled hair, which had been left natural as a break from her usual braids, Rorie didn't want to move, or think, or speak. She simply existed as Cecily worked her fingers along her scalp. When she reached the knotted muscles of her neck, Rorie sucked in her breath, breaking their kiss.

"You're the one who's tense this time."

Rorie sighed, her thoughts now thoroughly disengaged from any attempt at role playing. "It's not every day you fly halfway across the country to adopt a kid."

"Just lay your head on my shoulder and let me work out the knots."

Letting go, Rorie felt her body being rolled until she her full length was pressed atop Cecily's body as Cecily's hands expertly worked along the aching muscles of her back. Tension draining, she let her thighs part and drop to either side of Cecily's leg. She rocked her body gently, the friction of contact sending pleasant tremors through her, though she felt no need to rush toward the goal. Lost in bliss, her eyelids fluttered, and she'd nearly dozed off to sleep when Cecily's voice brought her back to the present.

"Hey, no falling asleep during the movie." Rorie moaned in protest as Cecily shook her shoulder insistently. "Come on, wake up or you're going to miss the best part."

She'd forgotten their game, but remembering it again, she felt the need to finish it. It had been her suggestion, after all. Following Cecily's guiding hands, she lifted herself up until she was on her knees, straddling Cecily, who remained in place on the bed. Rorie's pulse ticked wildly and she no longer felt any interest in sleep.

"Scoot closer."

With a wiggle of her hips, Rorie inched forward, but not fast enough for Cecily, who grasped her bottom and gave a strong tug until her knees rested above Cecily's shoulders. The sound of her heartbeat echoed in Rorie's ears. *This is something different.* She thought the words but her breath was coming too rapidly to speak. Cecily wasn't usually so *demanding*. It was really hot.

"Time to get back on script." So close was she to Cecily's lips that the words vibrated her core.

Rorie cried out as Cecily's mouth made contact, losing herself completely to the sensation until the muscles in her thighs quaked and she could hold herself upright no longer and had to use her arms to steady herself as the intensity of her orgasm tore through her. The last of her energy spent, she fell backward, gasping for air as she rested her head on Cecily's soft belly, every nerve in her body firing like the grand finale of a Fourth of July display.

"So, what did you think of the film?"

Rorie forced her brain to focus through its happy haze long enough to reply. "If the finished product is anything like tonight's preview, I think it'll get excellent reviews."

THE CRISP HOTEL sheets crept across Cecily's toes in the dark. Beside her, Rorie rotated infinitesimally to one side in an attempt not to wake her. Her precaution was unnecessary. Cecily could no more sleep than could Rorie. Sex had provided a powerful distraction from the reason for their trip, but the effect had been fleeting.

"Can't sleep?"

"No." The covers rippled in earnest as Rorie flipped the rest of the way onto her side. "I keep thinking about tomorrow. Or today, I guess."

Though she couldn't see the clock from where she lay, Cecily knew it was past midnight. In less than seven hours, the phone would ring with the wakeup call they had requested from the front desk. An hour later, they would begin the drive from Memphis to an unfamiliar dot on the map across the Mississippi border where the Fairmont Home was located. By this time tomorrow, Bryn would be theirs.

Or Rorie's, to put it more accurately. As her closest kin, the argument for guardianship had been easier for Rorie to attain on her own than it had would have been for Cecily, as an unmarried partner, to be included on the petition. Not that she wouldn't be just as involved, but as the legal guardian and a first-time parent, Cecily wasn't surprised that Rorie felt the pressure of the situation even more keenly than she did.

"You'll do fine." Cecily snaked her arm around Rorie's waist, pulling closer.

"What if she doesn't like me?" Rorie's voice cracked.

Cecily nudged Rorie's warm skin with her nose. "Of course she'll like you. Why wouldn't she?"

"I don't know anything about kids. What they like, how they think. Total mystery."

In her mind, Cecily could see Tyler as a little boy not much older than Bryn. Before they'd turned their basement in Connecticut into a private movie-screening room, it had been a playroom filled with a constant jumble of monster trucks and little boys. Her house had been the favorite destination of nearly every one of her son's classmates, and concern over whether they would like her had never once crossed her mind.

She patted Rorie reassuringly. "Kids aren't that complicated." In Cecily's experience, it was the moms that were to be feared, not the kids.

"Easy for you to say, Cici. You've done this before."

"And I'll be doing it again, right alongside you. Together, we can handle this."

A long, heavy sigh filled the room. "You're right." The statement lacked conviction.

Though her pregnancy had been unplanned, being a mom had come naturally to Cecily almost from the start. Caring for Tyler had been a welcome reprieve from the rest of her married life, for which she had shown far less aptitude. Sharing that fact wasn't going to help Rorie's worry, though, so she searched her memories for some useful advice that her partner might take to heart.

"Try to remember what you were like as a kid."

"What I was like? I don't know. Shorter?"

"Ha ha," Cecily said dryly. "But fine, that's a start. Think about how big the world seems to someone Bryn's age. How scary it is to be so vulnerable. And then—I don't know. Trust your instincts." It might be less than helpful, but it was the best she could do.

"What if I don't have any instincts?"

Then you never would have fought so hard to save her.

With her fingertips, Cecily traced circles along Rorie's back, her way of indicating that she was listening even as she refrained from giving a response. She was all out of advice, and this was something Rorie needed to puzzle through on her own.

After a short silence, Rorie spoke again. "I hated always being told what to do. When I was Bryn's age, that's all my dad seemed to do, like my opinion didn't matter."

"See? That's something you can work with."

"It's late." A loud yawn drew out her words, a signal that Rorie's body might finally be willing to attempt sleep.

Cecily gave her back a final pat. "Get some rest. Tomorrow's a big day."

Beside her, Rorie's body relaxed and her breathing slowed as she slipped into sleep, but Cecily's mind continued to whir. She'd done this before, it was true, and so she knew even better than Rorie did how much things were about to change.

Her biggest challenge this time would be helping Rorie ease into her new role, and how she could best accomplish that without taking over completely was what kept her awake until the wee hours of morning.

ELEVEN

THERE WAS silence in the car the next morning as they headed away from the city, both women preferring the gentle hum of tires on road to the country or gospel options on the local radio. The trip from Memphis took little more than an hour, but in half that time they'd left all cosmopolitan traces behind, and were instead immersed in a rural sliver of Dixie, a land of peeling paint and boarded storefronts. Prosperity had left the area behind long ago, if it had ever been there to begin with.

Rorie frowned as she turned onto the main street of the small town that her niece called home. "Can you check the GPS?"

"Almost there," Cecily replied with strained cheerfulness. "Five more miles, straight ahead."

Rorie's stomach clenched. Five more miles. "It's a lot different from LA." What type of life had Bryn had up until now? She couldn't begin to imagine what it would be like to spend childhood in a place as depressing as this.

"How they live doesn't matter as much to kids, you know,"

Cecily said, as if reading her mind. "Money and appearances and all that. They just care if they're loved."

It was meant to be reassuring, Rorie knew, but it only stoked her concerns more. Had Bryn been loved? What were the odds, with parents and a grandmother suffering from addiction, that she'd been raised in a nurturing environment, even before entering the foster care system? Her own childhood hadn't exactly been overflowing with tender emotion. Her father had done the best he could, but he'd fallen short frequently. And her mother hadn't been there at all. Even having reunited with them both in adulthood, it couldn't completely erase the damage of the past. What damage had already been done where Bryn was concerned, and was Rorie remotely equipped to handle it?

Cecily was right. Money in itself didn't matter. But money was something she knew she could offer. A bedroom filled with toys and a closet of clothes. Good schools and summer camp. But when it came to the type of love a child needed to thrive? She wasn't convinced she knew what that was. Her heart beat faster as a mild panic took hold. *What if I fail?*

The GPS announced the approach of their destination on the right. Rorie's hands shook as she turned the steering wheel. As she took in the facility in front of her, her worries about her capacity for parenting subsided, replaced with more immediate doubts. Her brow furrowed as she squinted at the sign in the parking lot. "This can't be it, can it?"

The Fairmont Home for Children didn't look at all the way Rorie had expected. In her mind, the group home where Bryn lived was a sprawling old mansion with towering white columns, a southern plantation grown shabby over the years, but retaining traces of its past glory. Sentimentally, she'd pictured a tire swing hanging from the thick branch of a tall tree, and a pond with a dock made from roughhewn pine where the children would swim on hot summer days. If she'd been designing it for a movie set, that's how it would have looked.

This idyllic vision had seen her through many sleepless nights since she'd found out about her niece's existence, but it bore little resemblance to the truth. In reality, the facility was a collection of squat brick buildings, dull tan with streaks of dirty brown. At first glance it appeared to be an elementary school, and perhaps that was how it had started out its existence.

It certainly hadn't been built for living in. There was nothing remotely homelike about the institutional structures and asphalt-covered grounds, where a few faded four-square courts drawn in flat yellow paint provided scant relief from a monochromatic landscape. Rorie shuddered. It was no place for a child to grow up.

"It's definitely the place."

All trace of cheerfulness had drained from Cecily's voice. Walking beside Rorie as they crossed the campus, her face was pale and drawn. Rorie grasped at Cecily's hand for reassurance but found it to be as cold and clammy as her own. The sooner they collected Bryn and got her out of this place, the happier they all would be.

The door marked reception was locked, with a buzzer on an intercom box beside it to summon a member of staff. Rorie pressed it and could hear the bell sound inside, making her nerves flutter at the finality of it. *No backing out now.* The door opened to reveal a young woman wearing a polo shirt with the Fairmont Home logo stitched at the breast, a harried look on her face.

"Are you the ones here for Bryn?" the woman asked. Rorie and Cecily nodded in reply. "You can check in at the desk. Half the east wing is down sick with the flu, so I have to run. Her social worker will be out to meet you as soon as she can." With that, she dashed off down a corridor, not giving them a chance to respond.

"Busy place," Cecily remarked as three more workers raced past them without a second glance.

Outside the window, Rorie saw a long yellow bus pull up and a line of children file along the sidewalk to board it, overseen by more staff in matching uniform shirts. The children themselves were dressed in a hodgepodge of typical play clothing, of the type that could be bought cheap at a discount department store. That was another thing, she realized, that she hadn't counted on.

In her imagination, though she'd never be willing to put it into words, the children had worn printed flour sack dresses and tweed newsboy caps, like the raggedy cast of a community theater production of *Annie*. Even admitting it to herself made her cheeks burn. It was ridiculous to picture modern children dressed like orphans in a Broadway musical, but it was the only frame of reference she had. *Well, it's not like I'm a professional costume designer.*

A nervous tremor passed through her as she contemplated once more how little she understood about her niece. Maybe the judge had been right to start with not to give her custody. There had to be someone out there who was better equipped for this. Someone who was a natural nurturer, who understood what children were like and what they needed.

Someone like Cecily. She glanced at the woman sitting beside her. *My partner.* She'd be there every step of the way. The realization came at just the right moment, calming

Rorie's jitters and bringing a faint smile to her face. *Thank God I'm not doing this alone.*

A heavy door closed with a bang and Rorie swiveled in the direction of the noise. A middle-aged woman approached the reception desk and offered her hand to Rorie and Cecily in turn. "Hi, I'm Cathy."

The sight of the social worker immediately put her at ease. She had gray hair and a plump belly, like a grandmother straight out of central casting. *At least one of my expectations was right.* Cathy's appearance was as comforting to Rorie as it must have been to the children she worked with each day, and it made her feel like maybe Bryn's time at the home hadn't been as dire as she'd feared. This was the type of woman who could pull a butterscotch from her pocket at a moment's notice. It couldn't have been all bad, right?

Cathy smiled. "The paperwork's all in order, so if you'll follow me, we'll collect Bryn's things from her room."

She led them across miles of linoleum flooring, through a sitting room with a television and a mismatched assortment of couches and bean bags grouped around an area rug. The furnishings wouldn't win any design awards, but they looked softer and more welcoming than Fairmont Home's entrance had, and more of Rorie's initial negativity toward the facility eased.

"Her bag's packed in the bedroom," Cathy explained, motioning them through a door into a dormitory containing eight twin beds.

When she saw the aforementioned bag, bile rose in her throat. Her change of heart had come too soon. Bryn's bag was literally that, a bulging black plastic trash bag, knotted at the top. Rorie shuddered. Beside her, Cecily drew in her breath sharply as she, too, caught sight of the way Bryn's belongings had been packed. How could it not make a child feel worthless to have their treasures treated like trash?

"I'm sorry about that," Cathy said hastily, perhaps sensing their shock. "We usually try to give them duffel bags when they leave, but our supply ran out and donations have been a little light this quarter. If you'd like to wait here, I'll go get her. She's in the dining area, saying goodbye to her friends."

Rorie nodded with as much confidence as she could manage, but her heart ricocheted like a stray bullet off her ribcage. For the first time it hit Rorie full force that her niece was a fully formed human with friends, and likes and dislikes, and a whole personality. And while she couldn't begin to understand what life in this home had been like, she knew Bryn's whole world was about to shift axis. *What if I mess this up? She might hate me.* Panic rose inside.

"I don't know anything about kids, Cici." Her breathing grew shallow as she spoke. "I don't know Bryn at all. I didn't even know her mother!" She steadied herself with a hand against the wall as the room took on a wobbly, spinning quality.

A calm hand squeezed her shoulder. "We can do this."

The quiet confidence that radiated from her calmed Rorie's racing heart and put her surroundings back into focus. Cecily had done all this before. *She knows the drill, even if I don't.*

"Okay." Rorie gave a thin, shaky laugh. "But you're officially the child expert in this family, just so you know."

"I'll do my best." Her words were humble, but Cecily beamed with pride at Rorie's vote of confidence. Then her expression grew serious. "I'm going to hang back, though, when she comes in. You need to get a chance to know her a little by yourself first."

Rorie swallowed roughly, but nodded. It was a wise plan.

Cecily strode to Bryn's bed and began picking at the knot on the plastic bag. "I'm just going to see if I can get a sense of what she already has and what we'll need to buy. Other than a suitcase, clearly," she added, glaring at the bag.

Rorie gave the bag a distasteful look. "Clearly."

"Ms. Mulloy?" Cathy had returned with a tiny girl in tow.

A shock of recognition made Rorie's spine tingle. There was no mistaking who she was. *Bryn.* So obviously her own flesh and blood, this child with her wild mane of curls and shockingly blue eyes. Eyes that studied Rorie and Cecily warily. Rorie swallowed again, sandpaper coating her throat.

"This is Bryn." The social worker let go of her hand and gave her shoulder an encouraging tap in Rorie's direction. "These are the ladies I told you about, who are going to take you to your new home. Can you go say hello to your aunt, sweetie?"

Though she walked bravely forward, Rorie sensed trepidation beneath her niece's surface that mirrored her own. *We're in the same boat, aren't we kiddo?* In a flash of understanding, it occurred to her how tall she must seem to someone so small, like the giant at the top of the bean stalk. On instinct, she touched one knee to the ground so that their eyes were level. "Hi, Bryn."

The child's eyes widened, then her eyebrows scrunched together as if confused. "Mama?"

Rorie's heart contracted, pain more bitter than she could have anticipated lancing through. "No, sweetie. I'm your Aunt Rorie."

The girl sniffled, uncertain. "You look like Mama, only she's in heaven with Daddy, and Father Greg at Sunday school says people don't come back from heaven. Is that true?"

Rorie's eyes stung, unnerved by the directness of the question. She nodded solemnly. "I'm afraid it is." She wished she could offer Bryn a more satisfying answer.

The corners of Bryn's eyes twitched, but she held back her tears. "Yeah, I thought so. But you *do* look like her." Whether a statement or an accusation, Rorie wasn't sure.

"She was my sister. And that's why—" She'd been about to say *you're going to come live with us*, but stopped short, awash in the memories of her father making similar declarations each time he was assigned to a different military base in some new state. *It sucks to be a kid and not have a choice where you go.* "That's why I was hoping you might come to California and live with me. That is, if you want to. I even have a bedroom all ready for you."

Bryn sniffed. "What color is it?"

"Seashell pink."

Bryn stayed silent, appearing to mull it over. Rorie's nerves tingled as she realized the hole she'd dug for herself. What if she hated pink and decided she didn't want to go? She'd been an idiot to make Bryn think she had that kind of power over the situation. *Such a rookie mistake!*

But finally, Bryn gave a nod. "I like pink."

Hallelujah! Rorie let out the breath she hadn't realized she was holding and flashed a smile. "Good. I'm glad. Now you should meet Cecily. She's my girlfriend. She lives with me, and she'll help take care of you, too."

Rorie took Bryn's hand and led her toward the bed, where Cecily had formed two piles of clothes from Bryn's bag. She was studying them with a critical expression, seemingly unaware of their approach.

"These are okay," she said, addressing Cathy, who stood beside her, and pointing to the smaller pile, "but the rest are so worn and dingy, I think we can just leave them behind."

"Those are mine!"

With a shriek that stopped Rorie's heart, Bryn raced to her bed and began snatching the clothing into her arms. Before any of the grown-ups could react, she'd shoved every item back into the bag, which she clutched against her chest like a life preserver. "These are MY THINGS!"

The child's voice echoed with the force of a lion's roar, and Cecily froze, her eyes wide. "Oh, no, Bryn...I didn't mean..." she stammered, clearly realizing her colossal misstep.

"I'm taking my things." Bryn's fierce stance left no room for argument.

"I was only thinking we could go shopping..." Cecily looked pleadingly at Rorie.

Stunned by her niece's response, Rorie's brain whirred into high gear. "How about we go to the store and get a suitcase. We'll need one for the plane. Big enough to hold *all* of your things," she added when Bryn failed to answer. Finally, Bryn mumbled her assent and Rorie's tense shoulders slumped in relief.

Their untamed new ward marched between them out of the group home and into the parking lot, stubbornly carrying her precious bag with both hands. Cecily reached for Bryn's hand when they got to the pavement, but Bryn simply glared and grasped her bag even tighter. Bryn's one concession was to allow her aunt to steer her gently around the parked cars with one hand on her shoulder.

Rorie's hands were slick with sweat as she helped Bryn into her booster seat and fastened the seatbelt across her lap, and the reason had nothing to do with the humid Mississippi air. In the blink of an eye, she had become the only one her niece seemed willing to trust. It was irrational, an absurd leap of faith based on nothing but raw emotion. But something told her that there would be no reasoning with this tiny person.

She reminds me of myself at this age. Strangely, the realization was calming. She'd never thought she had it in her, but somehow on a very basic level, she *got* this kid. She understood what made her tick. As she maneuvered the car onto the highway, a strange sense of serenity replaced Rorie's earlier concern, along with a rush of confidence.

Maybe I'm cut out for this motherhood thing after all.

TWELVE

RECLINING ON THE HOTEL BED, Cecily felt a satisfying pop as the joints in her limbs yielded to a deep stretch. It had been a long and grueling day, more awful than she'd ever expected it to be. The reason was as simple as it was confounding. *Bryn hates me.* Her heart dropped to a depth she hadn't known was possible even as the words flitted through her brain. How could one four-year-old be the source of so much emotional distress?

And talk about holding a grudge! After her blunder at the Fairmont Home, Cecily had done everything she could think of to make it right. A new suitcase had been procured immediately, purchased from the only big-box store for miles. It lay beside her now in all its bubble gum pink glory. She'd nearly wept with gratitude when she saw it in the store aisle. Just for good measure she'd thrown in a carry-on bag covered in the smiling faces of every cartoon princess ever created.

No, not every princess. Bryn had been quick, almost gleeful, to point that out. Her favorite princess was conspicuously absent. *Of course she was.* Aside from the outburst over her possessions, those had been the only words addressed to

Cecily from the child all day. Granted, she hadn't spoken much to Rorie, either. She was remarkably reserved for a preschooler, generally more interested in observing than prattling on. But though Bryn might be quiet by nature, when directed toward Cecily, the silence felt deliberate.

Cecily sighed, wondering if she would ever manage to win over the stubborn little creature who had refused so much as a goodnight kiss from her tonight. It was an alien experience to be so thoroughly rejected by a child, and it cut to the quick. She'd never known anything but a child's love and acceptance, at least perhaps until the teenage years had hit, and even then, Tyler had rarely sulked or rebelled the way so many teens do. Given that Bryn couldn't even tie her own shoes yet, Cecily had counted on having a little more time to acclimate before the difficult years set in.

With mounting dismay, she was forced to consider that maybe parenting wasn't her super power, after all. Maybe Tyler had just been an exceptionally easy kid and as a first-time parent, she'd had no idea. Maybe she'd just been lucky when it came to her son and his friends, and had never really been tested until now.

Was it because Tyler and his friends were all boys? She'd heard boys were easier but the feminist in her had staunchly refused to believe it. Even if it were true, could there be that big of a difference between boys and girls already at such a young age? Or had her gaffe been so much worse than she'd understood in order to earn this response? She pressed her hand to her forehead, trying to block out the memory of Bryn's ear-piercing scream when she'd heard Cecily suggest leaving her play-worn clothing behind. It was the type of superficial comment her own mother might have made, heartless and judgmental. *Why, why, why couldn't I have just kept my mouth shut?*

So many questions swirled around in her head, and yet not a single answer presented itself to Cecily's exhausted brain. Had it really been only the night before when she'd been declared the expert on parenting, and Rorie was the one struggling to keep her head above water? She'd be tempted to laugh, but knew if she started, she'd end up in tears instead.

Cecily cracked open one lid and peered at the door to the adjoining room where Rorie had been ensconced in the dry-run of their new bedtime routine. It was going on half an hour now, but based on how Rorie had looked each time Cecily had poked her head in to check on them, her partner had no complaints. In fact, pure bliss had been radiating from her the whole time like she'd stolen the facial expression from the model on a Mother's Day card. *My, how things change in twenty-four hours.*

From the other room came the low, melodic rumble of Rorie's voice reading a story. It was already the third story of the night. Cecily knew this not because she'd been invited to read one herself, or even listen, though buying the book had been her idea. No, she most assuredly had *not* been asked to join. But each story's ending had been punctuated by a plea for 'just one more'. It was the most she'd heard Bryn say all day.

Despite fearing their new ward had cast Cecily, without her consent, in the role of the evil stepmother and summarily banished her to the dungeon, Cecily couldn't help but smile as Bryn's small voice piped up for the fourth time, followed by the sound of Rorie launching into another story. *So patient.* Despite her concerns, Rorie was a natural with the child. Turned out she'd had nothing to worry about all along.

Closing her eyes, Cecily let the gentle hum of words wash over her. She couldn't make out the tale, but she didn't need to. Just the sound of Rorie's voice soothed her nearly as much as it did Bryn, though it filled her with melancholy, too. She'd never doubted herself like this before, not in this capacity. Her stomach tightened and her left foot began to twitch.

She'd had the in-over-her-head feeling in the workplace, sure. Her first time on stage at the Oakwood Theater, her first day at Grant Studios, or the moment she stepped on set at *Portland Blue*. God knows, starting her own company had kept her awake many a night, convinced she'd never be taken seriously as a producer. It still did, though a little less so now that it had been almost six months and their first web series was about to be underway. But those were rational, as she'd legitimately had no training or experience doing them before. Raising a child was supposed to be a skill that was firmly in her wheelhouse.

As her body struggled to relax, Cecily focused her troubled mind away from the stresses of home, allowing her thoughts to drift to work. For as much emotional turmoil as that usually caused, at the moment it was a subject of comparative calm. An email from Jill had arrived earlier, right around the time Bryn was explaining the ways in which Cecily's choice of princess luggage was not up to snuff. She'd barely glanced at it then, but curiosity tugged at her now. *Maybe I'll just check to see how the first day on set went.*

There were photos attached that sent Cecily's heart into high speed. *Beautiful!* Everything looked exactly the way she'd pictured it. But almost immediately, disappointment brought her spirits crashing back down to earth. She should have been there, overseeing every detail, because it was *hers*. Her heart lurched. Given what was taking place at the company she'd founded, today should have been one of professional triumph for her. Instead, it had been a personal disaster. Given how things were going with Bryn, would it not have been better if she'd just stayed home? As it was, she felt she'd abdicated responsibility at her job only to fail on the home front, too.

Silence buzzed in Cecily's ears. The hum of Rorie's voice had stopped, and this time no child's voice answered with a call for more. Moments later, the door creaked, and the mattress shifted as Rorie joined her on the king-size bed.

"She's finally asleep."

"You seem to have a way with her." *Unlike me.* Cecily glanced up from her phone, attempting to keep her tone neutral. It wasn't fair to ruin Rorie's triumph with her own insecurities.

"Maybe." Rorie nestled her body behind Cecily's, running her fingers along Cecily's spine in a way that chased away some of her gloom and filled her with the urge to arch, kitten-like, into the caresses. "Thanks to you."

"To me?" Her words came out as a purr, and as she succumbed to the need to stretch, she spied the black screen of the phone still clutched in her hand. She pushed it beneath her pillow so the blinking message light wouldn't be too tempting, and turned her attention to Rorie. "I think you figured this one out on your own."

"Not until our talk last night. It turns out you were right."

"About what?"

"Well, Bryn's a lot like me."

"You're saying when we met, you didn't like me either?" She tried to play it off as a jest, but some of her earlier sulkiness bled through.

Her bottom stung as Rorie gave it the teasing swat she deserved. "I'm not even going to dignify that with a response. I meant what you said last night about remembering what I was like at her age."

"And what was that?" Her own issues put aside, she

swiveled her head to look behind her, studying Rorie's face with genuine curiosity.

"By the time I was four, my mom was gone and I think we'd moved three times already for Pop's job. He never seemed to grasp how hard that was, either." Rorie gave a half-shrug. "You know how he is. Always just telling me what I had to do, what I had to leave behind."

Cecily swallowed hard around the lump in her throat. "Rorie, you know I didn't mean to make Bryn—"

"I know." She smoothed Cecily's hair back, wrapping a tendril around one finger.

"It's good that you can connect with her like that. That you understand her."

"It's hard to explain, but I feel like I do."

"It's only right. You're her auntie, after all."

"Auntie." Rorie smiled. "I guess I am. Although, it's funny. Tonight at bedtime—"

Cecily frowned at the sudden pause, like there was something Rorie was afraid to say. "At bedtime, what?"

"Nothing. It's just, I think she called me *Mama*. Maybe."

"That's..." Cecily tamped down the hint of jealousy that threatened to surface, instead wrapping her arms around Rorie and pulling her close until her head rested on Cecily's shoulder. "That's really great. Amazing, in fact. I know the social workers warned us about how difficult it might be for her to form attachments right away." For some reason, she'd never thought to apply that warning to herself.

Rorie sighed deeply. Her warm breath tickled Cecily's neck, and she could sense her partner's distress. "Are you still having doubts?"

Rorie shook her head. "No, it's not that. It's just, becoming her guardian was only the first hurdle. Adopting her could be a much bigger challenge. Between being a lesbian and a single mother, I'm not sure which one pisses off these Bible Belt judges more, and there's no guarantee your mom can repeat her magic next time."

"You're *not* a single mother." Cecily flinched at all the word implied, that maybe Rorie, too, doubted her ability to win Bryn over.

"Of course not. I know that. But I am as far as the court's concerned, since we're not—"

"Married. I know." She didn't mean to sound so snappy, but the stress of the day had taken its toll. "And I'm sorry if that would make things easier, but—"

"Cici, that's not what I meant."

"You *know* that being married wasn't a happy time for me." Her skin crawled at the memory of nights spent alone in an empty house, a crying baby her only company. The desperation, being convinced she was doing it all wrong. *Maybe it didn't come as easy to me as I thought it did. Nostalgia comes with a great pair of rose-tinted glasses.*

"Tell me," Rorie said, and it was clear she wanted to know.

"Once Tyler was born, and my parents were back in Louisiana, it was just me. Chet worked seven days a week. I felt trapped, and so isolated." Cecily's voice cracked.

In her mind she could hear his voice on the phone, calling yet again to say he wasn't coming home. His attention was the last thing she'd wanted, yet the chronic lack of it left her bruised inside. He had a family to support now, he'd always say, in that tone that implied somehow all of this had been her idea. Like she hadn't sacrificed everything, too.

"I'm not saying him being around more would have saved our marriage, but it sure didn't help." She squeezed her lids shut to block the tears. *God, no wonder I locked the memory of those years away.* "It's been so long since I let myself think about it, I'd forgotten how hard it was."

And it *had* been hard, being the reluctant wife of a neglectful husband. Perhaps it was only by comparison that motherhood had seemed so carefree. She opened her eyes again, but Rorie's expression was unreadable, and she feared she'd failed to explain herself in a way that Rorie could accept.

"I'm not asking you to get married."

Is she angry? Maybe if I lighten the mood. "Yeah, you're lack of a ring box and bended knee were two good clues."

"No, I mean, I'm not going to ask you, period. I think it's important we clear that up right now." There was seriousness in her tone, but not the anger Cecily had feared. "So, if you're afraid I will, that's not what's going to happen. If you ever change your mind about it, it's up to you to ask."

"But you don't hate me for feeling like I'll never want to?"

Relief washed over her as Rorie whispered 'of course not', though part of her squirmed at having the ball dropped so thoroughly in her court. *I'll think about how to deal with that later.* For now, she'd accept the victory.

Lacing her fingers behind Rorie's head, Cecily drew her close for a kiss. Her body tingled as the warmth of contact spread through her, but as she moved to deepen the kiss, a sobbing cry rang out from the next room.

"Mama? Mama!"

Rorie stiffened, a look of alarm crossing her face as she pulled her body away. "I'm sorry, I think I need to—"

"Go. It's okay. Go check on her."

Without Rorie there, Cecily felt the chill of the evening and crawled beneath the covers for warmth. It would be a while. From next door, Cecily heard mattress springs groan and could picture Rorie cuddling up beside the little girl.

Their little girl, though goodness knew when it would start to feel that way for real. Right now, Cecily had no doubt that her presence would not be welcome.

Swinging her legs to the floor, Cecily crossed the room and rifled through her bag, producing the Jada Larkin script that had remained there, untouched, until now. Returning to bed, she switched on the reading light and opened to the first page. It wasn't at all what she'd expected. *It's absolutely brilliant.* Transfixed, she continued to read as scene by scene the film played out in her imagination. Goosebumps covered her arms. It was everything she'd been looking for in their first feature film. Just when she'd started to fear she would fail at everything, this script offered salvation.

She reached the end and switched off the light, filled with a sense of destiny. *We have to do this.*

She'd be back in Los Angeles on Saturday, and had planned to take the next week off, but now? There seemed little point, like she'd only be in the way. And meanwhile, the first project she'd produced had already been rolling on without her for far too long, and she had a new project to plan. For the first time since that morning, her confidence came flooding back.

In the adjoining room, Rorie and Bryn slept soundly, and Cecily paid them no mind. She had other things to think about, decisions that had to be made. Sliding her hand beneath her pillow, Cecily pulled out her phone, the screen a sudden spot of brightness in the dimly lit room as she composed an email to Jill, letting her know that Monday morning she'd be in bright and early. They had work to do.

THIRTEEN

A CACOPHONY of sound assaulted Rorie's ears, a stark reminder that the quiet child they'd picked up in Mississippi had disappeared part way through the weekend, replaced by a nearly identical version whose volume switch was permanently stuck on high. Bryn still wasn't a big talker, but there were a seemingly infinite number of ways to make noise at the age of four. The plinking of a toy piano, the mooing of an electronic cow, and somewhat inexplicably, a trumpet fanfare, emanated from Bryn's bedroom in rapid succession.

What toy did we buy with a trumpet? Rorie frowned as she looked at the blurry numbers on the bedside clock. A little before seven. She massaged the sleep from behind her eyelids with one hand as the other tensed on the top of her duvet, preparing to rip it away with the same grim anticipation as a bandage from a wound. It still felt ungodly early, but at least Rorie had been allowed to stay in bed fifteen minutes longer than the day before.

Cecily was already gone, headed into the office earlier than usual. Again. Rorie took a deep breath, hoping as she released the air from her lungs that her frustration would flow out with the breath as well. This hadn't been the plan. Cecily had promised to take the week off, but instead she'd gone into the studio before the sun was up three days in a row. Cecily thought Rorie had a handle on the situation, but since returning to Los Angeles, most of Rorie's newfound confidence had evaporated and each day was more of an emotional struggle than the one before.

Rorie knew that Cecily was eager to return to her first big project at work. She didn't begrudge her that, but she'd been in the business long enough to understand that there would always be big, important, exciting projects in the pipeline. That was the nature of working in Hollywood, that every new endeavor took on an urgent, larger-than-life quality. But allowing their family to take a backseat was not a precedent Rorie was willing to establish. They'd have to discuss it soon, when Rorie knew how to express what she was feeling in a reasonable way. And if she weren't so exhausted by the end of the day when Cecily came home that all she could think about was sleep.

With no job to get ready for, Rorie had envisioned leisurely mornings spent perusing the news and sipping coffee while Bryn played quietly at her feet. None of this could have been further from the truth. Chasing after a four-year-old was a full-contact sport, and she'd barely managed to get Bryn's breakfast on the table and the clean dishes from the night before put away before it was already nine o'clock. Her task had been punctuated by an endless cycle of picking up things that didn't belong out, or scooping up items in sudden danger of destruction. Not that anything remained neat for long in the face of hurricane Bryn. Had she really spent two hours like this? If she'd needed any more evidence that she wasn't cut out for full-time motherhood, the past few days had added substantially to her list.

As she was wiping droplets of milk from the kitchen table, Rorie's cell phone rang, and the number on the screen made her heart skip a beat. It was the producer of the show she'd been hoping to land. The promise of returning to work, especially coming when it did, was almost too good to be true.

"Hello?"

"Rorie, it's Jim Douglas from Paramount."

"Yes, of course." She cringed as Bryn beat the inside of her cereal bowl with her spoon, producing a clanging sound that could wake the dead, along with a fresh shower of milk that obliterated her earlier efforts.

"Is this an okay time to talk?"

"Absolutely." She cradled the phone to her shoulder, freeing up one hand to operate the remote control while the other hand guided Bryn to a chair in the living room. She wasn't so much of a parenting novice as not to know it was a terrible idea to use screen time as a babysitter, but given the importance of the call, she was willing to play dumb on the issue. "What can I do for you, Jim?"

"Well, I'm hoping you'll say you can be my new production designer."

Rorie grinned into the phone. *Saved, at last!* "I would be thrilled to join the team!"

The whinny of a horse came from down the hall, and Rorie's head whipped toward the sound. *How did she get all the way over there?* In the second she'd turned her back, Bryn had managed to make it from the living room to her bedroom, and was now galloping full tilt down the hallway on a hobby horse, screaming *yeehaw!* Along with the cartoon characters on the screen. *This would never happen if Cici were here.*

To think, the fact that infernal object made real horse sounds had actually seemed like a selling point in the store. Rorie made a *shushing* sound that Bryn mostly ignored. Her muscles tensed. It wasn't the first time Rorie felt that Bryn didn't take her seriously, as if sensing her inexperience. A spot above Rorie's left eye throbbed like someone was trying to drive a dull stake into her skull. She cupped her hand around the phone, hoping to insulate it from the din.

"Look, it sounds like you have your hands full there."

"I'm so sorry, Jim. My niece—"

"No, no worries. Kids, right? As long as you're on board, that's good enough for now. Why don't I just give you a call later on this evening and we can discuss the details then."

Rorie's heart raced as reality set in. *I got the job!* Her excitement bubbled over, and suddenly none of her worries could keep her down. She was silly with glee, and galloped after Bryn, chasing her down the hall and around the living room until the little girl collapsed in a fit of giggles. Rorie tousled the child's curly locks, a smile on her face. Everything was going to work out after all. Soon Bryn would be settled in and Rorie would be back to doing the job she did best.

But January was only eight weeks away. The realization cooled her excitement. Was she crazy to think she'd be ready to return to work by then? She'd have to start looking for a nanny right away, and she'd heard enough horror stories from other parents to be wary. Given Bryn's history, and how she'd reacted to Cecily, Rorie knew it could be a challenge to find the right fit.

Luckily, an actress from her old show who'd recently had a baby had been kind enough to send her a referral to one of the premier child care agencies in Los Angeles. Rorie pulled up the number, crossing her fingers that her good fortune would continue. Not usually a fan of using these types of connections, Rorie would name drop until she was blue in the face if it meant finding some help.

"*Price Agency*," said the woman's voice on the other end

of the phone. It could've been Rorie's imagination, but just the way she said it seemed to convey what an honor it was to even have their number.

"Hello. My name is Rorie Mulloy and I was given your name—" Bryn raced through the room, her horse neighing at full volume. "Bryn, honey, please stop running in the house. Sorry, as I was saying, I'm calling about finding a full-time nanny. I have a referral."

"Let me just pull up a new file. Can you tell me a little bit about—"

"Bryn, no!" As the child careened around the coffee table, the end of her pony's stick swept its surface, leaving a heavy glass vase tottering on the edge as she galloped past. Tossing the phone to the ground, Rorie lunged as it crashed to the floor. The room went black around the edges of her vision as her big toe broke its fall.

"Ow, fuck! Damn it, Bryn!"

The child froze, then skittered into her room and shut the door. Rorie hobbled to retrieve her discarded phone. The line had gone dead, and she felt sick to her stomach as she replayed the chaotic scene the woman had overheard. She wouldn't be holding her breath for the Price Agency to return her inquiry about a nanny any time soon.

A bright spot of red caught her eye, and Rorie winced at the gash the vase had left on the top of her foot, which was oozing blood onto the carpet. Staunching the flow temporarily with a handful of tissues, Rorie limped into the kitchen in search of supplies to clean both herself and the rug. She stopped cold at the sight of Margaret crossing the lawn from the guesthouse, heading toward the patio door. As Margaret tapped on the glass, the wild thought of pretending no one was home shot through Rorie's brain. But of course, the door was made of glass, and Margaret was staring right at her.

"You look a sight."

"Good morning to you, too, Margaret. Come in, why don't you." Margaret's gaze was fixed on the floor, and Rorie glanced down to see that a fresh bit of red had seeped through her makeshift bandage. "There was a little accident with Bryn and a vase."

Margaret's eyes widened. "She's not hurt, is she?"

Rorie let loose a strangled laugh. "Hurt? That child's indestructible."

She'd expected judgment, but was surprised to see sympathy in the woman's eyes. "They usually are, much more so than adults or furniture. Where is she now?"

"In her bedroom. She had the good sense to disappear when she realized what she'd done." As she transferred her weight to the injured foot, Rorie hissed.

"You need to get a bandage on that. Is my daughter here?"

Rorie shook her head. "She's been at work for hours."

"I see. Again?"

Margaret pursed her lips disapprovingly and Rorie tried not to revel in self-vindication. Clearly, she wasn't the only one who found Cecily's sudden devotion to work excessive.

"Well, you go take care of that foot, and I'll keep an eye on the child. Take a shower, while you're at it. Looks like you could use one."

"Are you sure you don't mind?"

It had been the type of backhanded comment that she'd come to expect from Cecily's mother, but the offer was such a godsend, she wasn't about to take offense. And she had a point. In the sleep-deprived blur of the last few days, Rorie couldn't remember exactly when she'd last bathed. It was the type of thing mothers always referenced like a badge of honor: the lack of sleep, and showers, and never peeing by yourself without a child underfoot. Come to think of it, she hadn't managed to use the bathroom unaccompanied since the day they'd arrived home. It felt oddly reassuring, like she'd earned her credentials for membership in the motherhood club.

"I don't mind at all. It's hardly the first time I've entertained a rambunctious preschooler."

Margaret was the picture of efficiency as she marched toward Bryn's room, and any reservations Rorie might have held dissipated. Given Cecily's differences with her mother, it was easy to forget that this was a woman who had raised two children, plus grandchildren, and had earned her own fair share of parenting credentials over the years. *Thank God Margaret came by when she did, or I don't know what I would have done.*

Under a steamy spray of water, surrounded by the sweet scent of shampoo, Rorie's head began to clear and her spirits lifted. Her problems were nothing that a little help couldn't fix. And while she'd rather it had been Cecily doing the helping, she'd take anything she could get until a nanny was in place. She groaned at the reminder, but refused to let it bring her down. She'd call the Price Agency again tomorrow, and with any luck, the receptionist wouldn't remember her as the crazy woman who had screamed obscenities at a child and then thrown the phone across the room, and they could just start fresh.

Rorie finished showering quickly and toweled herself dry. She paused to carefully wrap gauze and tape around her injured toe, but chose to forgo the relative luxuries of shaving or her usual moisturizing routine, afraid to take too much advantage of Margaret's unexpected generosity. Silence greeted her from the direction of Bryn's room—a minor miracle!—but even if things were going smoothly, she didn't want to impose any longer than necessary. Margaret had stepped in today, but Rorie knew she couldn't count on that forever.

Cecily's mother would surely be leaving soon, though at the moment Rorie felt less inclined than ever to push for her departure date.

There was Cecily, too, of course, if her work schedule let up. *If that isn't just an excuse she's using to avoid spending time with Bryn.* It was an uncharitable thought, but it rang true. Though the worst of their falling out was slowly ebbing, her niece had yet to warm up to her other guardian the way she had to her aunt. While she routinely called Rorie *mama*, she refused so much as to call Cecily by name. It troubled Rorie to think that Cecily was withdrawing from them, but maybe she was wrong and Bryn wasn't the reason. If it really was just a busy work schedule, the last thing Rorie wanted was for Cecily to think that she didn't value her job.

Maybe their talk could wait, until Rorie had a better sense of her motivation. *Why, when it comes to Cecily, are these things always so hard?* A long-forgotten memory surfaced of their time together in college, working in the scene shop side by side. Things had been complicated then, too, but in a different way. An easier way. An unexpected longing for that time made Rorie's heart ache. Between career and family, would they ever see more of each other than ships passing in the night?

It was quiet as she emerged, dressed and refreshed, into the hallway. In Bryn's room, the little girl sat cross-legged on the floor as she and Margaret built a tower out of brightly colored foam blocks. The ache in her chest subsided. A new job, a happy child, and another step toward peaceful coexistence with Margaret. Not everything was perfect, but it wasn't bad for her first week as a parent, after all. The rest could be worked out in time.

SHE'D DOZED off in the living room chair, surrounded by the pillows and blankets that Bryn had used to build a fort. This time it wasn't a loud noise that woke her, but a moan, soft and low. It came again and she bolted upright, pillows spilling to the floor.

"Bryn?"

"I'm hot, Mama."

The muffled voice came from below her, and sweeping the floor with her eyes, Rorie saw a small hand sticking out from a lump of play cloths and sheets, more building supplies temporarily cast aside. It seemed that Bryn had decided to nap, too, she realized in relief.

"Of course you're hot, silly. You're completely buried under there!" Rorie pulled back the covers from Bryn's nest on the floor, frowning at the listless expression on the child's face. She brushed her fingers across Bryn's forehead, pulling them back in alarm as if she'd touched a hot stove. "Wait here a minute, sweetie."

Nerves jangling, Rorie made her way to the bathroom as she searched her memory for where she'd put the thermometer. If she even had one. She let out a breath as she found one with a digital display, still wrapped in plastic from the store, among the shopping bags Cecily had brought home from a shopping trip over the weekend. She'd cursed her partner then, running off to buy things they didn't need instead of spending time with her and Bryn, but her annoyance shifted to reluctant gratitude as she admitted they'd needed them after all.

"Put this under your tongue, sweetie." Rorie eased herself onto the floor beside Bryn and positioned the thermometer in place, holding a finger to Bryn's chin to keep her mouth closed long enough to get a reading. The heat radiating from Bryn's tiny body was enough to make Rorie start to sweat. *She's on fire.*

Seconds later, the device beeped, its display flashing red. Hand trembling, Rorie raised the thermometer to eye level to confirm what she already knew.

FOURTEEN

CECILY TENSED as the heavy script made contact with her desk, pages rippling. The breeze produced by its impact fanned stray strands of hair from her face. "Well? What did you think?"

"It's not at all what I was expecting." Jill shook her head slowly and Cecily's heart stopped. Had she guessed wrong? "You were right. It's completely brilliant."

Cecily grinned, exhaling in relief. "I knew it! I just knew you'd love it." Not that she needed Jill's permission. It was her company, after all. But Jill's approval meant a lot. She was on her way to mastering the role of producer. "We have to do it. I'll call Jada's office right now."

"Hold on there. Do you have any idea what time it is?"

Cecily checked her watch and frowned. Could it really be after five o'clock already? "I'm sure she's still in the office."

Jill's brow furrowed. "Maybe so, but first, it's a crappy thing to do to make her stay even later. This discussion could take hours. You can call tomorrow. And besides, shouldn't you be heading home? I thought you said you were going to try to get out of here earlier today."

Cecily conceded Jill's point with a sigh. After working late two nights in a row, she'd promised Rorie she'd be home on time. In fact, she'd meant to leave ages ago, but had gotten so caught up in her work that it slipped her mind. *I'm not avoiding going home*, she denied vehemently to herself, though no one but her guilty conscience had suggested anything of the sort. It was just that her work was so engrossing that all the hours of the workday flitted by before she had a chance to come up for air. Right?

She glanced down at her bag, hesitating. She needed to hear it from Jill once more before she'd be ready to leave. "It really is good?"

"It's more than good. It's Sundance festival good. This film is going to put us on the map. I had no idea Jada had it in her to write something like this. I mean, she has talent, but let's just say this is nothing like the films she showed at her party last weekend."

"Oh, yes, the party." Cecily's eyes sparkled teasingly, her bag forgotten. "How *was* the party, and your evening with Rhonda?"

"Spectacular." She paused, then flashed a wicked smile. "And yes, I mean both."

Cecily raised an eyebrow. "Oh, is that right? So, you mean, you and Rhonda..."

"Had a *very* good time. There's definitely some potential there." She pointed her finger at Cecily's face. "And don't look so surprised. Like you weren't playing matchmaker when you gave us the tickets."

"Okay, maybe I was. So, I want details." Cecily waved her hands rapidly, realizing the error of her words. "*Not* about you and Rhonda. I mean about Jada and the party."

"It was stunning, and I've been to my fair share of swanky Hollywood parties before. Everything about it, from the décor to the food, was like something out of a fairy tale. Literally. That was her theme for the evening, and if there's one thing Jada Larkin excels at, it's making her vision a reality."

Cecily felt chills as she thought of the script. "As I was reading it, I could see every detail in my mind, exactly the way it should appear on screen." It was a beautiful vision, but not an inexpensive one. Cecily bit her lip, thinking about the money. "Are you sure we can do it justice on our budget?"

"It'll be a challenge, but I think we're up to it. And judging by some of the other guests at that party, additional financing won't be an issue. The place was chock full of potential investors, and I came home with a *lot* of business cards."

Cecily laughed appreciatively at Jill's shrewd approach to business. "And *that's* why I can't live without you." It was true. There were times the realization would have twisted her in jealous knots, but not today. Jill was an amazing producer, and Cecily planned to learn everything she could. "So, let's talk about the next steps." She made to sit back in her chair.

"Tomorrow." Jill's tone was firm.

Cecily groaned as she realized that another twenty minutes had passed. If someone as driven as Jill was ready to leave, it had to be well past quitting time. "I really should get going. Rorie will be wondering where I am."

"And Bryn, too."

Cecily gave a snort. "Bryn couldn't care less."

"Still having adjustment issues?" Jill's expression was sympathetic.

"The kid can't stand me. She gives me the silent treatment, doesn't want me to play with her or tuck her in. She's just so..."

"Four?"

Cecily's shoulders slumped as the words sank in. "I was

going to say intimidating, but yeah, she's four. I'm letting a four-year-old call the shots in my own home."

"It does sound like it."

"I've let her get under my skin." She thought about how on edge she'd felt over the past few days and her heart sank as she admitted that she really had been afraid to go home. "I'm an adult, not to mention a seasoned mom. I should've been able to handle this better." She groaned. "I can't believe how foolishly I've been behaving."

"Don't be too hard on yourself. Kids can be scary. My own son's five, so trust me, I know."

Cecily looked at Jill in surprise at the mention of her son. She couldn't remember her talking about children before.

"He lives with Alex. My ex. I get him every other weekend."

Cecily nodded solemnly. Shared custody was no laughing matter, but in reality, it was the gender-neutral quality of her ex's name that was causing Cecily's consternation. After more than two months working together, the possibility of having to admit that she still didn't know such basic information about Jill as the gender of her ex or the fact that she had a child made her squirm with embarrassment. But they were usually so focused on business that more personal things tended to fall by the wayside. *Or maybe my constant state of envy over her talent has gotten in the way of becoming friends.*

"I'd like to meet him sometime. Your son, that is. Maybe you could bring him by the office and show him around." It was an impulsive suggestion, but she felt compelled to make more of an effort.

"I'd like that." Jill's smile was genuine. "You should bring Bryn and they could play together."

Cecily's stomach tightened but she kept her face composed. "That might be nice."

Jill looked at her thoughtfully for a moment before speaking. "We're a lot alike, you know. When it comes to work, we're both single-minded and determined."

Cecily felt a rush of pride settle around her like a warm blanket. "I'll take that as a compliment." When it came to being a businesswoman, Jill represented everything she aspired to be.

"I guess it is, in a way. What you've accomplished the past few months *is* impressive. But—" Jill's lips formed a thin line as she pressed them together thoughtfully. "This type of work that we do, it can be all-consuming. I'm speaking from experience. I let myself get so engrossed in it that I forgot to focus enough on my relationship and my family, and I paid a high price for it." It wasn't hard to guess that this was where Alex had shifted from partner to ex.

Cecily nodded grimly, picturing Rorie waiting for her at home. "I don't want that, but it's hard when it feels like there's so much here that needs my attention. I was gone less than a week and I missed so much."

"That may be, but no one's so indispensable at work that we can't get by for a few days without them. Not me, not you. At home, it's a different story."

Cecily's head drooped, knowing it was true. No matter how much Rorie seemed to have things under control, Cecily knew deep down that her partner would never let on if it wasn't as easy for her as it looked. She recalled all the late nights Chet had put in while she was a new mother and isolated. "I should take the rest of the week off, like I'd planned. Maybe you could call Jada tomorrow about optioning her script." She felt a pang of loss as she said the words, as though giving up even a little bit of control on the new project caused physical pain.

"Are you sure? It could wait until next week if you'd rather handle it."

She would rather handle it, but that was just her pride talking. If she planned to succeed in finding more balance, she'd have to learn to give up a little control. "No, you do it. You had a chance to build a rapport with her at the party. I know you'll get it right."

Though disappointment stung, Cecily had bigger issues to worry about as she headed home, like making up her absence to Rorie and building a connection with Bryn. Things she should have done already, but had lacked the courage until her talk with Jill reminded her of the consequences.

Will Rorie forgive me for leaving her alone this week?

---

104 DEGREES. *Can that be right?*

Rorie turned off the thermometer, gave it a violent shake, then turned it back on and tried again. The result was the same.

"My head hurts, Mama."

Rorie's chest constricted at the sound of the tiny voice. "I know it does, Baby. It's okay, though. We'll fix it." She had no idea how.

Somewhere in her contacts was the number of the pediatrician, a doctor she'd been referred to by another friend before the trip to Mississippi, but whom Bryn hadn't yet met. Her first appointment wasn't scheduled until the following week. Could she just call and ask to be seen? Is that what people did with sick kids? *Or maybe you take them to the hospital.* Rorie felt her own temperature rise as her pulse raced. *Just how high is 104 degrees, anyway?* It seemed impossibly high. She found the doctor's number and dialed.

"Dr. Garibaldi's office."

"Yes, hello. My daughter, er, well she's actually my niece..." Rorie's throat tightened as she struggled to explain the relationship, even while she sensed that it made no difference. But in her panic, her brain had turned to a sticky goo from which no clear thoughts could emerge. "She's sick. Really sick. I need you to tell me what to do."

"I'm sorry, but the office closed at five. This is the after-hours answering service. But I can page the on-call pediatrician and have them give you a call back, if you think it's an emergency."

Was it an emergency? Or was a sky-high fever something real moms took in stride? How the hell was she supposed to know these things? *Cecily would know, but she's not here. Big surprise.* She'd have to decide what to do on her own.

Rorie's jaw hardened. "Yes, please. It's an emergency."

With Bryn settled on the couch, cuddling the soft, plush head of her hobby horse, Rorie dashed across the yard to the guesthouse. Cecily might not be home, but her mother would be able to talk her through this. She pounded her fist against the door, which opened to reveal Margaret's startled face. Rorie fought the urge to kiss her wrinkled cheek.

"What is it?"

"It's Bryn. She's burning up. I don't know what to do."

"You called the doctor?"

Rorie nodded. "The office was closed, but they're calling me back." She jumped as her cell phone rang. "Hold on. That's them now. Hello?"

"*Rorie, it's Jim.*" She opened her mouth to speak, to let him know it was a bad time, but he continued without a pause. "*Look, there's been a change of schedule. There's a location in Georgia I need you to check out for us. Can you fly out in the morning?*"

"Georgia?" Rorie blinked, her head swimming. "I thought this was filming in LA, and not for another eight weeks."

"Yeah, well we just got a lead on a tax credit situation that could work in our favor, but we'd have to sign the contracts right away, before it expires. So, can you do a nine o'clock flight to Atlanta?"

"Jim, I just can't. My niece is sick. I mean, maybe next week?" It was the last thing she wanted to commit to at all under the circumstances, but she didn't want to lose the job. She was willing to figure out a compromise.

"Rorie, this is important."

"So is Bryn, Jim." Frustration sharpened her tone.

"Sure, of course. But don't you have a partner who can stay with her?"

"No, damn it, I don't have a partner who can stay with her, okay? I'm on my own." It felt true. Tears swelled behind her lids and threatened to overflow. She teetered on the edge of self-pitying despair until the beep of call waiting brought her back to her senses with a jerk. "That's the doctor. I've gotta go."

She dropped Jim's call without ceremony, breathlessly detailing Bryn's symptoms to the on-call pediatrician the second she heard his voice. As soon as she mentioned the high fever and aching head, the doctor stopped her.

"Has she been in a large group recently?"

"She was in a group home until last week. She's only just come to live with me."

"You've been traveling?"

"Um, yes. We flew from Mississippi. Doctor, what's going on?"

"I don't want to alarm you, but there's a chance it's bacterial meningitis. You need to get her to the ER for tests right away."

"Oh, Jesus." Stricken, Rorie ended the call and turned to Margaret, who watched her silently with that look of hers, the one where it was obvious she knew what had been said, but wanted to pretend she hadn't been eavesdropping. Sometimes, that look made Rorie furious, but right now she was bursting to speak.

"It could be meningitis. People die from that, and I have to get Bryn to the ER. And I think I just lost my new job before it even started. And your goddamn daughter is, well, I don't even know where, and it's a good thing she isn't here because if she were here, I'd kill her for not being here!"

What she'd said made no sense and she knew it, and didn't care. Anger boiled inside, and she'd needed to vent. She took several rapid breaths and waited for Margaret to tell her she was overreacting.

"She'd deserve it." Margaret wore a look of compassion mixed with respect.

Rorie's mouth gaped. Never in a million years had she expected Cecily's mother to come to her defense. Flustered, she worried how much she'd overstepped bounds. "She's just busy at work," she heard herself say in defense of her absent partner. "And Bryn was perfectly healthy when she left this morning. She didn't know."

"You don't need to defend her to me," Margaret said with a cluck of her tongue. "I know my daughter pretty well. You know who she's like? Her father. Pig-headed, both of them, and completely insensitive to the needs of others."

"Well..." Rorie clamped her mouth shut, not sure what to say. She couldn't disagree, but it felt disloyal of her to elaborate. And the truthful observation that Cecily had taken after her mother just as much as her father in those qualities seemed wholly inappropriate given Margaret's unexpected camaraderie. Silence was by far the best—and only—option.

"You go and take Bryn to the hospital. Make sure you have her insurance card and your phone charger, since you don't know how long you'll be there. Maybe a change of clothes for both of you, too. I'll deal with my daughter when she gets home."

She swept through the house, gathering up Bryn and as many things from Margaret's list as she could remember in her flustered state. Rorie could still see Margaret's look of grim determination in her mind. The prospect of taking Bryn to the ER alone terrified her, but given the reception that Cecily was likely to face when she arrived home, Rorie thought she might be getting the better end of the bargain.

FIFTEEN

THE HOUSE WAS dark as Cecily came up the walkway, her gait slowing as she reached the door. With a nervous glance through the front window, she reminded herself that the time change made it seem even later than it was. Still, it was so much later than she'd intended... and promised. Worry gnawed her insides. Rorie would be furious. She should have stopped for flowers, only it would have meant getting home even later.

Once inside the door, her chest clenched at the sight of her mother sitting alone in a chair in the living room, a single reading light trained on her stony face. Instantly she was transported back to her teenage years and the knowing gut-drop of being horribly in trouble. Cecily gulped, imagining the reading light directed at her instead. Given her mother's expression, it seemed an omen of things to come, like an interrogation scene out of a World War II movie. She opened her mouth to speak, but her mother beat her to the punch.

"Do you have any idea where your family is, young lady?"

Cecily's jaw snapped shut so fast that she bit her tongue, wincing at the sudden concentration of pain. "I..."

"Do you realize that Rorie and Bryn have been at the ER for over an hour?"

A chill washed over her. "They're at the hospital? What happened?"

"Bryn spiked a fever this afternoon. They're running tests." The judgment in her mother's expression was relentless. "It might be meningitis."

"Meningitis?" Cecily's voice was barely a whisper. People *died* from meningitis. She'd seen it on the news. "Bryn has meningitis?"

"She might. They won't know until the tests come back."

Hand pressed to her chest, Cecily sank into the chair opposite her mother. All she could see were images of Bryn, not the sassy Bryn that had terrified her the past several days, but the one who was a sweet little version of Rorie, sleeping peacefully or playing quietly with her toys. The child she should have been home with this week instead of at work. Guilt made her gut churn.

"I didn't mean to be away so long." She swallowed hard and regretted it as the metallic taste of blood filled her mouth from the spot where her tooth had grazed the tip and left a gash. That, along with the guilt, made her gag.

"But you were, weren't you?" Her mother showed no mercy. "While we're at it, I don't suppose you realize that Rorie probably gave up her job today, on account of not feeling like she could count on you."

"She *what*?" The news crashed around her ears. That job had meant everything to Rorie. If she were really to blame, nothing Cecily could do would ever make up for it.

"You'll have to do what you can, but I'm afraid it'll be impossible to live that one down, Cecily."

She'd just been thinking it herself, but under the added

weight of her mother's recrimination, Cecily snapped and turned on the messenger.

"What right do you have lecturing me on my relationship like you're some expert? Not after leaving Daddy the way you did. What do you know?"

"What do I know about putting career before family?" Her mother's voice was drenched in bitterness, and it made Cecily's stomach turn even more.

"Don't you dare accuse Daddy like that! Sure, he spent a lot of time working, but he was always there when I needed him."

Her mother sniffed, then let out a long sigh. "I wasn't talking about your father, Cecily. I was talking about me."

Cecily stared, uncomprehending.

"I have something to confess. I didn't leave your father, Cecily. He asked me to leave." Her mother waved a hand in the air, as if shooing a fly instead of dropping a major secret into Cecily's lap.

"What?"

"After you made your announcement over Thanksgiving dinner, he'd started to see a lot of things differently, changing his mind on a lot of issues. And that was fine in private, but if he kept it up in public, it was going to cost him the election. And I told him so."

"Mother." Cecily closed her eyes, not sure she wanted to hear any more.

"We'd worked too hard to let it go like that. He was determined to change his platform, and I demanded he not go through with it. His political career was my life. I never had a job, because *that* was my job, keeping your father in office. And he was going to lose, and then where did that leave me?"

Cecily's muscles ached from tension as she let the story sink in. "So, you're blaming me?"

"No." Her mother's shoulders slumped, her usually perfect posture deserting her. "But I did then. I wouldn't relent, and neither would he, and finally he said if I couldn't support him, I should just go. And I did. I knew of a lawyer here on the coast, and when I came here, I wasn't even planning to see you. I was so mad at you for what had happened. But then I saw you there, looking so sick on TV, and I couldn't stay away." She drew a breath and then added, pointedly, "Sick kids will do that to you."

Cecily nodded in convicted silence, thinking once again of Bryn.

"I know how rough a start you've had with that little girl. I really do. But you can't hide in your work, Cecily, or put it ahead of your family. And you need to make it right because in the time I've been staying with you, one thing's become pretty clear to me. I never thought I'd say it, but that woman and child are the best thing that's ever going happen to you."

Under the glare of the reading lamp, Cecily saw tears glint on her mother's cheeks, and her own started to flow. At that moment, she knew she would do anything to make things right with Rorie and Bryn. Losing either of them would destroy her.

"You know, I told Rorie you were like your father today, but you're not." Her mother smiled weakly through her tears. "You're a lot more like me. You hate being wrong, and the only thing you hate more is having to admit it."

Cecily chuckled mirthlessly at the apt assessment. She drew a breath, but her mother continued to speak.

"I was wrong."

Cecily's breath caught in her throat. Those were words she'd never expected to hear.

"And stubborn. Cecily, your father was right. Being here, seeing you and Rorie and this family you've begun to create,

I'd be lying if I said I didn't see how good it is for you. You never could have had this with Chet. I see that now. And just because it's not for me doesn't mean other people should be forced to miss out. I may be a lot of things, but I won't be a hypocrite. Even winning an election isn't worth that."

"Moth—" Cecily stopped herself. "Mom. Thank you."

"You should get to the hospital." Her mother sniffed loudly and blinked her lids, but didn't wipe away the tears, as if refusing to acknowledge the wetness of her cheeks.

"Are you sure she'll want to see me?" Cecily's heart thudded heavily at the prospect of being turned away. "What if I've already ruined everything?"

"You have no control over that, but you just have to try." She closed her eyes wearily, and Cecily knew she was speaking as much about herself and Cecily's father as she was about her daughter. "You might brush your hair first, though. And for God's sake put on some lipstick. I know I taught you better than that."

Their moment of bonding over, Cecily had been dismissed in typical fashion with a jab at her appearance, but this time she didn't mind. She'd dreamed of the day her mother would admit her mistakes, yet seeing the former dragon lady so utterly slain provided no comfort. In this moment of uncertainty, perhaps she preferred to see her mother's strength, no matter how ornery it made her, if only to remind her of the strength she came from. It might be possible to get Rorie to forgive her, but earning her trust again would be a long road of constant effort. Cecily would need all the strength she could muster, because she couldn't afford to grow tired on that journey.

She grabbed her purse, pausing at the door to dab on some tinted lip gloss in her mother's honor before heading to the hospital. All she could do now was try.

THE HOSPITAL ROOM was empty when she arrived, except for Bryn, asleep and looking impossibly small amid the white sheets of her bed, an IV obscuring most of her tiny hand. Rorie had texted her the room number, and Cecily had chosen to take it as a positive sign. At least she wasn't so opposed to seeing her that she didn't mind revealing their location. But Rorie must have stepped out just before she arrived, so Cecily approached the child on her own, rattled nerves slowing her steps.

She reached the bed and brushed her finger along the tape that ran across Bryn's hand, covering the spot where the clear plastic tube pierced her skin. Her hair splayed out on the pillow, framing a face like a cherub's, with cheeks too pink from fever. Cecily's heart was heavy with shame. The sound of the monitors beeped accusation at her. She'd failed to love this little girl who needed love so much, because she'd been so scared to fail. *Why couldn't I have been brave right away?*

Bryn moved ever so slightly as Cecily's finger slipped from the tape and brushed her skin. When the child's fingers curled around hers as she slept, Cecily's heart threatened to burst with a rush of every maternal feeling she'd feared she would never feel. It overwhelmed her, and filled her with a new resolve to win Bryn's affection no matter how long it took. Tenderly, she watched the child sleep, until the sound of a throat clearing made her look up.

"Rorie." Seeing her in the doorway, Cecily felt herself falling to pieces inside. There was no smile of relief, no motion for a welcoming embrace.

Rorie's emotions were shrouded in calm. "You came. Given this past week, I honestly wasn't sure if you would."

"I'm so sorry." Cecily's voice cracked. She yearned for

Rorie's arms to enfold her, to put her own arms around her, but her bravery deserted her. She was afraid to approach in case she was pushed away.

Rorie's gaze remained steady and level. "The whole time they were poking her with needles and hooking up the IV, and she was crying and begging for them to stop, I kept wondering if I was really going to have to do this alone."

Cecily hung her head, broken. "There's no excuse for how I've behaved this week. And Mother told me about the job. Did you really lose your chance at it over this?"

"I guess I'll find out soon enough. Honestly, right now I don't care. All I care about is you promising me that you'll never make me feel like this again." This time, it was Rorie's voice that wavered. "Now will you please get over here and hold me, because I can't stand by myself much longer."

She didn't have to say it twice. Cecily was across the room, arms holding her tight, before the words had dissipated from the air. It was only the sound of another person entering the room some time later that made them pull apart.

"Pardon my interruption. I'm Dr. Garibaldi, Bryn's pediatrician. I'm sorry I've only just arrived, but the doctor on call filled me in."

"How does it look?" Rorie asked, concern etching her face.

"Well, the good news is, it's not meningitis." He paused while Rorie and Cecily embraced through teary grins. "However, she did test positive for a particularly nasty strain of influenza."

Rorie nodded. "There was some type of flu going around at the group home when we picked her up."

"Well, fortunately while this one can be a real doozy for adults, it tends to pass quickly with kids. She should come through it okay soon enough. But her fever's still higher than

I'd like, and even with the IV, dehydration's a big concern. I'd recommend keeping her here overnight."

They agreed, and given the late hour, were soon settled into chairs near Bryn's bed to wait out the night. Some hours later, Margaret arrived to drop off toiletries and dinner for them both, then announced that as soon as Bryn was back home, she would be returning to Louisiana to see if it might not be too late to patch things up with Cecily's father.

"Every election night for the past forty-five years, I've stood by his side as he's given his acceptance speech," Margaret explained. "It wouldn't feel right if I weren't there this time when he concedes defeat."

"I'm really sorry, Mom." Cecily's heart felt heavy at the thought of her father losing.

"Don't be. He's doing it for the right reasons."

Cecily squeezed her mother in a tight embrace, bursting with more pride for both her parents than she could ever remember.

By the next morning, Bryn's fever had broken, and as sunlight streamed through the hospital room's windows, the little girl opened her eyes.

"Mama?"

"Right here, Sweetie," Rorie answered, stretching as she sat up from her chair and reached for the child's hand.

"Is Cecily here, too?"

Cecily's breath caught. It was the first time she could recall that Bryn had said her name. "I'm here." Bryn said nothing in response, but the shy smile she gave was enough to give Cecily hope that better days were ahead.

The doctor came in, and after examining Bryn, he declared her fit to go home. She'd already perked up considerably, and was visibly antsy to be unhooked from the IV so she could race around the room.

"She has a few days of recovery ahead, but she'll be better off at home," the doctor assured them.

With discharge papers signed, Cecily, Rorie, and Bryn were eager to be on their way. But as they walked into the hallway outside Bryn's room, Rorie stopped short, one hand braced against the wall while the other held Bryn's hand.

"Are you okay?" Cecily tensed, noting Rorie's flushed face and eyes that seemed mildly out of focus. She put a hand to Rorie's forehead and registered her heat with alarm. "You're burning up!"

Ushering Rorie and Bryn back into the room and into a chair, Cecily ran to get the doctor, who took Rorie's temperature and confirmed Cecily's fears. It was nearly as high as Bryn's had been.

The doctor shook his head as he read the thermometer. "Chances are that she probably has the same influenza as Bryn."

Cecily's brow creased as she recalled what he had said before. "Isn't this one worse in adults?"

Dr. Garabaldi nodded. "In my experience, yes. It's similar to the Spanish flu in that it hits healthy adults with strong immune systems unusually hard."

Cecily's heart contracted at the words *Spanish flu*. She was no history expert, but she'd watched enough episodes of Downton Abbey to remember the tragedy of that flu epidemic. "I want her admitted right away."

"Cici, no," Rorie argued, though her voice was small and lacking in conviction. "There's no need."

"That might be premature," the doctor agreed. "She mostly needs peace and quiet and plenty of rest."

Hands planted on hips, Cecily looked squarely at the doctor. "Those are three things she won't get at home with a four-year-old. I want her here, three nights, minimum."

"Insurance won't cover it," the doctor warned.

"Then send me the bill." She looked at Rorie. "I'm sorry, Sweetheart. I'd send you to the spa instead, but I doubt we can get reservations on such short notice, or that they'd appreciate you exposing the other guests."

Rorie chuckled softly, looking like even that small effort caused her pain. "But what about Bryn? You'll be all by yourself with her. Your mom won't even be there after tomorrow."

Cecily looked at the little girl, who rested quietly against Rorie's knee, and squared her shoulders. "You're forgetting that I'm an expert with children." She held out her hand, willing it not to tremble so much that Rorie would notice. "Bryn, will you come home with me now so your mama can get some rest and get better like you did?"

After a moment's hesitation, Bryn lifted herself from Rorie's knee and, with an imperceptible nod, she clasped Cecily's hand. Relief washed over Cecily like a warm wave.

"See? You have nothing to worry about. I've got it under control."

As she walked down the hall with Bryn's hand in her own, Cecily prayed with every fiber of her being that her bold assertion would turn out to be true.

SIXTEEN

"I'M HUNGRY."

Bryn's wide blue eyes stared, unblinking, as Cecily roused her head from the pillow. Her hands were on her hips, and her little red mouth formed a perfect pout.

It was an ominous start to the morning. Cecily had enjoyed a reprieve the night before. By the time they'd left the hospital and arrived home, Bryn had been passed out in the backseat, her body held upright only by the straps of her booster seat while her chin was buried deep in her chest. It hadn't been that late, only a little past five o'clock, as Cecily carried her limp body into the house, and Cecily had spent most of the night expecting to hear her stir or call out from her room. The child had slept fourteen hours straight. But she wasn't asleep any more.

"I want breakfast."

She seemed especially feisty this morning, without the slightest trace of the illness that had hospitalized her just twenty-four hours before. As Cecily slid her feet into some slippers and shuffled toward the kitchen, Bryn was already racing around the house, full tilt, astride her neighing stuffed horse. She was well rested and raring to go. Unlike Cecily, who hadn't had a wink of sleep all night in her big, empty bed.

Cecily smothered a yawn with the back of her hand. "How about cereal?"

"Peanut butter and jelly."

"For breakfast?" Cecily slumped in defeat as the pout reappeared. "Okay, okay."

Rummaging through the refrigerator for the jelly, Cecily heard the patio door slide open and jumped in alarm, picturing Bryn galloping off into the backyard. Instead, she saw her mother's head poking into the kitchen.

"Cecily? I've got a cab coming in ten minutes. Are you sure you don't need me to stay?"

"No, I'll be alright. Daddy needs you right now more than I do."

"If you're sure?"

"I am. Thanks, Mom." After years of calling her *mother*, it was strange how natural it felt to say *mom*. But they'd finally reached a point of understanding. Cecily wasn't naive enough to think the road ahead of them would be perfect, but she felt confident the mutual respect they'd gained would hold. It was a comforting feeling.

Bryn raced through the room and Margaret smiled fondly. "She sure loves that horse."

"Don't remind me. It's been whinnying all morning. Apparently, there's no way to shut it off."

"Well, she'll just need to learn to ride properly. That should fix the problem. You should buy her one."

Cecily laughed. "A horse? We'll see." She shook her head. Only her mother would think fixing the problem of a noisy toy by buying an animal that ate its weight in hay every day was a normal thing to suggest. *It must be her grandmother brain kicking in, she never would have indulged me that way when I was Bryn's age.*

"Bryn?" Margaret called as the girl passed by again. "Come give Gran a kiss goodbye. I'm leaving for the airport."

The child stopped and threw her arms around Cecily's mother, giving her a wet smack on the cheek. "Bye, Gran!"

As Cecily looked on, something like jealousy pricked her insides. *Rorie's called Mama, and Mother gets to be Gran, but what am I?*

After her mother had gone, Cecily turned back to the bread, peanut butter, and jelly that sat on the counter, and began to assemble a sandwich.

"Mama Rorie doesn't do it that way. She puts peanut butter on both pieces of bread."

"Oh." Cecily frowned at the slices of bread in front of her, one spread with peanut butter and the other with jelly. She considered spreading more butter on top of the jelly, but feared she would only make the situation worse. Instead she pressed the pieces together and set the sandwich on a plate.

"And she cuts them into butterflies."

"She what?" *Did she say butterflies?* "How about triangles?"

Bryn shrugged. Cecily cut the triangles and made an attempt to arrange them like a butterfly. "How's that? Does that look right?"

"I guess. But the strawberries need to be in four pieces."

Cecily sliced through the strawberries in silence, then reached for the bag of pretzels.

"No! I only like the fish ones. Mama Rorie knows."

Bryn's voice brimmed with accusation, and Cecily's blood starting to simmer. Wasn't there anything she could do to please this child? "Well, Mama Rorie's not here."

"Is she really coming home?" Bryn's voice was little more than a whisper and it made Cecily stop in her tracks.

Cecily's brow furrowed as she looked into Bryn's worried face. "Of course she is, as soon as she feels better."

Bryn fidgeted, staring at her feet. "My other Mama, when the doctors took her away, she didn't come home."

Cecily's heart lurched as it struck her just how much this little girl had suffered through. No matter how irritating Bryn's demands could be, this was probably the first time she was in a place safe enough to *make* those demands. That was something she must try never to forget again. Her earlier annoyance set aside, she knelt onto one knee and looked tenderly into Bryn's eyes.

"Mama Rorie is going to be just fine. In fact, we'll call her on the phone a little later, once she's had a chance to get some more sleep. Would you like that?" Bryn nodded, but her expression remained somber. *She needs something to distract her until we can call.* "I know, how about we have a floor picnic?"

Bryn's eyes widened. "What's that?"

"What's that? It's when you take your food and you eat it on a blanket on the living room floor. I used to do it all the time with my son."

Bryn frowned. "I haven't seen any little boys. Where is he?"

"He lives far away, in a place called Connecticut. And he's not a little boy anymore. He's all grown up." *Does that make him your brother?* She wasn't entirely certain if that's how it worked. Cecily held her breath, waiting for her to ask, but for once Bryn seemed satisfied with her answer.

They took a blanket from Bryn's bed and spread it out on the floor, then sat down with their plates and turned on the television. But when Bryn asked to watch her very favorite princess movie, Cecily's spirits plummeted. She'd promised to pick up the DVD at the store, but with all the turmoil of the past few days, it had slipped her mind. Still, she was determined not to lose the small foothold she'd fought so hard to win. *Damn it, Cecily, you're an actress—improvise something!*

"I have a better idea." It had come to her in a flash, and she grinned at her own brilliance. "Let's turn off the TV and act out the movie instead."

Bryn's face scrunched. "Act it out? How?"

"That's where you pretend to be the character from the movie." Cecily looked at her with surprise as she continued to seem confused. "You don't know what acting is? Well, just follow along with me, because that's my specialty! We'll start by finding costumes. The movie has two princess sisters, right? You be one and I'll be the other. Which one is your favorite?"

Bryn considered the question in silence, then shook her head. "Neither. I like the snowman the best."

"The snowman's a great choice. Do you like to play in the snow?"

Bryn shook her head again. "I've never seen real snow."

"Well, where I used to live in Connecticut, we got snow every winter." Cecily paused nervously before completing her thought. "Maybe you'd like to go there and see it sometime? And you could meet my son, Tyler, too."

Bryn weighed the question with as much seriousness as she had given to her favorite character. Finally, she gave a single, decisive nod and Cecily nearly hollered in triumph.

Soon, they had pulled together costumes and props from all around the house. When Bryn saw her reflection in the mirror, with three fluffy white pillows strapped to her body and a baby carrot affixed to her nose with a strand of elastic, she devolved into a giggling fit that Cecily found completely contagious.

"I look just like a snowman!"

"You really do, Pumpkin!" It was the name Cecily's father had used for her, but it felt so surprisingly natural, so completely right, that Cecily laughed out loud.

They sang the songs and improvised their way through the scenes well into the afternoon, and when they'd finally had their fill, they relaxed back on their blanket while Cecily popped in the one children's DVD she did own, that of her animated series from Grant Studios. When Cecily's character spoke her first line, Bryn clapped her hands in glee.

"That squirrel sounds just like you, Mimsy!"

Mimsy? Cecily cocked her head to one side in confusion. That wasn't her character's name. "Who's Mimsy, Bryn?"

Without turning her attention from the screen, Bryn replied, "You are. Mama Rorie's already Mama, so you can be Mimsy, because it sounds like mama and Cecily at the same time."

As Bryn continued to watch the show, unaware of the impact of her announcement, tears of joy burned in the corners of Cecily's eyes. She'd finally been given a name.

THE CHILDREN SAT with heads together, Bryn's sandy brown curls smashed against Jack's straight, jet black hair, as they engineered their skyscraper of foam blocks. Cecily smiled at Jill. "Thanks again for bringing him."

"Not a problem. It's the least I could do. Have you talked to Rorie this afternoon? How's she feeling?"

"Getting better, or so she claims. I'm still worried. They insisted on sending her home Saturday, but there's still a danger of it turning to pneumonia if she exerts herself too much."

"It sounds like you're all better off to have you and Bryn out of the house for the next couple of days. I can have Alex drop Jack off here tomorrow after school again if you think you're planning to come in."

"Yeah, I think I will." Though Cecily was committed to achieving a healthier balance between her work and home life after this health scare, Rorie would get better faster if she had the house to herself. Bringing Bryn to the office had been the perfect solution, and she was grateful to Jill for providing a playmate.

"So, you got a hold of Jada today?" Balance was all well and good, but since she was in the office, she might as well talk shop until it was time to go home.

"I did. Here, take this." Jill handed her a thick file.

"What is it?"

"Everything you need to get started. Just take it," Jill added as Cecily opened her mouth to protest. "I know you're dying to get your hands on it."

"I am, but it's not fair to you. You're the one who ran with the deal when I couldn't. This is a potentially award-winning project." Cecily's heart lurched at what she was about to say, but she forced herself to continue. "It should be yours."

"Just doing my job, Boss Lady," Jill joked. Then her face grew more serious. "If you need help, please ask, but I'm not fighting you for this one. Jada's film is all yours. After all, she approached you first, and Sapphicsticated is your baby."

Cecily took the folder, humbled both by Jill's generosity and the faith she had in her. It was true that she was technically the 'Boss Lady', but Jill was her mentor as well as her employee, and Cecily glowed with the pride of a senior on graduation day.

Leafing through the project file, excitement bubbled inside her. She felt the all-consuming need to take hold of this film and dive in completely, with the same intensity as she felt the need for food or water. If she let herself, she could hole up in her office for the rest of the night to work before resurfacing. She glanced uneasily at Bryn where she played, questioning once again her ability to maintain the balance she sought. *Why does it have to be so all-or-nothing with me?*

"Oh, here's Alex now," Jill announced as a tall man, with thick black hair just like his son's, came walking up the hall.

Well, that answers that, Cecily thought wryly as she shook hands with the man. There was no longer any doubt about the gender of Jill's mysterious ex. She knew it should have no bearing on anything, but she wondered how Rhonda had taken the confirmation of Jill's bisexuality. Given her particular hang-ups on that subject, it couldn't have been easy, but Cecily was proud of her friend for being willing to give Jill a shot.

As if summoned by thinking her name, Cecily heard the unmistakable clicking of Rhonda's heels approaching.

"Oh, and there's Rhonda." Jill's face was lit up like a kid at Christmas. "We have a date tonight."

"On a Monday?" Cecily smirked. "So that's how it is, huh?"

"I just need to make sure Jack's all set with his dad. Would you mind telling her I'll just be a minute?"

Cecily headed Rhonda off in the hall beside her office door. "Jill says to tell you she'll be ready in a minute."

Rhonda wore an oddly troubled expression as she looked toward where Jill stood. "Who's the guy?"

"Alex." Cecily's stomach formed a knot as the lines in Rhonda's brow deepened.

"Alex, the ex? That Alex?" Her eyes had the wild look of a panicked horse.

"Uh, yeah." Clearly, Rhonda had been as much in the dark about the gender of Jill's ex as she had been. "And the little one's Jack, her son." Cecily studied Rhonda's face, looking for signs of shock over that news, but thankfully, Rhonda simply nodded.

"Jack I've met. I guess I just assumed Alex was more of an *Alexandra*." Her eyes narrowed. "How could she keep this from me?"

Cecily's eyes widened at the notion that Jill would hide important information like this. "Did you ask?"

"Well, I..." Rhonda stuttered, her lips forming a pout. "Maybe I didn't really want to know. I just. I wanted this time to be different."

Betrayal and loss flashed across Rhonda's face, compelling Cecily to intervene. "Rhonda, this time *is* different."

"It's not." She gathered her bag close to her and started to turn. "I should go."

"Rhonda, wait. You can't just leave like that. What are you so afraid of?"

Rhonda's eyes flashed. "What am I afraid of? Isn't it obvious? I'm afraid she'll leave me for some *guy*," she nearly spat out the word, "just like all the others."

Cecily held her gaze steady, forcing Rhonda to listen carefully to her words. "But she's nothing like the others, is she?"

Rhonda squeezed her eyes shut, defeated. "It doesn't matter."

Cecily's face softened. "Of course it does. You've made mistakes in past relationships, and so has she. We all have. But if you like Jill, you should go out with her tonight and see where it goes. Don't let your fears, or her past, or yours, dictate what you do."

"But, Alex—"

"Forget Alex. So Jill was married to a man before. So what? I was, too. It doesn't make her any less likely to commit to you, just like it doesn't mean I'm any less committed to Rorie."

Rhonda swallowed, the muscles in her face and neck twitching. "Right. Which is why you've been so quick to tie the knot with Rorie."

"That's... completely different." But the pang of conviction stabbed Cecily's gut.

"Is it? God, you can be so condescending sometimes. Like that look of terror on your face every time someone even hints about marriage around you has nothing to do with fears from your past, because you're totally over that, and evolved, and all that shit? Or are you more like the rest of us than you think?"

Cecily slumped, bowed by the weighty astuteness of Rhonda's observation. "I didn't mean to sound like I had it all figured out."

Rhonda nodded silently, then tucked her bag under her arm. "Right. I've gotta go."

"Where are you going?" She tensed, not wanting to hear the answer.

With a roll of her eyes, Rhonda gave a half smile. "I've got a date, remember? I don't want to keep her waiting."

Cecily let out her breath in relief. "So, you're taking my advice, even though you think I'm condescending and full of shit?"

"Sure. It was good advice. You might consider listening to it yourself sometime. Twenty years is a long time to wait for someone to make up their mind, sweetie."

Cecily's muscles unclenched as Rhonda's endearment reassured her that her friend wasn't irreparably mad. But a different worry creased Cecily's brow. "Rorie told you that?" Rhonda was one of the few friends Rorie would trust enough to confide in.

"No, she'd never say it. But you know it's true."

Alone in her office, Cecily leaned back in her chair and shut her eyes. Of course it was true. She'd allowed the fears from her own past to guide her every bit as much as Rhonda had. Now Rhonda was fighting those fears and making a change. Cecily wondered if she would ever find the courage to do the same.

The Jada Larkin film called to her, but Cecily resisted. It was time to head home, and spending time with Rorie and Bryn called to her with the same intensity. *Why does this have to be so hard?* She stood to leave. Work would be there in the morning, and the struggle would start all over again to give everyone and everything in her life the time it needed. Her head ached, and the mention of marriage had set her right eye twitching. The stress was wearing on her.

I need a vacation. She brightened at the thought. Maybe a trip to Connecticut? It had been ages since she'd seen Tyler, and he'd yet to meet Bryn. Besides, it was going to be Christmas soon and her heart longed for home. Not that Connecticut felt like home to her anymore, but then, neither did California. With all the upheaval in her life, Cecily had yet to feel like more than a long-term visitor in the Westwood house. Plus, it was ungodly hot for December, and at least back east there would be snow.

But can I really get away? Cecily stared at Jada's script and instead of the thrill of excitement, she felt suffocated. It was a masterpiece, but to bring it to life would take every ounce of her being. And once it was finished, there would be another, and then another—with their own set of rewrites and casting, with investors to schmooze and agents to flatter—each new project demanding her unquestioned loyalty to succeed. How could she ever get away?

She struggled like an animal caught in a trap. *This is my life, damn it! And my business, and my family. I have to make it work.* She squared her shoulders. The film would get everything from her it needed, but only *after* she got her trip. She was determined to have it all. There was never the perfect time to get to leave work behind, but surely she could spare a week at Christmas for her and the family to get away.

SEVENTEEN

RORIE BLOTTED the dampness from her face with one hand as she sat in the shade of the patio's pergola. Kids shrieked as they played in the street out front, and a lawn-mower hummed in the distance—all the sounds of a lazy summer day, except there were scarcely two weeks to go until Christmas. It was a typical California winter heat wave, complete with the relentless Santa Ana winds, dry and scorching, that plagued the region this time of year. Under different circumstances, the so-called 'devil winds' would rub her nerves raw, but life was too good for that right now, and Rorie's spirits remained high despite the weather doing its best to provoke irritation.

Bryn had been with them for two months. It was hard for her to believe how quickly the time had passed, while at the same time it felt like she'd been a part of their lives forever. Rorie shaded her eyes and squinted to where Cecily helped Bryn maneuver a giant watering can over the thirsty flowers in their garden. They were buddies now, Cecily and Bryn—or Mimsy, as the child had christened her. And she was Mama Rorie. *Mama Rorie.* Spoken from the sweet lips of a child she'd never anticipated having. Who'd have ever thought she'd love it so much?

It wasn't the life she'd expected, yet each day brought them closer as a family, and it was everything Rorie could have hoped for, or almost. Sometimes this idyllic life they were building felt too tenuous, without any documents that would make their relationships to one another permanent and irrevocable under the law. The past few months were proof enough that change came quickly, and experience had taught Rorie that not all change was good. The last thing she wanted was for her happiness to be easily ripped away on a bureaucratic whim.

The dog next door erupted in a fit of barking that could only mean the imminent approach of the mailman. Rorie stood by reflex and headed inside, moving toward the front door. In her weeks away from work, she'd learned to recognize the rhythm of the neighborhood in a way she never had before. She knew, for example, that it was too early in the day for the regular mail, and so she opened the door in expectation of a package, startling the carrier who held a slim envelope in his hand marked *special delivery* in bright red letters across the front.

Rorie frowned as she signed the carrier's clipboard and was handed the envelope in return. It was addressed to her, yet she wasn't expecting anything urgent. The return address listed the law offices of Pierce and Franklin in Biloxi, and Rorie's insides grew cold despite the blazing heat as she took in the Mississippi address. Her fingers trembled as she pried open the seal and pulled out paper inside. After the first paragraph or two, her throat grew as dry and troubled as the hot air that assaulted her from the still-open front door.

Retreating to the coolness of the entry way and shutting the door, Rorie reached for her phone and dialed her attorney.

If she was going to make it through the whole letter, she would need professional help.

"Helen? I think we have a problem. I've just received a letter, and Gloria Alexander is suing for custody of Bryn."

On Helen's instructions, she scanned and sent the letter, waiting in tortured silence while the woman read it all the way through.

"Well, that's an unexpected development. It's her right as Bryn's grandmother, of course, to request custody, but frankly from what Murray found out about her, I didn't expect her to have the money or the inclination to pursue it on her own."

Rorie sank into a chair, her head swimming. "Why now? She could have challenged it at any time before Bryn came to live with us. Why wait until now, when she's finally so content to be here?"

The clicking of a keyboard sounded in Rorie's ear. *"This might explain it. It seems Pierce and Franklin have close ties to a conservative religious group that promotes so-called traditional family values in Mississippi. They have a history of taking on cases against LGBT adoptions, pro bono."*

"I don't remember Murray saying anything about Gloria being very religious. Wasn't she a drug addict?"

"Recovered. Clean and sober a year now, according to the letter. It's not uncommon for people to have a conversion experience while in rehab, but in this case, it's just as possible that Pierce and Franklin sought her out for their own agenda."

Fuck. This was exactly the type of capricious, political meddling to which the lack of those 'pieces of meaningless paper' that Cecily didn't seem to find important left them vulnerable. The wind whistled through a gap in the window and Rorie fidgeted at the angry tea kettle sound. "So, what do I do?"

"Well, this is interesting. You see, they basically had two

choices in how to approach this. They could have gone after you for being gay, but even in the current political climate, that's an uphill battle. There's too much case law in your favor for all but the most dedicated of judges to try to go against it on those grounds alone. So they took the opposite approach, and are arguing that the fact you're in an unmarried relationship with your partner creates a negative environment for the child."

"How so?"

"Were you recently in the hospital?"

"Yes, I had the flu."

"And your partner stayed with Bryn while you were indisposed?"

"Of course."

"That's the basis of their argument, that leaving her in the care of someone who wasn't her guardian for several days constituted child endangerment."

"Endangerment?" Rorie's blood grew hot with rage at all the word implied.

"But it's a slippery argument at best."

"Meaning?"

"Meaning, the charges of endangerment will never stand up under the circumstances, and if you and Ms. DuPont get married, their case evaporates. They say you should be married, and if you are, they can hardly change the argument midstream and then say the fact that you're married creates a negative environment, now can they? Any chance of tying the knot between now and the January court date?"

Rorie gave a weak laugh. "I don't think so."

"It was worth a shot, as that really would solve your problem."

Rorie's once-high spirits plummeted. "Isn't there some other way?"

"Don't worry. I'll come up with something."

After ending the call, Rorie read and reread the letter. How could anyone honestly believe that a person caring for a child when their partner was sick posed a danger? Rorie's temper flared anew, agitated by the incessant howling of the wind. *Does Gloria even care about Bryn? Do any of them? Or are we just cogs in some political driven machinery?*

Rorie's heart ached. Getting married would solve their problem, but she couldn't go back on her word, not even for this. She's sworn she would never ask Cecily to marry her, and she wouldn't. Not even for Bryn. In fact, perhaps especially not for Bryn, because Rorie knew how close the two had become after their rocky start, and that Cecily would marry her in a heartbeat if it meant keeping the child with them. But it would be for the wrong reason, and if they ever were to marry, Rorie refused to begin it that way. *Helen will figure it out.*

The sound of the patio door sliding on its track brought Rorie back to the present. She slid the letter back into the envelope and stuffed it behind the cushion of her chair as Cecily and Bryn entered the room. This was one discussion that she had no eagerness to launch into right away.

"There you are!" Cecily let go of Bryn's hand and gave Rorie's shoulder a squeeze. "Was the heat too much for you?"

"This damn wind. I hate when it kicks up right when the temperatures are finally supposed to be cooling off."

"I know," Cecily said with a pout. "I think I saw one of the inflatable snowmen from down the way blowing up the middle of the street earlier."

"A snowman?" Rorie shook her head. "Who can get into the Christmas spirit at all when it's like this?"

"I'm glad you said that. Because I had an idea." Cecily perched herself on Rorie's knee, wrapping her arms around

Rorie's neck. There was a mystery to her smile that made Rorie's stomach flip-flop in anticipation. "Let's go to Connecticut for Christmas."

"Connecticut?" Rorie frowned. She'd given next to no thought about how they would spend their first Christmas together as a family, but she'd assumed it would be close to home.

"It never feels like Christmas in LA, and especially not this year with all this heat. If we had a fireplace, we'd have to turn the air-conditioning on just to light a fire."

Rorie smiled indulgently at Cecily's logic. "True, but that's probably why we don't have a fireplace."

"You know what I mean. It's not Christmas without snow." Cecily batted her eyelashes with an exaggeration that made Rorie laugh out loud. "Bryn's dying to make a snowman, just like the one in her favorite movie."

Bryn. Her concern for their future with the little girl bubbled to the surface, but Rorie pushed it down, saving it for a better time. "Well..."

"I've still got the old place in Darien, where Tyler goes on weekends off from NYU. We could stay with Tyler in the house, and he could meet his new little sister. And we could all watch movies together in the screening room and drink hot cocoa, and have a real New England Christmas." Cecily flashed a victorious smile, clearly convinced she'd won already.

In truth, she had. The scene played out in Rorie's mind, and it was too perfect to resist. "You're sure you can spare the time away?"

Cecily nodded. "It may mean some late nights after we get back, but seriously, if you can't take time off for Christmas to spend with your family, what's the point?"

Rorie pulled Cecily closer and kissed her cheek. "Okay. Let's have Christmas in New England."

Whatever the future held for them, that's what Rorie wanted now, more than anything else. One perfect Christmas together.

"WHERE'S THE SNOW, MIMSY?" Bryn peered out from the small space beneath her knitted cap and above her thickly wrapped scarf that left mere inches of skin exposed to the cold.

Cecily blinked into harsh sunlight that yielded no warmth. Freezing winter temperatures had greeted them as soon as they stepped off the plane in Connecticut, but the promised snow was conspicuously absent, and Cecily struggled to hide her own disappointment in an effort to cheer up Bryn. "It'll be here soon, Pumpkin. We still have a few days until Christmas."

Driving up to the big, colonial house on its quiet suburban street, Cecily felt a rush of nostalgia as she caught sight of the familiar white clapboard siding and stately black shutters. It wasn't quite the feeling of coming home, but like the echo of a distant and half-forgotten memory.

This house had been home once, of course, but no longer. LA was where she lived now, and yet the house in Westwood failed to give her quite the same sense of belonging she'd hoped to find. Perhaps it would someday, when she'd been there longer and filled it with memories of her life with Rorie and Bryn. At this moment, her lack of a place to truly call home felt like a curious sort of limbo between past and future, a need as yet unfulfilled.

As the car pulled into the driveway, Tyler's shadowy

silhouette filled the open doorway. It wasn't late, but sunset came early in the dark days of winter this far north. Not bothering to grab the bags in her haste to greet her son, Cecily raced up the walkway and engulfed Tyler in a hearty bear hug as Rorie and Bryn followed some distance behind.

"Tyler!" Cecily beamed at her son, who'd settled into the old house since returning to the east coast for sophomore year. "Are you still growing?"

He rolled his eyes, the perfect mockery of teenage snobbery. "I doubt it, Mom. I'm almost twenty."

Cecily's brow furrowed as she squinted at her son. Something about him felt...different. Maybe not the height, but something. "Well, I don't know. You look taller to me."

Beyond him in the foyer, the shadows shifted, and Cecily's smile froze a little on her face as she recognized Tyler's girlfriend, Reese, approaching the door. She was the daughter of one of the meanest of the suburban moms who had tormented Cecily's life there for years. She knew the two had been dating for a year, much of that time in secret, but Cecily had half hoped they'd broken up and Tyler had simply failed to mention it.

"Oh, do you have company?" She asked it as innocently as she could manage, pretending not to recognize the girl. It was a petty ploy, but it made her feel more in control.

"You remember Reese, Mom." He said it in a matter-of-fact way that made it clear he'd caught her in her act, and wasn't buying it for a minute. Tyler slipped his arm around the young woman's waist and pulled her to his side with an air of possessiveness that was unmistakable, and made Cecily's stomach twist. *He's still so young!*

"Of course. Nice to see you again, Reese." *Even nicer that all your clothing is firmly in place this time.* The same could not be said the last time when she'd inadvertently walked in on Reese and Tyler in an uncomfortably intimate moment at Rorie's guesthouse back home.

"It's so nice to see you, Mrs. Parker. Oh! I mean Ms. DuPont." Reese's cheeks flushed noticeably at her error, even in the dim light.

A wicked thrill coursed through her as she realized that inspired as much terror in this girl as her own mother had in poor Rorie just a few months before. For a moment, the rush of power was deliciously intoxicating. Then she reminded herself that even her mother had redeemed herself eventually, and she might want to avoid the need to do the same.

"Please, call me Cecily."

When it came down to it, Cecily didn't want to be a completely evil bitch, but the fact she'd had a choice about it was nice. Reese flashed a sparkling white smile, and Cecily could see why her son was so smitten. She was a pretty girl, and seemed sweet enough. *I guess none of us can help who our parents are.*

"Can I get you something to drink while Tyler brings in the bags?" Reese looked from Cecily to Rorie, and then Bryn. "We don't have any alcohol, of course, but we have juice and water, or I could make coffee."

Cecily steadied her expression as she contemplated the use of the word *we* in that sentence. *We?* She'd said it twice. Some of the newfound goodwill she'd been filled with evaporated on the spot. Cecily stared after Reese as the girl made her way to the kitchen and opened up the cabinets like she owned the place. *Just how much time does she spend here, anyway?*

As she looked around her old home, Cecily's skin prickled. Like Tyler, it, too, had changed. There were new throw pillows on the couch. She'd taken the old ones to California with her, but what twenty-year-old boy would think to replace them? There were other changes, too, and all with a remarkably *feminine* feel to them.

Shaken, she moved through the kitchen, seeking refuge in her old sitting room. Of all the places on earth, that one felt most like hers. It was where she'd passed so many quiet evenings alone when Chet was working and Tyler was out with friends. In its doorway, she and Rorie had shared their first kiss after eighteen years, and it was where she had fled for comfort after her coming-out debacle at Thanksgiving dinner. But when she reached the doorway, she froze. Everything had changed.

"Tyler, what the hell happened in here?" Her voice shook with emotion.

Her son came running, and it was clear from his expression that he'd expected to find something at least as serious as a bear. When he saw what she was looking at, he laughed. "A little redecorating, Mom. I needed a music room."

Cecily trembled. Gone were her pastel sofa, the coffee table she'd chosen herself, her little television. Even the wallpaper had been stripped and replaced with some funky color of paint. There were bean bags. She shuddered. *Bean bags!*

"You're here on the occasional weekend, Tyler. You couldn't live without a music room?"

Tyler shifted, looking like his collar had grown too tight. "That's the thing, Mom. I've had fewer days with classes this semester, and a lot of films to watch for school that are so much better when I can use the room downstairs, so I've been here three or four days a week. Dad said it was okay," he added hastily as Cecily geared up to launch into a reprimand.

She stopped short, gritting her teeth. Until they sold the house and split the assets, technically it belonged equally to Chet and he had every right to let Tyler stay there. She would've done the same. *It's just...*

"It's not too lonely here, all by yourself? I'd think the dorms would be more fun."

Tyler gulped. "Nah. I like it."

But Cecily could see right through his deception. He liked it just fine, all right, because he wasn't living here alone. *How could he not tell me, or ask me what I thought?* She was crushed with the knowledge that her son didn't need her advice anymore. Jealousy wracked her as Reese entered the room. There was an awkward silence as she searched for something to say other than screaming 'How could you steal my little boy and take my place?', which she had the sense left to recognize as being a little melodramatic, even for her.

"How's Polly doing, Reese? I haven't seen her since my move." Cecily didn't really care, but it was the best topic she could come up with.

"Mom? She's..." Reese paused, looking uncertain. "She hasn't been herself for a few months, to be honest. I think she's depressed."

"Oh, I'm sorry to hear that." Despite herself, Cecily felt a trickle of concern, though more for Reese than Polly if she were completely honest about it. A depressed parent could be hard on a child, and she wondered if that was one reason, other than the wanton desire to shack up with her son, that Reese might not want to spend much time at home.

Reese's face brightened. "Although she's obsessed with planning a trip to Japan all of a sudden. Her friend—remember Amanda, with the curly red hair?"

Cecily gulped down a mouthful of water from the glass Reese had handed her. *Do I remember Amanda?* The sight of her frizzy head buried between Polly's skinny white thighs was a memory she was unlikely ever to purge. Of course, she doubted Reese was privy to any details about her mother's extramarital pursuits, and so she simply nodded in response.

"Well, Amanda moved to Tokyo this past summer when her husband was transferred, and you know mom. She can't stand it when other people get to do things she doesn't. She's been talking about touring Japan ever since."

Of course she has, but seeing Japan is hardly the reason. To Cecily's consternation, a wave of sympathy for her old rival engulfed her. Polly could be a nasty piece of work, but even so, her situation was all too relatable. Trapped in a loveless marriage, in love with a woman she couldn't be near. How easily that might have been Cecily if things hadn't worked out the way they did.

"Tell her I hope she enjoys the trip." And she really meant it, too. It was a rare moment of charity toward the woman, but Cecily felt inclined to it as she realized just how grateful she was for her the courage she'd eventually found to live life on her own terms.

By the time they'd gotten Bryn to bed that evening, Cecily felt utterly drained. She and Rorie retired to bed early, but Cecily was unable to sleep. Her emotions were in turmoil. This trip was supposed to be a cathartic coming home, her own few days of living out every tear-inducing, joy-filled scene promised by every cheesy, happy holiday movie ever made. Instead, she was choking back tears of frustration and loss.

Jesus, I'm on an emotional roller coaster today.

She made her way to the basement, turning on the lights at the dimmest setting available. She chose one of the leather couches at random and let her body sink into it, the deep cushions like an embrace, though one that fell far short of the warm human variety. Though the house was filled with people sleeping upstairs, the weight of loneliness haunted her in the basement. She needed company, if only from some friendly faces on screen. Flipping on the projector, she used the remote to scroll through a long menu of entertainment options in her son's digital film collection, finally settling on the mother of all Christmas movies, *It's a Wonderful Life*. She'd be crying like a baby by the end, painfully aware of the inevitable disappointment of real, unscripted life.

The movie had only just begun when she felt the couch shift. Sleepily, Rorie curled against her. Cecily relaxed into her, a measure of contentment taking hold at the welcoming feel of her partner's radiating body heat. She reached for Rorie's hand and frowned to find it cold to the touch.

"I thought you might be down here." Rorie said with a yawn. The reason for her chilly fingers became apparent as she produced a pristine pint of Cherry Garcia and two spoons. "Shall we?"

For the first time since coming home, some of the peace that had eluded her finally settled into her bones, calming her breathing and soothing her addled brain. She took a spoonful of the sweet, cold treat, her favorite, and let it melt into a puddle on her tongue before chomping into the chocolate chips with unabashed glee. "God, I love this stuff." In blissful contentment, she kissed Rorie's neck, whispering, "And, I love you."

Rorie, who had dug out another half-dozen chips with her own spoon as Cecily savored the first bite, turned slightly and took the opportunity to pop the spoon between Cecily's parted lips. "And I guess I must love you, or I wouldn't keep letting you eat all the chips."

They watched the movie in silence, and just as she'd predicted, Cecily's eyes grew misty at the end. But the disappointment she'd feared was absent. For an unscripted day, the ending had proven much better than expected. Even so, with all the stress it had already caused, she worried if this trip had been a good idea, after all.

EIGHTEEN

AS THEY JOSTLED their way through the wall of people in New York City's famed Herald Square, Cecily silently rethought the wisdom of her suggestion to visit Santa Claus in the Big Apple. She was far from the only person to have had the idea, and it seemed plausible that every human in a fifty-mile radius might have descended on the city that day. The line to enter the North Pole was marked with velvet ropes that extended well outside the department store's front doors.

"I don't remember it being this packed last time I was here," Cecily said as she reached out to grasp Rorie's shoulder. Her other hand held Bryn firmly between them, yet even so, the thought of the little one letting go and getting swallowed up in the crowd filled her with stark terror. "It's three days until Christmas! Surely everyone's already visited Santa by now."

"Well, we haven't," was Rorie's even-keeled response. "Besides, from what I understand, the weather's been rainy most of December. This is the first nice day in a while, and people have last minute shopping to do. Just try to relax."

Cecily glared at the surrounding people who had so

inconveniently failed to plan ahead with their shopping, until she recalled her son's girlfriend, whom she'd just been informed would be joining them for Christmas Eve. *Yes, informed.* By a somehow completely grown-up son who hadn't left her a choice.

She dug her nails into her hand to control her rising temper at the things in her life she could no longer control. "Ugh, that reminds me. I need to pick up a present for Reese."

"I hope you're planning to get it here, because I'm not sure we're going to make it anywhere else to shop today." Rorie extended her free hand as they approached the ropes and waved at a woman near the back of the line. "Look, there's Susan! She's saved us a spot."

Susan, the managing director at the Oakwood Theatre where Cecily and Rorie had reconnected two years before, nodded but did not return the wave, as both arms were busy trying to contain a squirming toddler in a red velvet coat that looked like something out of a Shirley Temple movie. It was the cutest thing she'd ever seen, and Cecily instantly wanted one. *A red velvet coat for Bryn, that is*, she clarified for her own benefit, *not a toddler*. Though she'd come to adore Bryn completely, one surprise child to raise in middle-age was quite enough.

The little girl belonged to Susan's sister, Beth, who also happened to be Rorie's ex. It was a fact that made Cecily squirm more than she cared to admit. There was no doubt that Beth, along with her recent show-stopping wedding to the world's most perfect woman, and the birth of a daughter who appeared to be in the running for most cherubic infant in history, would be a major topic of conversation. Cecily's muscles tensed as they drew closer, especially her cheek muscles in anticipation of a few hours spent smiling over Beth's many accomplishments while inwardly fretting over whether Rorie harbored any regrets. No matter how nice a life they were building together, it could never measure up to Beth's. Or at least to how Susan would portray her sister's life for their benefit.

"Susan! How are you?" Cecily forced her smile bigger, her jaw already starting to burn from the strain as they exchanged air-kisses.

"Oh, you wouldn't believe what's just happened on our production of A Christmas Carol."

Susan launched into the woes of the Oakwood's newest show as Cecily listened politely. The creeping spread of warm sentimentality caught her by surprise, even as Susan detailed trial after tribulation that should have made her grateful to be working anywhere but the theater. *Oh, how I miss those days!* Cecily could hardly believe her own thoughts. Her life was infinitely better since moving to the west coast and starting Sapphicsticated, Inc. *I'm a Hollywood producer now, and spend my days talking to stars and big-shot VIPs!* No doubt this was nothing more than one more symptom of the cycle of unrelenting nostalgia, and its subsequent disappointment, that had plagued her since arriving in Connecticut.

"And who's this precious little monkey?" Cecily asked when, finally, Susan left an opening to redirect the conversation.

"This is my niece, Clementine." Susan's face shone with pride. "She just turned one, and had such a nice party. I posted pictures online. Did you see them? Oh, and did I tell you that Beth and Anita had miniature ponies for all the children to ride?"

"They had ponies in their apartment?" Cecily frowned, recalling from one of Susan's many recent posts that the party had been held at their home.

"Mmhm," Susan responded with a nod. "Shetlands."

"Oh, that's nice." Actually, it was insane, considering the average Manhattan apartment didn't have room for a Chihuahua, let alone a whole herd of horses.

Regardless, envy washed over her at the thought of those two moms working together with such focus, an unquestionably united team, to create a special experience for their child. Even if they were completely nuts. With heaviness in her heart, she admitted that she and Rorie still lacked that all-in team spirit when it came to their own little family, and that it was mostly her fault. Her struggle to balance work and home left her little energy for spontaneous craziness these days, or for going the extra mile. She could manage good enough, but extraordinary eluded her.

"Remind me what Anita does for a living," Rorie asked, with perhaps a little too much interest for Cecily's taste.

Does Rorie regret not having a partner more like Anita, or Beth?

Cecily stifled a groan at the direction her thoughts were traveling. She was cognizant that her jealous streak was not her most attractive quality, and in the interest of keeping it under control, a short break from the conversation might be in order.

"I think I *will* just pop into the store to get that gift for Reese, if you don't mind staying here with Bryn?" When Rorie nodded, Cecily passed Bryn's hand to her girlfriend and slipped back under the velvet rope and into the main part of the store.

The line had advanced to just beyond the escalators on the second floor while they'd chatted, but a quick look around suggested her best bets for a gift were on the ground floor below. Perfume, scarves, small handbags with a strap for the wrist. Any of those would make an appropriate gift for Reese, right? *My son's girlfriend. Whom he's basically shacked up with. Right in the house where I used to change his diapers!* Cecily grimaced as her thoughts traveled down the path that led to an uncomfortable and increasingly undeniable truth, that her little boy was well and truly grown. No wonder she'd felt such a longing lately for the past.

"Can I help you, Miss?"

Cecily looked up with a start as she became aware of the woman behind the counter. "Oh, I..."

The saleswoman gave a knowing nod. "Hoping for a special gift under the tree from your gentleman friend?"

"Am I what?" Cecily's brain whirled confusion, until her eyes focused on the contents of the display case she'd inadvertently leaned against in her distraction. Diamond engagement rings, in nearly every shape and style. "Oh! Oh, no. Not me." Her eyes darted across the glass display top, landing on a butterfly-shaped pendant in a holiday gift box, complete with bow. It would do for Reese as well as anything else she was likely to find. She grabbed the necklace and pushed it toward the woman. "Just buying a present for my son's girlfriend."

The woman took the box, ringing it up and swiping Cecily's credit card without comment. When she handed the boutique shopping bag to Cecily, however, the woman pointed to the rings with a wink. "It's okay to admit it. Every woman secretly wants to get a diamond engagement ring for Christmas."

Do they? Cecily took an involuntary step away from the display. *Did Rorie?* She'd taken Rhonda's scolding to heart. And a proposal would certainly be a spontaneously crazy way to build some team spirit. Her nerves jangled in their familiar way. *But not because I'm afraid.* That had been unfair of Rhonda to say. Her feelings about marriage were totally different from Rhonda's irrational fear of dating bisexual women. Apples and oranges. *I'm not nervous about getting married again,* she reaffirmed to herself, conveniently ignoring the eye that had started to twitch. It was just that when it came to marriage, she didn't see the point. It was a legal formality that was more trouble than it was worth. What would a piece of paper really change?

Nothing. Absolutely nothing.

Even so, the sparkle of diamonds held her attention as she ascended the escalator, and briefly she wondered if she should have bought one to keep on hand... just in case. She shook her head at the idea, dismissing her foolishness. She and Rorie were fine the way they were. Besides, an engagement ring wasn't something you tossed in your purse for an emergency, like a bottle of hand sanitizer or a package of dental floss. And when it came to picking one out, she wouldn't know where to begin.

When Cecily rejoined the line, only a few people stood ahead. Bryn was bobbing and ducking, trying to catch sight of Santa through the forest of adult legs.

"Are you sure he'll know where I'm staying?" Bryn asked, tugging on Rorie's hand.

"Don't worry Bryn. It's his job to know these things," Susan reassured her.

"See? What did I tell you?" Rorie confirmed with a grateful look toward her friend.

"But we live in California, and now we're here," Bryn argued to Susan. "And besides, Mama Rorie and Mimsy aren't really my mommies."

Cecily drew in a sharp breath, while Rorie drew the little girl close to her and kissed her head.

"Oh, Bryn. Of course we are!" Cecily stretched her hand toward the little girl but couldn't quite reach, and she was trapped in place by the crowd. Her inability to smooth the child's forehead with her fingers and take away her worries caused her chest to tighten.

"Absolutely," Rorie affirmed, planting Bryn's forehead with another kiss. Cecily wriggled closer and did the same, but it failed to sooth her anxiety as much as she'd hoped.

"But, not really," Bryn continued matter-of-factly, looking Cecily squarely in the eyes. "Not until the judge says so, right?"

"Well, uh..." Cecily struggled for a reply. Her insides twisted. Even when the judge's gavel came down, it would be Rorie on the paperwork, but not her. *Will she still think I'm not really her mom?*

Just then, a girl dressed as an elf called out for the next in line, and Bryn raced toward the fat man in the red suit at top speed, dragging Rorie, whose hand was caught in hers, along for the ride.

"Oh, isn't that heartbreaking," Susan said as she and Cecily followed behind at a more leisurely pace. "Poor little thing. I'm sure it will be such a relief for you and Rorie when she's legally yours."

"Well, Rorie, anyway," Cecily corrected.

Susan gaped. "What do you mean? You're not both adopting her?"

Cecily frowned at Susan's incredulous tone, her discomfort over the situation growing exponentially. "It's just, it's easier that way...since we're not married." Even as she said it, she knew it sounded weak. *Have I made a huge mistake?*

"I just know how relieved Anita was when the adoption papers were finalized with Clemmie over the summer." The child in question had passed out in Susan's arms during the wait, and she tousled her sleeping niece's head as she spoke.

Cecily regarded her with surprise. "Why? Beth and Anita are married, and Clemmie's their biological daughter, right?"

"They're both listed on her birth certificate, yes. But she's *Beth's* biological daughter," Susan corrected.

"Seems like that's good enough." Despite the worry over her own situation, Cecily gave a chuckle at this couple she'd never met. *What worrywarts!* Beth and Anita must be the types who would dot every 'I' twice for safe measure. "What a lot of trouble to go to just for an extra piece of paper."

"You're right, being married *should* be enough."

Caught short by the doubt in Susan's words, Cecily paused in her tracks. "But?"

Susan arched an eyebrow at the question. "I forget how sheltered you've been, with your politician dad and your rich lawyer ex-husband. You've never had to think too seriously about things not going in your favor."

Cecily's brow crinkled as she frowned at the insult she was sure lay hidden in Susan's observation. Her body stiffened in defiance. "It's not like it's been easy the past two years. People's opinions lag behind sometimes, but at least the law's on our side now, mostly."

"Laws change." Susan shook her head, as if amazed at her obliviousness, and Cecily's chest clenched as the potentially disastrous consequences of her naiveté dawned on her. "Sure, a name on a birth certificate's good enough now, but what about after the next election, or when some new judge gets appointed to the bench? Beth and Anita wanted every protection they could get. You can't gamble with family."

Susan walked off to set her sleeping niece in Santa's lap for a picture, but Cecily remained in place, fear contorting her insides. Susan was right. Until recently, Cecily had lived the type of privileged life that lulled her into thinking she was immune to trouble. She'd felt she lived a charmed life. But the very choices she'd made that contributed to her happiness also put her at risk. *Had she put the people she loved at risk, too, by failing to recognize it?*

Cecily's gaze was drawn to where Bryn, still bouncing at the end of Rorie's arm, waited for Santa's elf to hand over her picture and candy cane. Her heart squeezed, like a vice tightening around her ribcage, at the thought of someone being able to take her away. She hadn't seen their purpose before, but now Cecily see with increasing clarity that pieces of paper sometimes served a vital purpose, after all.

NINETEEN

"WHAT'S IN THIS ONE?" Bryn grabbed a wrapped present from beneath the seven-foot spruce in the living room and gave it a shake as Cecily dove in for a last minute save.

"You'll have to wait until tomorrow morning to find out." She set the box, which thankfully contained nothing more breakable than a few packages of new underwear for Tyler, back beneath the tree. Yes, underwear for Christmas, and some heavy winter socks, too. Somehow over the years, she'd become *that* mother.

"Do we really have to wait?" Bryn pouted at Cecily's nodding head. "Then how come you said we're celebrating tonight?"

"Because we are. We'll have food, and Christmas carols, and a fire in the fireplace."

"But no presents." For a four-year-old, this was clearly an unthinkable oversight.

"Tomorrow." Cecily stood firm. "But Tyler has to go spend the day with his dad in the morning. It's his baby brother's first Christmas. And Reese has to be with her family, too.

So they can open their presents tonight, but we'll wait until Santa comes in the morning."

Bryn's scrunched and sour face left little doubt how she felt about that. *Maybe she'll be a little less antsy for hers when she sees all her brother got was socks.*

"Hey, Peanut," Tyler said, entering the room and sweeping the little girl up until she dangled, upside down, in his arms several feet above the ground. "Let's go watch a Christmas movie downstairs. Reese is making popcorn. Hey, Mom, you don't mind if I make some cupcakes later, do you?"

"Cupcakes?"

"Yeah. Just some red velvet. They're Reese's favorite."

Since when does Tyler bake? Baking had always been her domain. Cecily shook her head in amazement at this grown boy of hers, who was a natural with kids and apparently knew how to bake, and she found herself at a loss as to when he'd become so domestically accomplished. But the agony she'd first experienced over his growing up was slowly turning to pride. "Have at it, kiddo. It's your kitchen now, I guess."

Baking his girlfriend's favorite cupcakes. Things really were serious between them if Tyler was willing to do that. For at least the millionth time since their arrival, Cecily felt torn. Reese was a nice girl, and once the shock of the changes in her son had worn off, Cecily could at least grudgingly admit that it was Reese's influence that had spurred them. It was just the girl's mother that gave Cecily pause. Being related to Polly Schroeder was a fate worse than death as far as Cecily was concerned. *Even as an in-law...* Cecily chuckled at how far ahead of herself she was getting. At least *that* was something too far off in the future to bother getting worked up about right now.

The opening strains of a classic Christmas cartoon boomed from the screening room downstairs and Cecily turned toward the kitchen to check on Rorie. She'd left her to assemble platters of sandwich fixings a good twenty minutes before, and had yet to return. It was just that Reese had been popping the popcorn with such *ownership*, and emotionally, Cecily still struggled with that. It was so obvious now that the girl was only returning to her parents' house to sleep at night for their benefit that Cecily almost wondered if she should tell them she was onto their secret and put them out of their misery. Almost.

Was it always this hard on a parent to see their kids leave the nest? Perhaps it wasn't leaving the nest in this case, since Tyler still occupied his childhood home, but he'd certainly made the nest his own. Cecily snorted. *Complete with chick.* Maybe by the end of their visit, she'd have the strength to bring it up with her son.

As her foot hit the kitchen tile, Cecily stopped dead in her tracks. Facing her from across the room was Rorie, studiously examining a diamond ring that sparkled in an open ring box in her hands. She looked up, startled, as Cecily let out a squeak.

"Oh my God," Cecily breathed, heart thumping wildly. "Is that what I think it is?" Excitement, terror, and joy. She could barely speak with so many emotions swirling inside, sending her soaring. *I didn't think she would, but now that she is...*

Calm and collected, Rorie blinked in a detached, almost cat-like way, before replying. "Depends. Do you think it's an engagement ring that your son was planning to give his girlfriend for Christmas?"

Cecily's head spun as it came plummeting down from the clouds. *What did Rorie say? What's going on?* "What?"

She searched Rorie's face for a clue, but came up short. She'd thought... well she'd thought Rorie was going to propose. *Obviously. Who wouldn't have thought it, with her holding a ring like that?* And in that moment, she'd realized how shockingly, how desperately, and how completely she wanted her to. There was no doubt about it. Her hammering, dancing heart didn't lie. *But that's not what's happening, is it?* A crushing weight hit her as the words Rorie said caught up with Cecily's runaway emotions. That's not what was happening at all.

An overlooked detail knocked against her skull. *Wait, what was that about Tyler?*

"I'm sorry, did you say that ring belongs to my son?"

"I think so," Rorie answered, her calm and steady voice a counterpoint to the chaos Cecily was drowning in as she contemplated the reasons for her son to buy a diamond ring. *How the hell is she so calm at a time like this?* "I found it hidden in the drawer when I was looking for a spatula, although why he'd hide it in with the baking utensils is beyond me."

Understanding dawned. "Oh, Jesus. The cupcakes! He was going to bake it into her favorite cupcake."

Rorie gave an appreciative nod. "I like it. Your boy's got style."

Emotions crashing, Cecily's eyes burned and stung. They were weepy, about to overflow, and there was nothing she could do about it. She blinked and rubbed them with the base of her palm, but the more she tried to hold it back, the more powerful the sob building inside of her became, until she couldn't hold it back.

Rorie's eyes widened at the avalanche-like breakdown. "Cici, are you okay? I mean, I know Tyler and Reese are young, but—"

"It's not that!" Her words came out in a wail, like a cat with an injured tail. "When I saw that ring, for a second I thought *you* were going to..." The word 'propose' was mostly lost in another wracking sob.

At first, Rorie laughed. "What, here, in the kitchen? Wearing an apron and putting lunchmeat on a platter?" But as Cecily continued to cry, Rorie's demeanor became less joking. Through the wavy wetness of her tears, Cecily could sense Rorie's eyes searching hers. When she spoke again, her tone was soft but serious. "I told you before, I'm not going to do that. If you want to get married, you're going to have to ask me."

"Okay." Something clicked, like the key piece of a puzzle that had refused to fit, until it did. She was home. She'd been looking for it everywhere, but in all the wrong places. It wasn't a place. If she searched all her life, she'd never find more of a sense of belonging, of home, than she did when she was with Rorie. It wouldn't matter where she was—Connecticut, California, or the ends of the earth. As long as she had Rorie, she'd always be home.

And suddenly, Cecily, too was filled with calm. She knew what she had to do to put things right. Drawing a deep breath, she let the words rush out before she could chicken out. "So, will you?"

A battle raged on Rorie's face as she struggled to maintain a neutral expression, as if she wasn't able to trust what she thought she'd heard. "Will I what?"

"Seriously?" Cecily crossed her arms, exasperated. "You're going to make me say it?"

Rorie choked a little, the sound of a laugh forcing its way past a lump that had suddenly formed to block its way. "Uh, yeah. Yeah, I am. Can you blame me?"

"Fine." Cecily breathed in again and made fists to steel her nerves. "Rorie Mulloy, will you marry me?" The ring shimmered in its velvet-lined box. She took it from Rorie's hand and tilted it back and forth so it caught the light. "Even though we're in a kitchen, and you're wearing an apron and putting lunchmeat on a tray, and I don't even have a ring for you?" *Damn it, I should have bought that emergency ring after all.*

"Yes. Yes, I will." Rorie's mouth split into a grin. "Even without the ring. Although you could have knelt."

Cecily's heart filled to bursting. "Don't push your luck." Her voice shook with all the emotion she was trying to hide beneath the joke.

Rorie held her arms wide and Cecily fell into them, the clumsy connection of their lips enhancing rather than diminishing the sweetness of the moment. It was just as good, if not better, as their first kiss after reuniting had been, just a few steps from where they now stood. They broke apart as they heard footsteps on hard tile.

"Whoa." Tyler stared at them, wide eyed, and as his eyes fully focused on the open ring box in Cecily's hand, something between guilt and panic crossed his face. "Uh, what's going on?"

Cecily looked solemnly at her son, remembering what had set off this unlikely series of events. "Rorie and I are getting married. And *you* and I are going to have a talk about this." She held up the ring and the color drained from Tyler's face.

"I'll just leave you two alone for a minute," Rorie mumbled as she walked briskly toward the door.

Cecily squared her shoulders and faced her son. Now was the time. Considering what she'd just accomplished, this conversation shouldn't feel so difficult, and yet she wasn't sure if she could make it through. "Tyler—"

"Mom, I can explain."

She waved her hand, cutting him off. "There's nothing to

explain. Tyler, you're twenty years old. That's too young to get married."

"You weren't much older." His face set into a scowl. It reminded her of the way Bryn looked when she was told she had to wait to open presents, a comparison that bolstered the firmness of Cecily's stance.

"And I paid for that mistake for years. But I was an idiot, and pregnant, and—" Cecily blanched. "Oh, god. Reese isn't—"

"Mom, no! It's just, we love each other and we want to be together."

Relief that she wasn't about to become a grandmother flooded her, but she needed to drive her point home. "Tyler, I know you..."

She'd been about to say 'I know you think you love each other,' but she swallowed the words. She'd seen the way he looked at Reese, and she recognized it as the same look Rorie gave her, and had from almost the moment they'd met. And she recognized it in his face now, when she looked beyond the defiance on the surface. *He's found his home, too, with her.* Even if the future could bring a change, that was his truth at this moment. And she wouldn't insult him by minimizing it.

She blinked back the tears that stung her eyes. "I know you do. But you have so much time ahead of you. Don't rush. It's fine to be together, but you don't have to get married. Maybe just have her move in first? Officially, I mean. It's not like she isn't basically living here already anyway, right?"

He looked like he was going to argue, but then thought better of it. "Well, maybe that's true. But if she actually moved in and we weren't at least engaged, Dad would flip. It looks bad for his campaign."

Of course. *Isn't that always what it comes down to with us?* She felt a wave of disgust for the family business that too often consumed them. "You know what, I've had about enough of living our lives around voter polls. *I'll* talk to your father about this one. Just promise me you'll wait until after you've both graduated from college. If you still feel the same way, you've got my blessing."

She smiled at the feel of her son's strong arms embracing her, but when she stepped back, a fresh look of panic had darkened his eyes.

"That ring was her present. Mom, if I don't give it to her, I've got nothing for Christmas!"

"Well, that's hardly a good enough reason to make me change my mind about proposing." Cecily laughed as a solution came to her. "I bought her a butterfly necklace the other day, would that do?"

"Perfect." The panic drained, leaving behind his usual goofy grin. But then he frowned. "But that leaves you with nothing to give her."

"It's one of the many sacrifices a mother is willing to make." Cecily smiled ruefully. "Looks like you're going to have to go without one of those packages of wool socks I got for you. Oh man, she's going to think I'm the lamest mother in the world."

"She might, but I won't." His words were sincere and pierced straight through her heart, spreading a warmth that felt better than any Christmas miracle. "Thanks, Mom. And congratulations."

Cecily blinked back the fresh round of tears forming in her eyes. "Alright, kiddo. Let me go switch the tags on those presents."

They didn't make an official announcement of their engagement, nor did they have to. By the time the movie was over and the three young people had emerged from the basement, Tyler had spilled the beans.

Bryn ran to Cecily the moment she reached the top of the stairs. "Mimsy, are you and Mama Rorie really getting married?"

"We are." Cecily left it at that and ushered the little girl into the living room where everything was laid out for the evening's celebration, but Bryn wasn't satisfied to let it be.

"But when? Are you going to have dresses? Do I get to be a flower girl? Rachel at the group home was a flower girl for her cousin, and she got to have a basket and flowers in her hair."

Cecily swallowed, the barrage of questions causing her throat to go dry. "Well, I don't know yet."

After they'd had cocoa and sandwiches by the fire, Reese disappeared into the other room, reemerging with a stack of glossy magazines filled with brides on every cover. "Ms. DuPont, would you like to borrow these?"

Hands shaking slightly, Cecily took them, pausing just long enough to ponder whether the young woman felt any disappointment over receiving the butterfly pendant this evening instead of an engagement ring. She hoped not. Reese was growing on her, and when the time came, she thought she really would be ready to welcome her into the family with open arms. *I've got to get her to call me Cecily instead of Ms. DuPont.* But then she rethought. She'd probably need to retrain Reese to call her mom soon enough, anyway.

But as she leafed through the magazines, instead of stoking her excitement, a growing dread crept over her. In full truth, the idea of a wedding freaked her out— picking a dress, ordering flowers, hiring a caterer. It was everything she'd hated about entertaining Chet's and her father's business associates, times a million. As if sensing her distress, Rorie settled beside her on the couch and clasped her hand as they watched the fire.

"You okay?" Rorie whispered.

"Yeah. I'm just getting a little—"

"Cold feet?" Rorie squeezed her hand with a sigh. "Look, I understand if you need more time to think this through. We don't need to tell anyone yet. It was an impulse, after all, so if you change your mind—"

"No!" Cecily shook her head vehemently. "No, I was serious about getting married. It's just the wedding part that's making me woozy. I did this whole white wedding thing once before." Cecily gave a wobbly laugh as she pushed the magazines away. "Twelve weeks pregnant, basically a shotgun wedding, and my mother still turned it into the social event of the season."

Rorie chuckled, too. Knowing Cecily's mother as well as she did, it was no wonder she easily joined in Cecily's somewhat bitter amusement. "I'll bet she did. Well, when you tell her we're engaged, just let her know we're not interested in all that this time."

Cecily's brow furrowed as she looked into Rorie's eyes, seeking the truth. "Are you sure? You've never done it before, even if I have. It's not fair of me to take that from you."

Rorie shook her head, and Cecily was relieved to find no hesitation lurking in her gaze. "I couldn't care less. We can just go to the courthouse, if you'd like."

"My mother will never go for that. As soon as she hears—" Cecily stopped abruptly, a brilliant idea forming in her brain. "Unless she doesn't hear."

Rorie frowned, confused. "You'll have to tell her, Cici."

"Not if we elope!" Cecily grinned. "I mean, yes, I'll tell her, but it'll already be done. It's perfect!"

Rorie tilted her head in consideration. "I suppose when we get back, we could drive to Vegas."

But Cecily was already reaching for her phone. "I have a better idea." She waited as the phone rang.

"Cecily? What a surprise to hear from you. Merry Christmas!"

"Hi, Bailey! Merry Christmas." Cecily giggled, embarrassed. In her excitement, she'd forgotten it was Christmas Eve. "Hey, I need a favor. Do you still have that list you put together when you and Phinn were planning your wedding? The one of all the places around the country where you could have eloped if you just couldn't take it another minute?"

Bailey had shared the list with Cecily when they worked together on *Portland Blue*. She'd been at her wits' end numerous times that autumn, and creating a comprehensive list of elopement possibilities in every part of the country had helped her keep a grasp on her sanity.

"You mean my Wedding Hell Escape Plan? Why?" Bailey paused a beat, then gasped. *"Wait, you're not getting married, are you?"*

Cecily tensed, knowing she'd have to tell the truth and praying she could count on Bailey to be discreet. "Yes, but don't tell anyone, okay? It sort of just happened, and even my parents don't know yet."

"My lips are sealed, I promise. Where are you now, LA?"

"No, Connecticut. We're spending Christmas with Tyler."

"Oh, that's perfect. I think I know just the place. How far are you from New Hampshire?"

Cecily considered. "A few hours, I think."

"There's an inn in the White Mountains that I'm positive you'll fall in love with, and they literally do all the work. Sometimes I still wish we'd done it that way. I'm emailing it to you now. Good luck!"

When she opened the link to the website, Cecily's heart

leaped at the first sight of the romantic country inn, and as a slideshow of photos streamed across her phone, her conviction that this was the place just grew. She nudged Rorie, who was on board with the plan the second an image of the huge stone inn, its gabled rooftops blanketed in snow, filled the screen.

"It's three hours by car, and they offer a package that takes care of everything. The owner's even a Justice of the Peace," Cecily explained as she read the details from the web page. "Wanna see if we can get a reservation for tomorrow night?"

"On Christmas?" Rorie questioned teasingly.

"Okay, fine. The day after, then."

Rorie arched an eyebrow. "That's not too fast? We really do need to call our families, and they may want to fly out for it, and—"

"Hold it right there." Cecily's stomach lurched. None of that fit into her plan. "This is starting to sound more like a wedding. Eloping is supposed to be quick and secret. We'll tell everyone when we get back to California."

Rorie looked prepared to argue, but changed her mind. "Okay. If you're really sure."

As if to confirm how certain she was, Cecily dialed the inn's number and waited as it rang, hoping someone would be there to answer the phone on the night before a holiday. Even more fervently, she prayed they'd be able to fit them in before their return trip to California at the end of the week. After an eternity of dragging her feet about getting married, now that she'd made up her mind to do it, it couldn't happen fast enough.

TWENTY

RORIE SCOWLED at the slick black pavement, or what little of it she could see through the snow that swirled around the windshield of their rented SUV. Its wipers fought valiantly to keep the onslaught of saucer-sized flakes at bay, but were losing ground by the minute. The storm that had delighted Bryn when it started—her first glimpse of real snow!—was intensifying rapidly the closer they got to New Hampshire's White Mountains, and Rorie gripped the steering wheel tighter at the sensation of tires slipping along ice.

"How much farther to the inn?" she asked, not wanting to remove her eyes from the road for the seconds it would take to check the GPS herself.

"It says ten miles," Cecily replied, "but in this weather, that's closer to twenty minutes. I'm glad you suggested stopping for the license when we did."

That really did happen, didn't it? Despite her nervousness from driving, the knowledge that a fully filled out and legally valid marriage license from the State of New Hampshire lay tucked in a folder in the trunk brought a smile to Rorie's lips. The truth was that she'd suggested stopping at the first town hall they encountered after crossing the state line mostly out of panic that Cecily might decide to bail if they waited too long.

Scarcely two days had passed since the surprise proposal on Christmas Eve, yet here they were on a winding mountain road, Tyler reading a book in the backseat while Bryn napped, eloping in secret to a country inn. Their forty-eight-hour whirlwind of an engagement had left little time for it to sink in that Cecily had proposed for real, and Rorie remained half convinced that if they paused for even a moment, the momentum would be lost and the whole thing would prove as real as a puff of smoke. That's why she'd volunteered to drive, despite having absolutely zero experience with winter weather compared to Cecily's two decades in the northeast, just to minimize the chance of Cecily turning the car around and heading back.

"Ten more miles." Rorie squinted at a road sign, trying to make out the words beneath a layer of snow. "There may be an exit ahead. Is there anything we need?"

"Let's see. The reservations are made, we have the license, and the inn will do the rest." Cecily ticked off the items so efficiently that Rorie marveled at her calm. Was this really the same woman who had been committed to avoiding marriage for the rest of her life, listing off the details of a wedding that would take place later that afternoon with the same steady voice she would use for a list of groceries?

Rorie struggled to remain equally well composed. "What about rings, and flowers? Do you even know what you're going to wear?" Her own wardrobe choice had been easy enough. She'd packed the same assortment of elegant, monochromatic clothing that she always wore, suitable for any occasion, even a wedding. But she knew Cecily would never be satisfied with just any old thing, even for a spur of the moment elopement. It shouldn't worry her, but she couldn't shake it.

"All taken care of. Flowers are part of the inn's elopement package, and I spent last night ordering rings, and something new to wear from the after-Christmas sales online. I had everything shipped overnight express, so they should already be there when we arrive."

Some of her tension eased. "You've really thought of everything. I'll admit, I'm impressed."

Cecily beamed. "Once I got over being terrified, it turns out planning a wedding in two days can be fun! I can't wait for you to see everything."

Rorie spotted the inn's roadside sign at the same time the GPS alerted her to the turn, and as she carefully guided the vehicle up the drive, her first glimpse of the inn confirmed that if everything turned out as amazingly as this, they'd have the perfect wedding. The building was constructed of large stone blocks and exposed wood timbers, with a slate roof whose multiple peaks and dips were coated in a charming layer of snowy fluff, exactly like the picture. Though snow was all around, and still falling steadily, the storm appeared to be less intense on the inn's tree-lined property than it had been on the open road.

Rorie struggled to catch her breath. "Cici, this stunning!" Her hands tightened on the wheel, though this time it was from sheer exhilaration instead of anxiety.

When they arrived inside, their reservation was already complete and the innkeeper showed them to their rooms, one with two beds for Bryn and Tyler to share, and a larger but still cozy suite with a pile of logs all set to light in the fireplace whenever they chose. With immense relief, Rorie noted that the boxes from Cecily's order sat in a neat pile at the foot of the bed.

"Oh, good. Everything's here." Cecily clapped her hands with no attempt to conceal her glee, and Rorie laughed.

"I'll go check that Bryn and Tyler and settling in while you open all those boxes."

When she returned to the room a few minutes later, the first box lay empty as Cecily held up the garment it had contained.

"For Bryn," she said, and Rorie could scarcely contain the urge to clap herself when she saw the red velvet coat with its fur trimmed hood. "When I saw the one Clemmie was wearing, I knew I had to get one for Bryn. There's a dress to go with it, too, and a wreath for her hair."

"I can't believe it," Rorie said as she ran her finger along the soft fabric. "I was thinking the same thing when I saw Clemmie's, that Bryn had to have one."

"You always could read my mind."

Rorie nodded in agreement at this longstanding truth, though it wasn't always as accurate a talent as she'd like. When it came to getting married, for instance, she'd have spent far less time worrying about it if she'd been able to look inside Cecily's brain and see that she really wanted to propose all along. It had caused more than one sleepless night, most recently because of the impact her unmarried state might have on Bryn's adoption. It was a detail she hadn't shared with Cecily, and for the first time it truly hit her that in another few hours, it wouldn't matter. They would be married, and the legal issue would dissolve as quickly as the snowflakes that landed on their bedroom window and melted away against its heat.

"Okay, this next one's the one I really want you to see."

Rorie snapped back to attention at the sound of Cecily's voice and the rustling of paper. She'd already broken open the packaging tape and was scattering tissue wrapping all across the bed with abandon. Then she frowned with such an intensity that Rorie's heart skipped a beat.

"What is it? What's wrong."

Cecily shook her head so hard that her dark brown bob seemed ready to fly off her scalp. "This isn't right. This isn't right at all. This is the company I ordered my outfit from for the wedding, but..." Rendered speechless, she held up what the box contained for Rorie to see for herself.

"It's..." Rorie tilted her head one way and then the other. "It's a Christmas sweater."

That was putting it mildly. It was, in fact, one of the ugliest Christmas sweaters Rorie had ever seen. *Is it more gaudy or glitzy?* She wasn't sure which word fit it better. It was the type of thing you bought to wear for your office's ugly sweater party, expecting to come home with the grand prize.

"I ordered it for my mom on clearance from the after-Christmas sale."

Okay, or it was the type of sweater you ordered for an aging politician's wife in the Deep South. Though, if there was a difference between the two, Rorie wasn't sure she knew what it was.

Rorie felt the urge to laugh until she saw Cecily's stricken expression, and the glint of a tear on her cheek. "Oh, Cici. It's okay." Helplessness overwhelmed her as it always did when Cecily cried.

"No, it's not. This is supposed to be a beige cashmere suit. I can't get married in this."

"Then wear what you have on!" Rorie cowered under the force of Cecily's glare. Clearly, the suggestion was not the correct one. "I only meant, it doesn't matter to me. That's not why I'm here."

"This is a disaster." Her face was a dead-ringer for the frowning tragedy mask that graced the cover of every theater playbill, and Rorie could see she was on the brink of her breaking point.

All of Cecily's easy-breezy confidence had deserted her, and Rorie could sense the return of this much more familiar version of Cecily, the one she loved so dearly for her passion, but whose strong emotions could sometimes get the better of her. And when they did, Rorie felt it was her duty to step in.

"Come on, let's go." Rorie's commanding tone surprised even herself, and immediately succeeded in stopping Cecily's tears.

"Where?" she asked, a flush of pink returning to her sallow cheeks.

The truth was, Rorie had spoken on impulse and wasn't entirely sure, but she could hardly admit it now. Instead, she borrowed a sheet from Cecily's usual playbook and decided to improvise. "Shopping. There's gotta be a place to buy a dress around here."

TWENTY-ONE

"YOU WANT TO GO SHOPPING?" The innkeeper, who was also their Justice of the Peace, stared curiously at them from behind the registration desk. "In the mountains? I'm afraid there were more stores to choose from where you came from than you'll find here. Besides, aren't I supposed to be doing your wedding in a few hours?"

"Well, that's just it. My fiancée," Rorie pointed to Cecily, a thrill rushing through her at the sound of that word despite their desperate situation, "had a little mix-up and doesn't have anything to wear."

The innkeeper chewed his lip, "Well, there is one store, but you can't really get there from here."

Rorie had heard that old rural New England joke a dozen times, but this time she felt little desire to laugh. He appeared to be dead serious.

"Roads are too bad from the storm," he added by way of explanation. A woman, Rorie presumed it was his wife, came up behind him with a look of concern.

"What's that?" she asked.

"These ladies need to go shopping for a wedding dress, but I told them the roads are closed."

"Oh dear!" A deep furrow formed in the woman's brow as she seemed to grasp the seriousness of the situation in a way that her husband had not. "That *is* a problem. I'm afraid my husband's right about the roads." She paused a moment, lost in thought. "Does it have to be a wedding dress?"

Rorie looked searchingly at Cecily, who finally shook her head. "No, any nice dress would do," she added, a hint of hopefulness in her tone.

The innkeeper's wife smiled broadly. "Then I might have an idea. What size are you?"

"A four," Cecily replied with utter conviction.

Rorie raised an eyebrow at the Hollywood vanity size. Every actress claimed to be a four, and only their wardrobe mistresses—and fiancées—knew the truth.

Cecily's cheeks colored as she mumbled, "Okay, a six." She smoothed her hand along one hip and sighed. "Maybe an eight."

The woman rummaged through a drawer, pulling out a handful of keys. "My family's been running this inn for as long as I can remember, and over the years a lot of guests have left things behind. Our policy was to keep everything for a year and then donate it, but my mother was too frugal to give anything away, so when my husband and I took over the place last year, we discovered decades of lost and found in the attic." She sorted through the keys until she found the right one. "Here it is. I've been putting everything by size into bins for the town rummage sale this spring. I'll bring the ones most likely to fit up to your room and you can look through and see if something might work for you."

Rorie smiled broadly at the woman, her heart once more

feeling light at the crisis averted. "Thank you. You don't know how much this means."

"Yes, thank you." Cecily bit her lip as if in debate. "You might bring up a few tens, just in case."

A short while later, the innkeeper delivered two large plastic tubs to their door. Rorie opened hers first, prying off the lid with a loud snap, followed by a snort.

"When she said decades worth of clothing, she wasn't joking." Rorie held up a floor length dress in a floral print in a style that hadn't been popular since before Reagan became president.

Cecily's face fell. "Oh, no. If that's the best we do, I may end up getting married in my bathrobe."

"Not that Jada Larkin one? I could live with that. We could just move the ceremony up here to the bedroom, and save ourselves some time, after." Rorie waggled her eyebrows, and Cecily responded by sticking out her tongue.

"Dream on. Oh, this isn't bad." She held up a formal dress in a modern style, arranging it so that it fell from her shoulders to the floor. Way too far onto the floor. "Damn. This thing must have been worn by a giant."

Rorie dug around in her own box again, searching through the layers of fabric until she spied a piece of white lace. Her pulse quickened. "Look at this. I think it's an actual wedding gown." She unfurled the gown, which had a lace bodice and a long skirt that ended in a train.

"Oh!" Cecily gave the dress an odd look, and Rorie couldn't tell if it was good or bad. "That's certainly very traditional."

"Try it on?"

A series of conflicting emotions played across Cecily's face, once more leaving Rorie in the dark as to their meaning. "Okay, I'll give it a try."

As Cecily stripped off the sweater and jeans she'd traveled in, Rorie mostly managed to keep her eyes from roaming and her thoughts pure. They'd arranged to have the ceremony at four o'clock, and it left them with little time for distraction, no matter how tempting. There would be time for that later. *Thank God for wedding nights.*

Cecily fastened the dress with a quick zip and turned to see her reflection, a wistful look on her face. She twisted and turned, catching every angle as best she could in the narrow full length mirror. It was an old-fashioned style, but more charming than out-of-date, with a sweetheart neckline and small cap sleeves. The lace had yellowed just the slightest bit around the edges, but overall, Rorie couldn't help but be struck by its perfection. Or perhaps it just seemed so perfect because of the woman who was wearing it.

Rorie stared, mesmerized, her heart nearly standing still. "You've never looked more beautiful. I love it!"

Cecily continued to stare at the dress in silence, her mouth trembling slightly. Rorie's brow creased as she realized that Cecily didn't seem to share her approval of the dress. "Cici? What is it?"

Finally, Cecily spoke. "I know you love it, but will you hate me if I keep looking?"

Disappointment washed over her. "But, why? It's like it was made for you."

"I know." Cecily's eyes were downcast. "And maybe it's perfect and I'm just being stupid. But I've done it this way before, and I don't want anything to remind me of mistakes today."

"I don't love the dress, Cici. I love you. We'll keep looking."

The disappointment hadn't completely dissolved, but Rorie understood. If things had been different, she would have loved to see Cecily wearing a dress just like that one. Maybe she would have worn one too, and they would have invited all of their friends and family to celebrate with them. It might have been nice, had things been different, but their pasts were their pasts. She pushed any remaining disappointment aside. It was their future she cared most about now.

A few minutes later, Cecily sucked in her breath loudly in obvious excitement, and Rorie paused in her searching, looking up to see Cecily pulling a dove-gray skirt and jacket from her bin.

"It's so Jackie-O!" Cecily said with a grin of unmistakable, conflict-free glee. "It looks vintage. You don't think it's a real Chanel, do you?"

Rorie gave a noncommittal shrug, unable to think why anyone would ever travel to the White Mountains in a designer suit, but unwilling to burst Cecily's bubble. "Do you think it will fit?"

Cecily looked at the clock with a grimace. "It better, because we're running out of time. I think it'll be fine. Why don't you head down and see if Tyler and Bryn are set, and I'll be there as soon as I'm dressed."

At the base of the stairs, Rorie stopped, her eyes tearing up as she caught a glimpse of Bryn, in a dress made for a princess and her beautiful velvet coat, holding onto Tyler's finger and twirling like Cinderella at the ball. Her soon to be stepson was tall and handsome in a dark suit, and Rorie couldn't help but think what a fine prince he made, and what a beautiful family she now had. She blinked hard, swallowing down a lump in her throat with the knowledge that if she had even a single drop of joy added to her heart, it would probably burst.

When the toe of Cecily's shoe showed at the top of the stairs, Rorie realized exactly how desperate her situation had become. She was going to cry, that's all there was to it. *At the sight of a goddamn shoe!* What would she do when the rest of her gorgeous wife-to-be came into view? *Probably die.* She ducked into the parlor where the ceremony would take place to avoid making a complete spectacle of herself.

The parlor had a quaint, timeless feel to it—not too modern and not too old—just classic and comfortable, with a solid wooden mantel, painted white, surrounding a roaring fire. It was draped in freshly cut fir, and the pungent scent of it tickled Rorie's nose and filled the room with the essence of the holidays. Though there were a few other guests staying at the inn, the room was empty and she hadn't seen a soul except the innkeepers and her own family, and so she had the sense of being in a private space of their own. If she'd designed the setting herself, it would have been exactly like this.

The innkeeper, taking on his role as Justice of the Peace, came into the room. It was undeniably the same man from behind the desk, but he'd donned a black robe for the occasion, and it transformed him so completely that Rorie was taken aback. The lump in her throat doubled in size, and she struggled for composure, sternly reminding herself of the vital truth that Mulloys do not cry in public, even while knowing it was probably useless.

There was a commotion in the foyer as, presumably, Cecily reached the first floor. Rorie heard the innkeeper's wife exclaim, and the sound of footsteps retreating. Finally Tyler and Bryn came in, joining Rorie where she stood by the fireplace, but even after several moments, Cecily still had not entered the room.

"She hasn't pulled a runaway bride, has she?" Rorie whispered to Tyler, mostly as a joke. He snickered under his breath and immediately she relaxed.

"Nah. The innkeeper lady said she had something for her.

She'll be right in." Tyler held out his hand, a red rose with a spray of baby's breath in his palm. "Here. You're supposed to wear this."

She took the flower, but the pin shook so much in her fingers that she couldn't get it through the heavily taped stem. She jabbed the sharp tip into her finger and hissed at the sharp pain. *At least now I have a good reason to cry.* She looked to Tyler with uncharacteristic helplessness. "Can you do it?"

With steady fingers, Tyler pinned the flower to her black jacket. He'd become such an accomplished young man. Pride swelled in her chest. He was Cecily's son, but they'd grown close during the time he'd lived with her in LA. He belonged to her, too, and performing this simple task for her had the effect of a blessing. The flower in place, she felt transformed.

"Mama Rorie?" Bryn, tugged hard at her hand, whispering in her ear. At least, she tried to whisper. Rorie had heard Tyler admonishing the child about proper wedding etiquette as they'd entered the room. But she was four, an age where whispering is an elusive skill. The result was a rush of hot, wet air accompanying words loud enough to set her ears ringing.

"Yes, sweetie?" She pulled her head a safe distance from Bryn's mouth while resisting the urge to scrub her ear canal with her pinky finger.

"You have a boo-boo on your finger. Does it need a kiss?"

Rorie looked down at the drop of red blood that had welled on the tip, and lacking other options, licked it away with the tip of her tongue. "You know what, I think it does."

Bryn gave her finger a kiss, then grinned with obvious pride at her contribution. The kiss helped more than Rorie might have guessed. At last, her nerves had settled and she was ready to get married, if only Cecily would arrive.

She didn't have to wait long, and when she saw the final touch the innkeeper's wife had provided, it was more than worth the wait. Atop Cecily's head was a dove-gray pillbox hat of a similar vintage as the suit, with a tiny strip of veiling that dipped over her forehead. It was just the right touch, that little nod to the fact that Cecily was, indeed a bride. But it was the final straw, seeing that tiny veil, and nothing could hold back the hot, wet trail of tears that started down Rorie's cheeks.

Cecily walked across the room with a natural gait, no pomp and circumstance or the step-together-step that brides moved to in the movies. For the first time Rorie realized how grateful she should be that there was no music, no church aisle, and no crowd of family and friends. She'd never have made it through, and from the iron grip with which Cecily took her hand when she joined her at the hearth, Rorie knew she wasn't the only one.

"Hi," Cecily whispered, and Rorie laughed through her steady stream of tears.

"Hi." She touched a finger to Cecily's forehead, running it along the edge of the narrow veil, then leaned closer and kissed her cheek just beside her ear.

The JP cleared his throat. "We'll get to that part in a minute." His voice was stern but his eyes twinkled, and their laughter relieved the tension of the moment. "Let's get started. Do you have anything you'd like to say, or would you like me to read the standard vows?"

Rorie's mouth hung open. In all their rush, they'd never once discussed the vows! She didn't have a single word prepared, and had no idea what she would say. "Um..." She looked to Cecily for an answer, suspecting that once again, the traditional path would bring back too much of the past. "What do you think?"

Cecily drew in a breath, pressing her lips into a thin line as she weighed the choices. "Do you mind if we just do the traditional vows? I'm not sure I can find the right words."

Rorie grinned. "Once again, you've read my mind."

There was an unexpected comfort in repeating the words that so many couples had said before. The awareness of all those who had succeeded in keeping these promises wrapped around her like a warm quilt as she promised to do the same. Love, honor, cherish. Honestly, there was a point where she'd lost track of the words. It didn't matter, the intention was there regardless.

"Well, that's good enough for me," their JP announced in his no-nonsense, Yankee way. "And what's good enough for me is good enough for the State of New Hampshire. Congratulations, you're married!"

"Not quite," Rorie corrected him. She might not have remembered all the words, but she knew when something was missing. She pulled Cecily close, drawing her lips into the one kiss she'd waited over twenty years for.

From the day she'd wandered back to the tool closet in their dusty university theater, looking for the source of a noise in the darkness, she'd never doubted that she'd met her match in Cecily DuPont. It had brought a brief moment of joy, and tormented her for the next eighteen years, but she'd never doubted that this one person competed her in a way that no one else ever would. And as she looked from her new wife, to her stepson, and the little girl they could soon call their own, that was the only word that came close to describing her state of being. Complete.

Outside the evening had grown dark, the sky filled with the last hint of purple, as the jingling of sleigh bells echoed in the still winter air. A horse drawn sleigh came into view through the parlor window, and Bryn, who had been remarkably quiet throughout the ceremony, let out a shout.

"It's Santa's sleigh!"

Rorie laughed and took Cecily by one hand and the child by the other. "Not quite." It seemed like magic, even so. She smiled at Cecily. "Time for a ride?"

"I wanna go! I wanna go!"

Tyler placed a hand on Bryn's shoulder and whispered *hush*. "Bryn, this is just for Mama Rorie and Mimsy, okay? This is their special day."

But Rorie shook her head. "It's okay. Why don't we all go?"

There would be time enough to be alone when they returned, with dinner for two, and champagne and cake in the suite. Right now, what Rorie craved most was to have her whole family beside her for the ride.

TWENTY-TWO

THE THRUM of the engine vibrated her seat as Cecily flipped through the stack of documents she'd printed for the flight. Normally, she'd be frantic over all the work that had remained undone in her absence, but the dimly lit cabin and persistent white noise lent themselves more to sleepiness than motivation. She'd been away from the office for more than a week, yet this was the first time she'd even attempted to work, an unprecedented situation that should have worried her more than it did. The solid band of white gold on her left ring finger glinted in the light of the overhead lamp.

Then again, it had been an unusually eventful week.

She pressed her fingers, cool and dry from the pressurized air, firmly against her temples, trying to massage her brain awake enough to focus on her task. They were simple employment contracts that required little more of her than a signature. Why was she was finding it so difficult to immerse herself in the details? But she knew the reason. Beside her in the window seat, a sleeping Bryn shifted, hugging the teddy bear that had been a going away gift from Tyler and Reese close to her chest. Her adoption review would be coming up soon, giving Cecily more pressing legal issues to fret over.

Her temples throbbed every time she thought about it, worried that her impulsive decision to elope would somehow mean they'd have to start from scratch. But now that they were married, she wanted to be Bryn's parent officially. Taking the leap to get one piece of paper wouldn't be complete without the other. Susan had been right. She needed to protect what was hers.

But how do I tell Rorie, if it could mean a long delay?

Cecily shifted uncomfortably in her narrow middle seat, and Rorie glanced up from book with empathy in her eyes. "Is that uncomfortable seat making it hard for you to work? I'm willing to switch."

"No, it's not that." Cecily clenched her fingers. Now was the time. "It's something else. It's Bryn."

"What about her?" Rorie's expression had become guarded, and Cecily worried that she'd already crossed a line.

"It's the adoption. I hope haven't screwed things up, but now that we're married, I'd really like to add my name to the paperwork. If it's not too late?"

"Too late?" Her obvious relief caught Cecily by surprise. "Just the opposite! It's right on time. There's something I hadn't told you, but I guess you should probably know." She went on to explain the letter she'd received from the law firm in Biloxi that represented Bryn's paternal grandmother, the basis of which was an objection to their unmarried state. "According to Helen, our best bet to fight it was, well, to get married."

Cecily's jaw dropped. "And you're just telling me this now?"

Rorie's expression grew sheepish. "I know, but Helen

assured me she could find a different solution that would be nearly as good, so—"

"Nearly as good?" Cecily paused for a breath to calm her exasperation. What-ifs, even if no longer warranted, flashed on repeat in her mind. "That's not good enough! Not if it could've meant losing Bryn."

Rorie's shoulders slumped. "I probably should've told you. I just didn't want it to be the reason. You already did that once, got married because of a kid. I didn't want it to be that way for us."

"Huh. I wouldn't have thought of it that way." Cecily turned her head to check on Bryn, who continued to sleep peacefully, unaware of how close she may have come to being sent back to Mississippi. "But now that we're married, it'll be okay?"

As Rorie nodded, the weight lifted from Cecily's chest. "It was a flimsy argument, anyway, but the way things are these days, I guess they figured it was worth a shot. There's no way California would've given their suit the time of day, but Mississippi has to sign off on it, too, and you never know."

"Oh, I know." Cecily snorted derisively. "There's no shortage of good folks down there who think they'd be doing Bryn a favor by taking her away from us."

Rorie let out a breath but didn't respond. They both know what Cecily had said was true.

"It'll change someday," Cecily said, giving Rorie's hand a squeeze. "If my mother can come around, the whole south will, eventually."

"I hope you're right. In the meantime, we're protected. So you can stop worrying, and get back to your work." Rorie smiled teasingly. "I know you're dying to."

Cecily laughed. "I know, you'd think so, wouldn't you? But I can barely get through the little bit I brought on board."

"Feeling nervous to get back?"

"A bit. I know the stack of year-end paperwork on my desk is going to be halfway to the moon." Cecily frowned as she realized that the new year was only a couple days away, and Rorie hadn't yet secured a new job. "But, what do you think your plan will be?"

Rorie sighed. "I wish I knew. Although, did I tell you the rumor that's going around on that *Paramount* show?" Cecily shook her head. "Well, the Georgia idea fell through, and the whole thing ended up being delayed until the new year like they'd originally planned."

Cecily brightened at the news. "Then you might still have a shot? I know they wanted you."

Rorie shrugged. "I don't know. Maybe. If they haven't hired someone else already."

Cecily raised an eyebrow at the lack of enthusiasm. "Would you want it, if they offered it to you again?"

"I'm not sure," Rorie said thoughtfully, her gaze resting on Bryn. "These past few months being at home with her have flown by. I haven't fully adjusted to the idea of leaving her with someone."

Pushing the armrest up that was between them. Cecily snuggled closer to Rorie and slipped an arm around her, guiding Rorie's head to her shoulder. "It's okay, you know," she reassured her, giving the top of her head a kiss. "There's no rush. You can stay home as long as you'd like, even forever, if that's what you want."

It was an opportunity she'd been lucky to have with Tyler, and as she offered the same to Rorie, she experienced a new sense of appreciation for her ex-husband. Whatever else, she could never let herself forget to be thankful for that gift that Chet had given her. She felt humbled to be in a position where she could make it possible for Rorie to do the same, if that's what she chose.

She could feel Rorie's head shake gently against her shoulder. "No, not forever. But it's even more important to feel like I have a real passion for whatever job I choose."

As Rorie drifted off to sleep, Cecily turned her attention back to the pile of work that awaited her. Rorie's response struck a chord. *Is this my passion?* She wondered as she tried to muster up her usual enthusiasm, which was still flagging. Right now it didn't feel like it, with her energy focused homeward, but experience told her that her excitement for the work would return soon enough, and probably with a vengeance. With a sigh, she tucked the papers away and turned off the overhead light. Resting her free hand on Bryn, and pulling Rorie closer, she wondered if she'd ever really achieve the state of having her personal and professional lives truly in balance, or if it would always be a struggle.

HER NECK WAS stiff and sore as Cecily rolled two suitcases up the driveway, Rorie following behind with Bryn who was still passed out in slumber, flung over her shoulder like a rag doll. It was only just past nine in the evening, west coast time, but it was past midnight in Connecticut, and every sinew in Cecily's body cried out for bed. She fumbled with the front door lock, then used her shoulder to give the door a shove, and regretted it immediately as pain shot through the already strained muscles of her neck.

"Ow, fuck, that hurt," Cecily muttered, her voice much louder in the silent entryway than she'd intended.

"Language, Cecily."

Cecily froze at the sound of her mother's voice. *Did I just imagine that?* God, she must be even more tired than she thought if she couldn't tell the difference between reality and the perpetually nagging voice of her mother in her head.

"It's really such a vulgar word."

She heard it again, followed by a sniff, and this time there was little doubt that the voice was very real, and coming from her living room. "Mother?"

"You need some help with the luggage, Pumpkin?"

Daddy?

Dropping the handles and leaving the luggage to fall where it may, Cecily turned the corner and stared, horrified, at her living room couch, where her mother and father sat. They were not alone.

"Cici, did you mean to—"

Rorie stopped dead behind her as she, too, tried to make quick sense of the scene. "Mama? Pop?" For indeed, it had not been a hallucination, and Rorie's parents were really, truly, seated beside Cecily's, four people jammed onto a three-person couch like a can of silver-haired sardines. "What's going on?"

"Funny, that's what we were wondering, too," it was Rorie's father who spoke, "right around the time we got a call from Senator DuPont and his lovely wife, wanting to know if we'd heard the news."

Cecily's insides twisted. *The news?* There was no need to ask what news they meant. Somehow, they'd heard about the wedding. "How did you—"

Cecily's mother held up one of her favorite tabloids from a few days before, pointing to her picture in a box near the top next to the headline 'Secret Wedding!' The allure of fame being what it was, under any other circumstances, it might have felt flattering. While not the main story of the day, rumors of her elopement had still made the front page, and unlike all of the cougar and love triangle nonsense, this happened to be true. However, having her parents read about her nuptials in some tell-all tattler wasn't exactly what she'd had in mind for breaking the joyous news.

"Mom, I'm really sorry. We were planning to tell you as soon as we got home. I don't know how they found out."

Actually, she could make a fairly reasonable guess. *Bailey.* With a sinking feeling inside, Cecily was forced to acknowledge that her friend might not have been as discreet as she'd been counting on. It's not that she would tell anyone on purpose, but thinking before speaking wasn't necessarily Bailey's greatest strength.

"Your mother was beside herself when she read it." Though he mimicked his wife's serious tone, Cecily could tell it was an act. Her dad was a softy at heart. "She made me call Flip, here, and see if he'd heard any more than we had."

"Which I had *not*," Rorie's dad boomed. He may have been upset, or it may have just been his years of military training that lent such sternness to his voice. It was difficult to tell, but the effect was startling.

Roused by the noise from where she still slumbered in Rorie's arms, Bryn opened her eyes and gave a yawn. At the sight of her Pop-pop, Grammy Grace, Gran, plus one kind-looking gentlemen she hadn't yet met, all piled onto one sofa, she wiggled to the floor and launched herself into the midst of eight eager arms.

"There's our girl!" Rorie's mother said, coming up the winner in the race to see who could get Bryn on their lap first. She hadn't said a word about their marriage, and it was sometimes difficult to tell how many of those types of details made it through in her delicate state, but the connection she'd forged with her granddaughter during the visits Rorie had made with Bryn to her mother's facility over the weeks were evident.

"Now Grace, don't be greedy," Cecily's mother complained when, after several seconds, Rorie's mother had failed to release the little girl from her embrace.

"You just wait your turn, Margaret," Grace shot back, and Cecily had perhaps the biggest shock of the night when instead of taking offense, her mother let out a good-natured laugh, as if she and Grace were lifelong pals.

"Exactly how long have you all been here?" Cecily asked.

"Oh, long enough to get *very* well acquainted," her mother replied. "Your father and I came in from Baton Rouge yesterday afternoon, and Flip and Grace were kind enough to drive up from San Diego so we could get to the bottom of this in person. In fact, we've all hit it off so well that we'd almost forgotten why we're here. Almost."

Oh God, they've been conspiring with one another. Cecily's heart sank at the possibilities. Sure, it was nice in theory for everyone to get along, but what did this mean for her and Rorie in the future? *They've got us completely outnumbered.*

"So, why are you all here, exactly?" Rorie asked, finally seeming to emerge from her shock. "Not that we're not happy to see you, but you could have just called."

"Well," Rorie's father answered, "we figured if the rumors were true, there'd be a couple of newlyweds in need of a babysitter for their honeymoon."

"Oh," Rorie said. "That's thoughtful, but we didn't really have plans. I mean, Cici needs to get back to work, and—"

"Nonsense," Cecily's dad joined in heartily, as if providing backup for his new best buddy. "Tomorrow's New Year's Eve. There's no reason work can't wait a few more days. You should take the chance to get away."

"Daddy, that's sweet, but I don't even know where we'd

go." It's not that the idea of a honeymoon didn't hold some appeal, but after a week away and a full day spent on a plane, it was more than Cecily's sleepy brain could process.

"Well, Pumpkin, your mother had a thought about that. Margaret, show them what you brought."

Cecily frowned as her mother took out a thick envelope and handed it to her. "What is it?"

"It's not a wedding gift, just to be clear, since you haven't even officially confirmed that you got married. It's just a little something we happened to get for Bryn. A Christmas gift."

"A Christmas gift?"

Her mother nodded. "Oh, and I meant to say thank you for that beautiful suit you two sent for Christmas. I can't remember the last time you sent me a gift," she added awkwardly.

"I'm glad you liked it." Cecily was touched by her mother's genuine thanks, even as she thought wistfully of her lost wedding suit. At least now she knew for certain where it had ended up. Besides, it had all worked out in the end, and probably earned her more points than the tacky Christmas sweater would have done.

Cecily reached into the envelope and drew out a key, which she examined in puzzlement. What kind of child's gift required a key? Bryn was years away from needing a car. She pulled out the papers inside, but they made little sense to her. Finally, she turned to her mother and declared, "I give up. What is it?"

"It's a ranch." Her mother answered.

"In Malibu," her father added helpfully.

Cecily blinked. "A ranch."

"In Malibu?" Rorie looked as dazed as Cecily felt.

"It was a summer camp," Cecily's mother said, as if that explained it all.

"I'm sorry, Margaret," Rorie finally managed to say, "I think you're going to need to give us a few more details. Why did you get a four-year-old her own summer camp?"

"I was looking for a place for Bryn to take riding lessons this summer. I told Cecily I thought a horse would be good for her, remember?"

Cecily nodded at the sound of her name, but didn't know what else to say. *She bought her a camp so she could ride a pony?* Sometimes, her mother astonished her.

"It was a lovely camp," Margaret asserted, "and came highly recommended, only it was closing and being put up for sale. It seemed like such a shame to see it turned into one of your ugly California strip malls. So, I bought it. It seemed like the perfect project."

Cecily gaped. "You and Daddy and are going to run a summer horse camp in Malibu?"

"What?" Cecily's father interjected. "No, not us, Pumpkin. You."

"But..." Cecily's head spun. "But I have a job. I have my own business! I can barely find balance the way it is."

"Well, not you so much," Cecily's mother added. "I was thinking it might give Rorie something to do, since she's between jobs."

Too much confusion swirled inside for Cecily to know where to begin. *My mother, Typhoon Margaret.* Did she really think you could just buy something like a ranch for a hobby? Her mother, who'd never worked a real job, who'd taken up *politics* as a hobby, for chrissake. What would make her even think for a second that this was a normal thing to do?

She turned to Rorie, mortified on her mother's behalf. "I'm so sorry. Clearly my mother is—"

"Onto something."

There was a ghost of excitement in Rorie's exhausted face

that Cecily found shocking. *Is she really considering this?* "Babe, it's okay for you to say it's a crazy idea."

"It *is* a little crazy," Rorie conceded, then flashed a crooked grin. "But it's worth having a look, don't you think? I mean, I don't have much else going on. Why don't we take our parents up on the babysitting offer and go check out this ranch?"

Cecily stared around the room, dumbfounded as both sets of parents smiled, and her own wife joined in. It was insanity, but...

Five against one. I'm doomed.

TWENTY-THREE

THOUGH MALIBU WAS SCARCELY an hour's drive up the coast, it was a world away. Just beyond the neighborhood of Pacific Palisades and the crowded beach towns was a stretch of Pacific Coast Highway where the sea on one side and the towering, craggy hills on the other had prevented the usual overbuilding that plagued the majority of the California coast. From that point of the journey on, it was easy for Rorie and Cecily to imagine that they'd been transported far from the city of Los Angeles.

"Turn here," Cecily said, looking up from the map and pointing to her right. And it was, indeed, a paper map that she was using, which they'd scrounged from a no-name convenience store in desperation when both their cell phone signals failed and the GPS cut out. One of its folded panels was so faded from years of sitting in direct sunlight that it was nearly unreadable, and all indications were that the thing hailed from the Carter administration. They prayed not too much had changed in the area since then.

Rorie studied the nondescript road Cecily had pointed to, then the buildings that surrounded it, and reasoned that their prayers appeared to have been answered. They were on a small stretch of land that was flat and wide enough to host a tiny cluster of buildings, the most interesting of which was a seafood shack with a neon rimmed white sign on its roof that rivaled the Hollywood sign in size. The whole street seemed a homey throwback to the 1950s, cheerful and welcoming. Given Malibu's reputation for snooty celebrities and multi-million dollar mansions, it was not at all what she'd expected to find just a few miles from their destination. Time hadn't left a mark here in decades.

Their chosen road twisted and narrowed to the point that it could scarcely continue to claim to have two lanes when Cecily announced that they'd reached the final turn. Rorie frowned. Stretching ahead of them was nothing but dry grass and scrub brush in shades of blue-green, bordered with a white picket fence. She pulled the car over and stopped, letting the engine idle, as she reached for the map herself.

"Are you positive?" She shook the map, turning it one way and then the other before pushing it away in disgust. Who the hell knew how to read a map anymore, anyway? "This doesn't look right."

"How did you think a ranch was going to look?" Cecily asked, arching one eyebrow as she effortlessly returned the map to its original folds.

"I—" Rorie paused to mull it over and realized she didn't have an answer. Her strongest mental image involved horseshoes and a wagon wheel. When it came to ranches, and summer camps for that matter, she had no frame of reference that wasn't drawn from a movie starring either John Wayne or Hayley Mills. Movies were the source material of her imagination, and how she interpreted new surroundings, but they weren't always on target. The romantic images in her mind didn't always square with reality, and could lead to disappointment. Even so, something about the concept of the place had captured her imagination from the moment Margaret had handed over the envelope. "I guess I just didn't know there was so much space left so close to LA."

"Yeah. I thought there'd at least be a nail salon and a couple of drive-thru fast food places. But this is definitely the turn. It shouldn't be more than another mile."

As Rorie started down the road again, Cecily leafed through the papers her mother had given her. "The notes from the realtor say the ranch is one hundred acres, with a house, several camp cabins, plus a barn and stables."

"One hundred acres?" Rorie let out a low whistle at that staggering figure. "I still can't believe your parents bought Bryn a ranch."

"I think my mother's losing her mind now that Daddy's retired. Oh, and did I tell you the latest? Daddy wants them to buy an RV and drive across the United States. My father. My Mother. In an RV. See what happens when you stop working? All this free time is going to their heads."

No work obligations and miles of open road, just you and the person you love the most in the world? Rorie didn't think it sounded too shabby. A sudden memory of long nights in the scene shop, working side by side with Cecily, provoked a quiet sigh. They certainly didn't spend time together like that now, and retirement was years away, not that there was any use complaining about it now.

"Our child's on her way to being a real estate mogul," she said instead.

Cecily laughed. "Don't get too excited. Most of it is conservation land with low resale value, although there are a few acres with development potential. When we put it back on the market, her college fund won't be an issue."

"Her college fund isn't really an issue now."

The observation came out more testily than she'd intended, but what Cecily had just said cut to the quick. *Put it back on the market.* That meant that Cecily had already made up her mind not to keep the ranch. Which was the most sensible decision, by far, and yet Rorie's palpable disappointment in the moment surprised her. Deep down, she already thought of the place as theirs.

"Here's the driveway," Cecily said, and Rorie grinned, the sight erasing the previous sting of Cecily's comment.

"Now *that* looks like a ranch," she said as they drove beneath the rusty wrought iron arch that marked the entrance to the property. An oversized horseshoe hung from its middle, and a wagon wheel was propped up decoratively on one side, exactly as she might have imagined.

They parked outside the main house, a sprawling two-story structure in the Spanish Colonial Revival style that had been all the rage in the early twentieth century. It looked old but sturdy, with freshly painted white stucco walls, red clay tile on the roof, and vines that crept along the balcony railings of the upper floor. According to the records, it had been built as a weekend retreat for a silent film star in the 1920s, and the exterior appeared little changed since those days.

"It's so old-Hollywood!" Rorie exclaimed as she rested her hand on the heavily carved front door and waited for Cecily to produce the key.

The interior was devoid of furnishings, but Rorie could see them in her imagination as they explored every room. A pair of well-worn leather club chairs would be perfect near the massive fireplace, with a simple antique church pew opposite the long wall of windows that overlooked the canyon view. They'd remodel the kitchen, and add a table to that sun-drenched nook for breakfasts of farm-fresh eggs and orange juice squeezed from their own trees. That she knew nothing about the care of chickens or citrus trees was of little importance in her fantasy scenario.

"I love it!" She declared when they'd completed the full tour.

Cecily's enthusiasm was more contained, but undeniably present, nonetheless. "It *is* pretty amazing, I'll admit. It's not as rustic as I pictured it being."

"I wonder if the schools nearby are good. With a little fixing up, we could live here comfortably year-round."

Cecily's somewhat nervous laugh rang through the empty space, but beyond that she neither confirmed nor denied Rorie's assessment. "Shall we explore the rest of the grounds?"

The barn and stables were built a distance from the house itself for privacy, along with the cabins that were added to house the children when the property was turned into a camp after the second world war. They unlocked the stables and walked through its broad center, noting the highly polished western style saddles, bridles, and other tack that hung neatly from the walls.

Rorie breathed in the satisfying smell of oiled leather. "The equipment's all still here, but where are the animals?"

"Animals?" Cecily gaped. "It didn't come with animals."

Rorie's brow furrowed as she contemplated this unexpected complication. "I guess I just assumed it would, being a ranch and all."

"Babe, someone would have had to feed them, and give them water, and muck out the stalls all this time. The camp's been closed since August."

"Oh." Of course, it should have been obvious how much work and care would be involved, but then again, as a city kid, Rorie'd never owned anything more demanding than a guinea pig. "So, we'd have to buy all new horses?"

"Buying the horses would be easy compared to hiring the

staff to care for them. In case you hadn't noticed, we're hardly experts on running a ranch."

Standing outside the stables once more, the sky was flushed pink as the sun set into the vast ocean, the smallest sliver of which was barely visible in the very far-off distance. Though it was in Malibu, the ranch had no oceanfront property. If it had, buying it would've been well beyond the reach even of Senator DuPont and his wife. It would be dark soon, Rorie noted, and there were still several buildings left to discover.

"Do you want to check the cabins?" Rorie asked when Cecily had locked the stable and tucked the key back into her pocket.

Cecily nodded. "They're supposed to have come furnished, so I thought we might be able to stay there tonight."

The cabins were squat and square, little more than wooden boxes with a pointy roof on top, like a child's drawing of a house had been used as the blueprint. Rorie reached for the door handle on the nearest cabin, a simple metal latch without a lock. The door groaned on its hinges, protesting her efforts to pry it open, before finally giving up and swinging open all at once. Inside were four sets of bunk beds on rough-hewn pine floors, and that was all.

Cecily's face fell as she looked around. "The realtor's packet said these were furnished."

"Technically, they are."

Cecily wrinkled her nose. "They don't even have mattresses on them."

"Thank God." Rorie shuddered at the thought of dusty, moldy mattresses. "Would you really want to sleep on them after hundreds of kids? There might have been bed-wetters," she added when Cecily was slow to respond.

"Yuck. Good point." It was Cecily's turn to shudder. "But

what will we do about tonight? I thought we'd be able to sleep at the ranch, but clearly that isn't going to work."

"Just wait here a second." Rorie flashed an enigmatic smile as she thought back to the items she'd packed in the trunk that morning. Unlike Cecily, she'd considered the possibility that they'd need to bring their own comforts along. She raced back to the car and reemerged with a stack of thick wool blankets and a picnic basket. "See? Food and warmth. We have everything we need."

Cecily eyed Rorie's armload of supplies dubiously. "Is there a tent somewhere in there, too? We'll need someplace to sleep, unless you want to look for a hotel."

"Nope." A thrill of anticipation coursed through her at the thought of the night ahead. "I thought we'd spend our honeymoon under the stars. Preferably naked. Sleep optional."

Cecily threw her head back and laughed her clear, sweet laugh that never failed to make Rorie tingle from head to toe. "In that case, I hope you packed that picnic basket full. We'll need to keep up our strength."

"THAT WAS SO GOOD," Cecily moaned, licking the spots on her fingers where bits of crunchy breading still clung. "I know it isn't fancy, but cold fried chicken is my favorite picnic food. I loved it as a kid."

"Somehow," Rorie spoke as she dug through the basket in the dark, "I can't picture your family having a picnic. Or, I can, but with a table and chairs, and a maid serving all the food to you on china plates."

"You mean, that isn't how everyone does it?" Cecily deadpanned.

"I did bring something fancier, just for your benefit,"

Rorie said, pulling out a champagne bottle and two flutes, and setting them between them on the blanket. She popped the cork expertly, not spilling a drop, and poured the bubbly liquid, filling each in turn.

Half sitting, half lounging with their limbs entwined, they clinked the rims together before taking a sip.

"To us?" Cecily suggested. It was simple and yet the most perfect toast for the two of them.

Rorie nodded in agreement. "To us."

Smooth and dry, the champagne went down quickly—maybe a little too quickly—and soon Rorie set her glass aside and stretched out on the felted surface of the blanket with arms behind her head. Cecily lay down beside her, angling her body almost by instinct so that all along the length of their bodies, there was no spot where they didn't touch. Using Rorie's extended elbow as a pillow, Cecily tilted her head upward and they both took in the twinkling starlight above.

"It's so beautiful here," Rorie said with a sigh after they'd remained in quiet appreciation long enough. "I never knew there were so many stars." Even through the thick layer of clouds that had started to form overhead, they were a million times brighter than in LA.

"You're so beautiful," Cecily whispered, turning her head and waiting to catch Rorie's gaze. "I can see about a million stars reflected in your eyes."

The thrill of desire coursed through her, making her ache, but there was something Rorie needed to say now, before she lost her nerve. "I was serious before, Cici. We could live here. It already feels like home."

"We know nothing about ranching." It was a knee-jerk response, but she didn't laugh, so at least Rorie knew that she had taken the statement seriously.

Rorie tried a new approach. "So, we'll reopen it as a camp. It would be good for Bryn."

"A camp?" This time Cecily couldn't hold back a snort. "You don't like kids."

"I do now! I just didn't know it, before." Rorie might be willing to admit that a horse camp wasn't ideal, but it would be worth finding the right staff to run it if it meant they could live here throughout the year. Something about the old ranch called to her, and she wanted to stay.

Cecily snuggled closer, pressing her mouth against Rorie's neck, then grasping her earlobe naughtily with her teeth. "Maybe you can convince me," she suggested.

With a quick flip, Rorie was poised above her, her hands sweeping Cecily's arms upward, clasping her wrists and pinning them above her head as she bent to devour her mouth. Cecily's lips tasted of champagne, and were equally intoxicating. Rorie longed to lose herself in them, and drink them dry.

Eventually, a rumbling noise in the distance made them come up for air.

"Was that thunder?" Cecily asked between drawing in deep gulps of air.

Rorie frowned. She could have sworn the forecast had been clear when she'd checked that morning. "There must be a storm in the mountains. It'll pass us by."

She lowered her head, mouths meeting again as their fingers laced and gripped each other tightly. Through closed eyes, Rorie detected a weak flash of light, followed by another distant rumble, but she ignored it in favor of focusing her attention on Cecily's lips.

"Remember that storm the night we first kissed?" Cecily asked when their mouths finally parted.

How could she forget? It was the first time she'd kissed someone she'd truly been in love with. "You were so confused and vulnerable. I didn't know whether to pull you close and protect you or take complete advantage."

"I know which one I was hoping for," Cecily's laugh was low and wanton. "But you were very honorable." Twenty years later, there was still a hint of disappointment in her tone, turning the words into a scolding.

"Not really," Rorie said in her defense, the memory of her own vulnerability still lingering. "I was just pretty sure I was a passing fad to you, and I'd end up with a broken heart. Even then, I knew you were the only one who would ever have that type of power over me."

"You tried to sleep on the floor that night, too, as I recall. And look at us tonight. I'm starting to wonder if you have something against beds." Cecily gave her a seductive, cheeky grin.

"They're overrated. I'm perfectly comfortable right here." Taking advantage of her position on top, she allowed her weight to rest on Cecily's body increasingly, until she let out a giggle and squirmed in a delightfully frantic way, just as Rorie had been hoping she would.

"You know," Rorie confided, easing her body to the side until her weight rested on the ground, "I don't think I slept a wink that whole night, with those silk pajamas you'd given me to wear slipping all over my skin and making me think all sorts of things, and you sleeping so blissfully unaware in my arms." Cecily giggled again, and Rorie knew it was her favorite sound in the whole world. "If you'd had any idea what I wanted to do to you that night…"

"Show me now," she commanded, her voice husky, raw with desire.

So many years had passed, and they were an old married couple now, besides, but Rorie could still feel the desperate need of that night spurring her fingers on as they flew along the buttons of Cecily's shirt, pushing the fabric aside, pulling down the cup of her bra because she had no patience for the clasp. Rorie grasped Cecily's nipple between her fingers like a vice until it puckered, then drew it in between her lips. There was no need to pretend, as it truly felt that she'd never done it before.

Sucking a breath between her teeth, Cecily's fingers grasped Rorie's hair, their subtle pressure urging her lower. Dragging her tongue across Cecily's abdomen, she knew that it was fleshier now than she would have found it in the dormitory twenty years before, but it was no less perfect.

The day had been a warm one for winter, made warmer by the biting cold they'd left behind back east, and Cecily had worn a light cotton skirt on their drive. Glimpses of her bare legs then had been a distraction, and caressing them now, Rorie found them to be every bit as silky as those infernal pajamas had been against her skin so long ago, and driving her just as wild.

By now the thunder had grown louder and more insistent, but it failed to grab Rorie's attention half as much as did the panting moans of anticipation as she pushed the crotch of Cecily's panties aside, dipping her head to caress the exposed flesh with her tongue. As she pulled her into her mouth, and Cecily's back arched and hips bucked in response, they were each so lost in one another that they barely noticed as the first drops of rain began to fall.

In the next moment, the sky opened. It began pouring with an intensity that cooled the passion of their youth, bringing them swiftly back to the present, where they were two middle-aged women who really should know enough by now to come in out of the rain. Leaving the blanket and basket on the ground, they made a mad dash for the nearest building, a huge barn they hadn't yet had a chance to explore.

They key was somewhere in Cecily's skirt pocket, but the skirt had become tangled and twisted, and the pocket wasn't exactly where she'd expected it to be. As Cecily continued the search, a steady stream of rain pouring off the tip of her nose, it came to Rorie's attention that the barn door had no lock. With all the strength she had, she gave the barn door a shove, and it yielded under the force and slid open along its rusted tracks. They scurried inside and Rorie fumbled along one wall for a light switch while Cecily tried the other. Then with a loud click, one of them made contact, bright light flooding the space, and leaving them awestruck at what was revealed.

TWENTY-FOUR

IT WAS like no barn interior Cecily had ever imagined. Rows of folding wooden seats on cast-iron frames sloped toward a full-sized stage at the far end, its stylized proscenium arch an impressive work of classic Art Deco design. The lighting, too, which glowed from walls and ceiling, was straight from the era of silent films. The heavy velvet curtain that framed the stage was visibly worn in places, and the screen that likely once hung to project movies on was missing, but otherwise the space appeared perfectly preserved and ready for a show. The only things missing were the actors.

"Is this real?" Cecily breathed, trying to take it all in. "I feel like I must be dreaming."

For the second time in an hour, she had the feeling of being transported to another time and place. She'd been a college senior again, from the moment Rorie's lips had brushed hers on the blanket outside, the stars shining in her eyes. Suddenly, she'd been certain they were twenty-two, with their whole lives ahead of them, and this time they wouldn't make the same mistakes. Still basking in that glow, they'd stumbled through a time portal and emerged in the golden age of Hollywood. It was beyond belief.

Rorie looked around in wonder. "The packet from the realtor didn't mention a theater?"

Cecily shook her head, still in a daze. "No, just a barn somewhere on the list of outbuildings. Since it's a ranch, I assumed it was just a plain old barn. Do you think it was built for the camp?"

"No, this is older. You said the camp wasn't built until the late forties, and this has to be from the 1920s, although it's in such good condition that they must have kept it up to use for the kids."

"I bet it was put in by the original owner." Cecily thought back to the history of the property she'd read on the drive. "She was a silent film star, remember? Although I can't remember her name. And a Vaudeville performer before that, I think."

"Can you imagine this ranch in its heyday?" Rorie's eyes grew dreamy. "The tuxedos and flapper dresses, flowing with bootleg champagne. I'll bet they threw some amazing parties up at the house, and came in here to watch a movie or have someone put on a show."

"It's the perfect place for it. We should think about doing a screening here."

"We should?" Rorie asked, eyebrows raised high. "Then you don't want to sell the place, after all?"

"Sell it?" Cecily started to laugh, wondering where Rorie had come up with such an idea, until she remembered what she'd said on the drive. But that had been before the property's charm had worked its magic. "Not after finding *this*. Besides, it might be nice to have a place in the country where we could take Bryn on weekends. As long as we buy her a pony. That should placate Mother."

Rorie had wandered closer to the stage while Cecily talked, and stood now with one hand resting on the stage above. Hoisting herself onto the edge of the apron, she rose to her feet on the stage and looked. "We could do more than spend weekends watching movies, Cici." She reached out and grasped Cecily's hand, helping her up. "Look at all this space! Whoever put this in meant for it to be used for real shows. This could be a serious venue for live theater, with a little fixing up."

Cecily looked around dubiously at first. It might be fine for some friends, but inviting in the public would mean a lot of repairs. Still, she'd come to trust Rorie's creative vision on issues such as this much more than her own. "I suppose we could reach out to some local performance troupes and see if anyone is looking for space."

"Think bigger." She looked as if her head was still lost among the stars they'd watched outside. "We don't need to rent the space. We need to build the program ourselves!"

"Our own theater company?" Cecily felt herself being caught up in the contagion of Rorie's vision, but one of them had to be the cautious one. "But we know nothing about the market here."

"We know more about that than we do about running this place as a ranch or a camp. Although, in summer, it could be a theater camp if we wanted it to be." Rorie seemed swept away by the possibilities. "We could do anything!"

After the months of melancholy surrounding the cancellation of her show, and the struggle finding a new job, it made Cecily's heart sing to see her wife so caught up in something new. But there was just one problem, though she hesitated to bring it up and send Rorie crashing back down to earth so soon. "But, I already have a job."

Rorie was undeterred. "But Cici, this could be so much

more. Tell me this, when were you the happiest in your life? And don't say right now."

Cecily clamped her lips shut, having planned to say exactly that. She thought hard, then said, "Senior year, I guess. After we met."

Rorie grinned triumphantly, as if she'd known exactly what Cecily would say. "And think about what we used to do. We worked together every day, collaborating on the show. If there's one thing missing from our lives right now, don't you think it's that?"

Cecily frowned. She hadn't thought about it in years, but at that moment she could feel the hole. Maybe it was because of how vividly she'd relived it earlier that night, but if there was one thing she could retrieve from their past, she knew that would be it. But that was impossible.

"Rorie, I don't just have a job, I have a company to run, and people counting on me. What you're suggesting is a huge undertaking. I couldn't do both."

"Then choose the one where we can work together. We'll live here with Bryn, and spend our days together working, and have nights like tonight out under the stars whenever we want."

Cecily's chest ached and she yearned with her whole heart to give the woman she loved everything she asked for, but how could she? Not without giving up on her own dream that she'd worked so hard to build.

But is it still my dream? There'd been an ambivalence to her work that had started on their trip home from Connecticut, and had yet to abate. The thought of returning to the office after their impromptu honeymoon filled her with apathy. Even mustering passion for the stunning Jada Larkin film that should've felt like an honor to produce was more of a struggle than she'd thought possible, and it stood in stark contrast to the enthusiasm on her wife's face.

"I've never seen you so animated." Cecily reached for Rorie's hand, lacing their fingers together. "This is clearly what you've been searching for all this time. No matter what I decide, you should do it."

Rorie frowned. "But we're better together. You know that."

"Of course we are. And you'll always have me and my support."

"But?" Oh, how well Rorie knew her, well enough to know it wouldn't be as easy as she'd hoped.

"I'm not saying no." Cecily took a deep breath, hoping she could figure out herself what she *was* saying. "I'll admit that the past several weeks, I haven't felt the same excitement about my job that I used to." Her voice shook. Just saying out loud had turned this from a vague feeling to a problem she would have to address. "But it's my company, Rorie. I have to think long and hard about it, and give it my all before I could walk away."

Rorie's jaw tightened. "But when you put everything into your job, it doesn't leave a lot leftover for me, or for Bryn."

"I know." The truth of the accusation stung, but Cecily tried to focus on finding a compromise. "Look, this has all happened so suddenly, and I just can't drop everything right now. But I'll promise to think about it, and in the meantime, you should do everything you need to do to make your vision a reality."

Rorie nodded, resigned. "How long do you think you need to think about it?"

"Let me make the movie," Cecily proposed. After all, it was the chance of a lifetime, and her baby from the start. "If anything will make me figure out whether Sapphicsticated is the right place for me, or whether it's here with you, it'll be that. When Jada's film is done, I'll give you an answer."

Continue where she was, or take one more leap of faith and see where it would lead? If only she could know right now which was the better path, and if only she knew that the right choice for her could also be the one that would keep the stars flickering in Rorie's eyes.

"MAMA RORIE? MAMA RORIE?" Bryn tugged on the hem of her blouse so hard she felt it slip from her shoulders on one side "Are the ponies here?"

Rorie stifled a groan and plastered a bright smile on her face for Bryn's benefit. "Soon, sweetie. You know that Mimsy will come and find you as soon as they get here. She always does."

As Bryn ran off again, Rorie's smile faded. If she never heard another word about ponies, it would be too soon, but Cecily had become obsessed. Cecily had bought three. Three! Rorie blamed Margaret, mostly, for ever suggesting them. Since they were usually only at the house on weekends, they boarded them on a neighboring property during the week, and the beasts had caused so much trouble already, being transported back and forth, that Rorie marveled that she'd ever been crazy enough to entertain the idea of running this place as a horse camp. She might have become a kid person, but now she knew that she was *not* a horse person. Besides, she had her eye on the empty stable to store extra sets once the theater was up and running. Whenever that turned out to be.

"Cici?" Her voice echoed against the timbered ceiling of the ranch house's great room. Slowly over the past six months, the vision in her head for the home had started to become a reality, but the furnishings were still a bit sparse. That was fine for a weekend getaway, but deep down, Rorie still longed to make it their home.

Receiving no answer, Rorie went in search of Cecily at the stables, skirting around two caterers as they set up tables and chairs. Their guests were due to arrive soon. All around the outside of the barn, preparations were being made for the party, which would be two celebrations in one. The photos of Bryn on each table hinted at the first reason, which was that in a courtroom in Los Angeles the week before, after a judge in Mississippi had dismissed all remaining objections and given his assent, Bryn had finally, officially, been declared theirs. Rorie's eyes watered even at the memory, the general rule that Mulloys don't cry having been suspended more and more lately.

Passing by the open barn door, Rorie peered inside where a brand-new screen had been installed for the second momentous occasion of the night. After six months of dedicated work, Sapphicsticated, Inc., had completed principal filming on Jada Larkin's film. Though there were months of additional work ahead of it before completion, the trailer for their first feature film would be debuted tonight once all the children in attendance were snugly tucked into their cabins with the nannies that had been hired for the night.

Rorie's stomach tightened into a knot. They hadn't discussed it since that night they discovered the barn, but they both knew that, with the film reaching this critical stage, Cecily would be close to having an answer to the proposal Rorie had given her. *Will the answer come tonight?* She couldn't have been more nervous if it were a marriage proposal she was waiting for an answer on. Glancing at her left hand, Rorie felt some tension ease. At least that was one thing she didn't have to be concerned about any more, thanks to Cecily's impulsive elopement scheme. She'd never been so grateful to be knocked off her feet by a surprise.

The truth was, her proposal to run the theater together had been just as unplanned and, she feared, not as welcome. She sighed. What had she been thinking? Cecily was not the type of woman to appreciate having her life turned upside down out of the blue, no matter how great the idea. She was committed to her Sapphicsticated, and to the Hollywood scene. In fact, she thrived on it. The huge party they were about to throw, attended by dozens of Hollywood elite, was testament to that. Cecily would never throw that all away for a quiet life on a ranch in Malibu and overseeing a tiny community theater. Rorie wasn't even sure why doing it appealed so much to her. She only knew that it did, making even her marrow yearn for it.

Since their discovery of the theater, Rorie had been on the phone with every theater group and program in Southern California, working on ideas for the space. There were several groups interested in renting it, but her preferred plan was to develop a regional repertory theater that offered top-quality, original programming. To do that, she needed Cecily by her side. She swallowed roughly. Looking out across the tables where hundreds of Hollywood VIPs would soon be seated to celebrate her wife's greatest career achievement to date, Rorie prepared herself for disappointment.

She spotted Cecily as she neared the stables. The ponies had arrived, and so had Bryn. Cecily was just helping Bryn into her tiny saddle when Rorie got close enough to speak without shouting.

"There you are," she said, her voice quiet. The last thing she wanted to do was spook the pony while it carried such precious cargo.

But it was Cecily who looked spooked, jumping and

whirling at a surprisingly nimble speed. "Have the guests started to arrive? Is Jada here?"

"No, no one's here yet. I just came to see what you were up to."

"Quietly freaking out," Cecily replied. She handed the pony's reins to one of the assistants who was helping with the horses. "Have a good ride, Bryn!" she called, both she and Rorie waving as their tiny equestrian took off for her ride. When they'd turned the corner and were no longer in sight, Cecily turned her attention back to Rorie. "Remember how I used to get stage fright?"

Rorie nodded.

"Well, this is worse. I'm under so much pressure for everything to go right. All the investors, so many Hollywood VIPs..." Cecily blanched. "What if they hate it?"

Cecily was right. Rorie hadn't seen her this nervous since the night she'd been forced to go out on the Oakwood's stage in Bailey's place. "It's going to be fine," she said, giving Cecily's hand a reassuring pat. "They're going to love it." Though, Rorie thought with a wry smile, their loving it wouldn't help her own selfish case.

And as the guests arrived and the evening wore on, Rorie was proven correct. Everyone at every table was buzzing about Sapphicsticated, or Jada's film, or both. Just before dinner, Rorie spied Jill, who was sitting with Rhonda, watching the crowd.

"How do you think it's going?" Rorie asked, and Jill grinned like the Cheshire Cat.

"I've never seen a crowd so enthusiastic," Jill replied. "Tonight's preview is going to be all anyone can talk about this week!"

It confirmed what Rorie knew to be true, and she was filled with pride for Cecily, but couldn't help feeling a tinge of regret. She'd wished so badly that Cecily would want to leave this behind, but how could she now? She sighed, resigned to the fact that life could never go back to how it had been when they were young.

After dinner, they filed into the theater until it was standing room only, and Rorie slipped into a corner in the back, out of the way, to watch as Cecily stood and addressed the crowd.

"Friends," she began, "thank you all for coming tonight to celebrate with us and see the preview of Sapphicsticated's very first film. It's truly been a labor of love for all involved." She waited for the applause to die down, then continued. "It's meant so much to me to have the opportunity to work on this project, and that's why it's especially difficult for me to announce that while I'll remain on the board as an executive producer, I'll be stepping down from day-to-day operations as of today, and leaving things in the very capable hands of Jill Davidson."

Rorie stood frozen as Cecily handed the microphone over to Jill and left the stage. Had she really just heard what she thought she'd heard? In shock, she slipped out of the barn and found Cecily standing alone outside, visibly shaken.

"Cici?"

Cecily had tears in her eyes, but when she looked at Rorie, her face split into a wide grin. "I did it. I got through it."

"Yeah, I heard." Rorie searched her face, trying to read the conflicting emotions at play. "But, are you sure? Tonight's been such a success. You hadn't said before what you had decided, but I guess I assumed—"

"I know. I couldn't talk to you about it earlier because I still wasn't sure, but now I know I'm making the right choice. Tonight's been exactly what I needed to figure it out."

"Why?" Trembling, hardly believing it was real, Rorie had to know.

Cecily took a deep breath, blinking back tears. "Because I like my work. It's thrilling. Sometimes, when everything falls into place just right, like it did with Jada's film, it's even important. But I love you. And I love being out here on the ranch with you each weekend, and watching Bryn ride. Every weekend when we leave, it hurts a little more to be away. Work takes me away, and to do it right, it takes more than I'm willing to give. I want to be here, to be home with you."

Rorie understood because she felt the same, but she wasn't blind to what Cecily would be leaving behind. Her brow furrowed. "It's quiet out here, and the theater's never going to be very big or prestigious, even if my wildest dreams for it come true. What will be enough?"

Cecily nodded her head solemnly. "With the exception of maybe an Academy Award, this experience here tonight was probably the biggest thing I could ever hope for in my career and you know what? It's not worth how much I have to sacrifice to keep it going. I'd rather have a quiet life here, and the chance to build something together." She wrapped her arms around Rorie and kissed her tenderly, and Rorie felt surrounded by love. "Let's move to the ranch and see if we can make those wildest dreams of your come true."

EPILOGUE

SEVEN YEARS Later

Crickets chirped in the dry grass just beyond the barn door that stood open back stage. It was a hot night, as the opening night of the summer season so often was, and Cecily mopped her brow with the handkerchief that was always in her possession these days. She blamed the weather, and tonight it was probably true, but as the end of her forties drew closer, she frequently found herself sweating for no discernible reason.

She peeked into the dimly lit wing just behind the curtain where Bryn paced in tiny circles, practicing her lines. At twelve years old, she was as tall and slender as Rorie, but Cecily flushed with pleasure at the knowledge that their daughter's flair for drama was her contribution.

Yes, that flush is pleasure, and not menopause.

She refrained from waving or otherwise trying to get Bryn's attention, not wanting to break her concentration. It had been years since Cecily had been on stage herself, but just waiting in the wings was enough to make her hands grow clammy and her stomach start to churn with the old ghost of stage fright. Not Bryn, though. She was a natural, and Cecily was in awe of the assurance this little girl had when it came to the stage. Although 'little' was hardly the word to describe her any more. When did she get so grown up? Then again, Rorie had already turned fifty, and Cecily's big milestone was only a few months away.

Ten years.

It had been ten years ago, almost to the day, that the Oakwood Theater had called, looking for volunteers. And in an uncharacteristic move, Cecily had decided to bring some excitement back to her life, maybe relieve some of the drudgery of her suburban existence and miserable marriage. She'd been such a wreck at the prospect of turning forty. She smiled at the memory, though it wasn't a happy one. Without that midlife crisis, she'd never have gotten where she was today. She'd been convinced her life was nearly over, when it turned out it hadn't even begun. That one small leap of faith had started it all. The first of many.

"Mom?" Tyler's deep voice reverberated in her ear, startling her out of her thoughts. "It's almost curtain. You need to get to your seat or you'll miss Bryn's first scene."

She nodded at her son, who was in from New York to direct the summer show, as had become his habit over the past several years. No matter how busy the documentary film business became, he never missed the chance to direct a play on the Malibu ranch. "I know. I'm just waiting for Rorie."

Cecily had eyes on her from where she stood, a shadowy outline barely distinguishable as her black clothing blended into the darkness. But the silhouette of her trademark braids, now laced with gray, piled on her head, made her stand out just enough so Cecily knew it was her. Beside her was another shadow, whom Cecily recognized as her daughter-in-law, Reese. She was working as the assistant stage manager tonight. Her face was hidden in the dark, but the swollen, pregnant belly was a dead giveaway that it was her. It was only Cecily's total elation at the news that kept her from having a heart attack over the prospect of turning fifty and becoming a grandmother all in the same month.

"Five minutes to curtain," she heard a voice say, and then Rorie turned and started walking her way.

"You ready?" Rorie asked when she'd reached Cecily's side. "Everyone else is already in their seats."

Cecily knew. She'd seen them as she came in, her mother and father, plus Grace and Flip. They'd arrived an hour early, afraid to miss a moment of their granddaughter in her starring role, and grateful for the chance to catch up with old friends. They'd slowed down over the past few years, but she was thankful they were still going strong. She'd stopped to chat on her way backstage.

"I was just waiting for you." She held out her arm, elbow bent, and Rorie linked it with hers. It was tradition. Other nights they might each have their own responsibilities to attend to, but it wouldn't be opening night if they didn't walk from backstage together, arm in arm, to take their seats in the front row.

"Look, there's Rhonda," Rorie whispered. "And Jill."

Cecily squinted to find them as they emerged into the relative brightness of the auditorium, then waved her fingers slightly in their direction. They were regulars at opening night, too.

Jill continued to run Sapphicsticated, Inc., keeping it true to the mission that Cecily had envisioned when it began, and winning numerous awards in the process. Rhonda had grown in her understanding of the business over the years as well, and now made a formidable second in command. Together, the two were an unstoppable force. They were making great strides in bringing positive lesbian stories to the world, and Cecily was proud to be a part of it behind the scenes, but never once since leaving had she missed it enough to consider going back. She'd found her place.

She and Rorie had only just slid into their seats when the house lights dimmed. A swell of music announced the start of the show, but then it stopped and Tyler came out on stage.

Cecily's brow furrowed. Was there a problem? A memory of the night she'd gone on stage as an understudy after Bailey got sick flashed through her mind. Another serendipitous moment that changed the course of her life. If it hadn't been for that, she might never have ended up pursuing acting, or gathering the courage to move to LA. Even so, she fervently hoped no one was sick tonight. Her muscles tensed as Tyler began to speak.

"Good evening, ladies and gentlemen. Tonight marks the start of our sixth season here at the Horseshoe Ranch Theater."

Cecily leaned close to Rorie and whispered, "Do you know what he's going to say?"

Rorie shook her head, and Cecily could sense her tension. "I thought you put him up to it." Cecily reached for her hand as Tyler continued to speak.

"Before our show opens tonight, I wanted to take a moment to recognize the two people without whom our show would not be possible tonight. Mom, Rorie, can you stand up for a minute?"

Without a clue why he was making such a fuss, they both stood as the audience applauded. After a few moments, they moved to sit, but Tyler stopped them.

"Now, they don't know this yet, but I just got a call backstage, from Sacramento. It was a representative of the Governor's office, calling to let us know that these two ladies, Rorie

Mulloy and Cecily DuPont—who also happen to be my moms, by the way—have been chosen to receive this year's Cultural Commission award in recognition of having the top small repertory theater in the state of California."

Cecily gasped as the audience burst into a cheer. She flung her arms around Rorie and felt her body tremble as she pulled her into a tight embrace.

"Congratulations, darling," she said, speaking close to her ear at full volume to be heard over the applause. "You always said you'd make this theater the very best, and you were right."

Tears glistened in Rorie's eyes as she shook her head. "I said that *we'd* make it the best. I couldn't have done it without you."

Finally, the audience settled down, and as Tyler left the stage, the renewed swell of music signaled the show was about to begin.

"Did you see him grinning up there, that sneaky boy?" Cecily whispered to Rorie before the curtain went up.

"Can you blame him? It's not often he gets to deliver a surprise like that."

Cecily kissed her cheek. "I'm so proud of you. The award's a huge honor."

Rorie smiled, but shook her head. "You know, I'm proud too, but not because of an award. I've passed on something I love to our kids, and to the people in this community, and I've gotten to do that every day, side by side, with the person I love most. That's worth more than any award."

Hot tears ran down Cecily's cheeks as she pressed her mouth to Rorie's lips. She'd said everything Cecily would have if she'd been able to put the thoughts together fast enough, and as they kissed she focused on every emotion inside, hoping they, too, would come through without the words. She knew they would. Rorie had always been able to read her thoughts.

"You've become very wise in your old age," Cecily joked. "Do you think I'll be as wise as you when I'm fifty?"

"I doubt it, but we'll find out *very* soon, won't we?" Rorie smiled slyly, clearly enjoying the chance to tease.

Cecily jabbed her lightly with an elbow to her side. "Don't remind me."

With a whoosh, the curtain went up, and they both turned to watch the stage, eager not to miss Bryn's first big scene. And their daughter nailed it, completely, just as they both had known she would. Cecily was filled to overflowing. Rorie was right, no award in the world, no honor or fortune, could match the joy she experienced just being part of Bryn's life and watching her grow, or of being Tyler's mother, and Rorie's wife, and spending each day surrounded by their love.

Maybe she'd gained some wisdom, after all, as she'd aged. As lessons went, that might have been the most important she'd ever learned. *And it only took me fifty years to really master it.* She'd been so dense sometimes that the memories made her shake her head at her own foolishness. And she'd had to risk losing everything enough times to reach the point where she could truly appreciate what it meant to have that elemental love in her life every day.

She longed to tell Rorie how grateful she was to her for never giving up on her, but it would have to wait. They were in the middle of the show, and it wasn't polite to talk, even if you did happen to own the theater. Instead, she rested her head on Rorie's shoulder and tried to commit to memory exactly how she felt at that moment, to file away for when she needed to remember.

There had been so many times over the years that she'd regretted her past, especially the years when she and Rorie had been apart, but she felt peace in her heart even over that. She'd overcome heartache and fear, found courage, and learned to see through the glitter and illusion of life in Hollywood to find something real and lasting on the other side.

Cecily had no more than thought of her need to be touched when Rorie's fingers closed around hers. It was instinctive, their ability to fulfill the other's needs when it mattered most. The warmth of being loved so completely flowed over her, and Cecily knew that Rorie felt it, too. And in silence they sat together, basking in the peace that was the reward for their greatest and at times most difficult achievement, simply living the life that they were always meant to lead, together.

A MESSAGE FROM MIRANDA

Dear Reader,

Thank you from the bottom of my heart for sticking with Rorie and Cecily's journey to the end. Their story, like all of ours, was truly a road through mountains, twisting and turning to the end as they sought their hearts' desires, and ultimately found their happily ever after together. May each of us find the same!

Best Wishes,
    Miranda

Printed in Great Britain
by Amazon